Discovery

by

Rishi Mishra

Dedicated to

my family,

the Poozhikunnel family,

and the Thacker family

Table of Contents

Prologue

"Calm down. Please listen to me," he said to his sister.

His sister's breathing was heavy.

"Calm down. They killed our mother and father. How can you ask me to calm down?" she screamed.

"I know, but these people – they are not the same," he said. "They know nothing of what really happened back then."

He hovered in the air a few feet above the ground between his sister and the sky above.

"They don't even remember what our parents did for them. They are ungrateful and they will regret the day they killed our parents," she said. "Now get out of my way."

"They are a peaceful people who have become what our parents envisioned. I cannot let you harm them," he said still blocking her way.

"I will not tell you again. Get out of my way," she said.

Silence ensued for a minute and neither of them moved as they stared at each other.

"Their ancestors did a terrible thing and I will never forget that, but I have forgiven them. They are not the same people. Please, understand," he said again.

His sister moved with great speed trying to get around him, but he stopped her. She glared at him.

"No matter where you go, I will stop you. Our parents would not want you to do this to them. What they did to our parents…it would make us no better than they were if we were to take revenge on them," he said.

She tried to move around him again, but he moved in front of her. This time she attacked him with a large wave of energy, but he was able to deflect her attack and keep her from getting past him.

"Please stop," he said.

"You'll have to kill me to stop me," she screamed

She continued to attack him with numerous waves of energy, each one larger than the previous one. He continued to deflect the attacks without tiring.

"I will not kill you. Please, just calm down," he said.

His sister wore down the more and more she tried to attack him. After a few minutes passed, she stopped her attacks.

"These people will remember what they did. You protect them all you want, but I will remember what you did today," she said before storming away and vanishing.

He looked on at where his sister had been and took a deep breath.

"I'm sorry," he whispered. He closed his eyes and a tear fell down his face.

Chapter 1: The Rogue Spaceman

"Are you sure you don't want it?" Elias asked.

"Yeah," his mother replied from the car. "I give it to them every year for the garage sale and it always just ends up back here. I think it's time to just throw it away."

"Okay," said Elias.

"I'll see you in a few hours," his mother said as she waved goodbye.

Elias watched her drive down the street that separated their house from the affluent town, both of which were in a somewhat isolated woodland area. She was going to their friend's house in the neighborhood which was a few minutes' drive away, but they always invited her inside to stay and chat. Elias closed the large, mahogany-colored front door and went back inside his house.

He walked through his living room sliding his socks along the polished, light-colored hardwood floor as he passed the all-in-one technology system and soft, brown, leather couches while making his way to the kitchen. There, he put the old Bluetooth speakers he had been holding into the trash. He sat down at the table and picked up a chew toy from the tiled floor, looking at it while sighing.

Elias missed his golden retriever, Fuzzy, who had been gone for a few days now. Kayla, Elias' little cousin, had come by to take Fuzzy to her house for the week. She couldn't have her own dog because her father was allergic, but every year Kayla's parents let her have Fuzzy in the house when her father had to go away to his annual dental conference.

He put the toy back down on the floor and went out into his vast backyard. It was a pleasant summer day and the sun was setting as Elias walked through the uncut, discolored grass towards a sparse forest and lake that lay next to his backyard.

Elias reached the edge of the forest and sought out his favorite rock. He lay down on it and the soft patch of green moss on top of it created a perfect cushion for him as he rested while looking up at the sky. A few minutes passed before Elias looked back towards his house.

He and his mother lived in a simple two-story home that had been built by his father, who had passed away when Elias was very young. Other than a few old appliances and the vast backyard, their home was like most other suburban homes in the United States. The one unique thing about their home were the doors that his father had built. They were all mahogany-colored and each of them had been made with intricate artwork crafted into them.

The sun disappeared from view and Elias closed his eyes. He could feel the soft wind flowing through the tall grasses and hear the revving of engines as the few people fishing on the nearby lake left for their homes. He let out a deep breath. He was still exhausted from loading the car for his mother and he could also feel the meatloaf and broccoli he had eaten for dinner settling in his stomach.

Night had fallen and it was quiet outside. Elias never usually got to stay out by the woods too late into the night, but his mother, who would normally call him back inside, was still at their neighbors dropping off her things. Elias' eyelids began to droop and he drifted to sleep on his favorite rock out in the woods.

◆

Alera had done this many times before. Slip past the guard, fly by the Planet of Underground Settlers, and shoot down to the Planet of Untouched Ones, or as the people there called it, Earth.

Alera was always bored on the ship and unbeknownst to her parents, she would sometimes sneak out of the ship to go to the Planet of Untouched Ones where she could fly around or practice her technique without anyone bothering her.

She hid between some of the boxes in the shipping bay waiting for the guardsman to fly back to the ship from his post. Traveling to the Planet of Untouched Ones was forbidden because Alera's people didn't want the Untouched Ones to know they existed. She didn't understand why. Her people and the Untouched Ones were both human species with similar languages and the only major difference between the two was that the people on the Planet of Untouched Ones didn't possess any energy.

The guardsman watched the ring of decoy transports from his transport guard station just outside the ship as he shuttled the smaller ships in and out of the area ensuring they all used the rocks to hide behind as was required by law. The law had been put in place because Untouched

Ones' probes looking for life were becoming a nuisance and the Standards did not like dealing with them. With the new law in place, the Untouched Ones would think there was a meteor shower or that one of the rocks would be orbiting near their planet.

Alera continued to watch the large ring of transports that floated around the Planet of Underground Settlers for her chance to escape. She saw the guardsman leave and fly by on a transport to the ship and Kabec was flying out to take his position at the transport guard station. Kabec was a few years older than Alera and not as adept to sensing as the guardsman who had just left his post. Alera flew into a half empty box and waited while the transport being used for bringing goods to the local Underground Settlers was sent off. Before approaching the red planet, she got out of the box and broke off a small chunk of the transport for herself so she could split from the original shipment.

The first few times she had tried going to the Planet of Untouched Ones, she had feared that the Underground Settlers would spot her as she passed by, but in time she realized that they were not too focused on watching the transported goods since nobody except themselves ever travelled inside the ring of transports. Alera's people lived in a small sector of space called the Lighthouse Sector where not much of relevance took place other than an occasional visit from a delegate of the Orbital Sector.

Alera flew slowly as she made her way there as the law required required that speeds be cut down. Alera learned that the reason for this law was because the Untouched Ones would see streaks of light when one who possessed energy moved fast enough, causing them to become suspicious of the activity happening outside their planet. She had even learned that on the rare occurrence that one moved at near top speeds, the Untouched Ones would see dark voids left behind. Alera found it odd that the Untouched Ones saw such things since she could see no such signs when looking at her people.

She guided her small chunk of transport to the ocean on the Planet of Underground Settlers. She pulled up just above the water, released the transport, and created a splash that disturbed the water below, creating small ripples. She wasn't worried about being spotted by the Untouched Ones on the planet because her energy prevented her from being sensed by their technology. She also knew that none of them would be out in the ocean to see her while it was dark outside.

Alera was now free to roam around as she pleased. Having reached the Planet of Untouched Ones, Alera continued on her mission to escape from the boredom of the ship and Lighthouse Sector life. Her first stop was to see the funny walking birds at the cold place the Untouched Ones called Antarctica.

◆

It was 25:32 standard Sanize time on Vertur, the third day of the week. Captain Renalt was reading over the daily ship updates on his hologram projector. He stopped watching the updates and looked towards the entrance when he saw that Kerlan had just flown into the captain's ship deck, irked by something. Kerlan was a Standard and as regulators for the Clierns, Standards would receive reports of all activities in the local galaxies around them as well as reports on any major activities in the Universe. Between Kerlan and Raina, the other Standard on board, the Lighthouse Sector was kept up to date with the rest of the happenings in the Universe.

"What seems to be bothering you?" asked Captain Renalt in a calm and concerned voice.

"Captain Renalt, I just received bad news from the Orbital Sector. It appears as though one of their yellow diamonds was unlocked," Kerlan said with a look of seriousness on his face.

"Was it one of Jaru's dark hands?" asked a worried Captain Renalt.

"No. This particular one was unlocked by a rogue spaceman from the outskirts of their sector. They're still looking into why he did it, but for now they don't expect any foul play."

"What happened to the yellow diamond?"

"The usual. He went crazy as soon as he felt the energy, and since nobody was there he freaked out. He flew out of his planet and when he saw himself flying in the middle of space he freaked out even more. He ended up flying back into his planet, but," Kerlan sighed and then shook his head, "he ended up killing three others when he crashed into a small building and tried to use all his energy to stop the fall. He was so traumatized from everything that happened that he can't think straight now."

"What was the guardsman on watch doing?"

"He was too busy with so many incoming galactic transports. The spaceman went right by him without the guard noticing."

"I've told Yelay to post more guardsmen in his sector," Captain Renalt said in frustration. He took a deep breath and sighed. "He just doesn't listen."

"There's not much he can do about that. They don't have the money to pay for both the extra guardsmen to watch over the sector and the security forces they need to fend off attacks," said Kerlan, as he sat down on a hover chair. "With Jaru's forces being spread out in the local galaxy group and his actions unpredictable, the bigger sectors are more difficult to control."

"I suppose. Luckily we only possess one yellow diamond to guard and one with little energy at that," said Captain Renalt.

"Yes, the boy on the Planet of Untouched Ones. I doubt there's any risk of Jaru trying to unlock him."

"Well, it's only a matter of time before the Clierns deal with Jaru. They've slowly been depleting his forces." Captain Renalt stopped looking at the hologram map and looked out a window into the vastness of the Universe. "Eventually he'll have to stop unlocking yellow diamonds and focus on defending the areas he controls."

"That's what we've been told, but it's been two yeldings since the Clierns said that. Jaru's control grows no bigger, but he still causes havoc around the local galaxies," Kerlan said.

A notification sound came from the HoloTele in Kerlan's suit and he took it out and looked at it.

Captain Renalt was unhappy about the news he had received from Kerlan and he began to glide around his ship deck. The news would bring worry to the people in his sector. While he knew Jaru's dark hands would come nowhere near his small sector, the people on board the ship still feared that one day one of them would visit. With no report on why the yellow diamond in the Orbital Sector was unlocked, the news would make people speculate that Jaru forced the rogue spaceman to do it, and that would cause even more panic throughout the Lighthouse Sector. The representatives of the people in the sector had been growing restless at their weekly meetings. They wanted to spend the few credits their sector had saved to hire a small security force to protect them from any possible threat Jaru's dark hands might pose.

"The general meeting is in a week, Kerlan. We must find a way to give this news to the representatives without worrying them," Captain Renalt said finally.

"Yes, I agree," said Kerlan as he finished reading his HoloTele. "Haireg is off duty now. We shall talk more about this over dinner."

Kerlan left the captain's ship deck to get the daily report from Haireg and Captain Renalt turned on the teletron, waiting for the news to break out about the yellow diamond.

Chapter 2: Alera's Mistake

After having seen the birds, Alera was now gliding above the ocean, well north of Antarctica. She always liked to visit the animals on the Planet of Untouched Ones because they didn't have any on the ship she lived on. Her parents had told her that keeping animals were an unnecessary luxury.

Having flown around enough to see her fair share of animals, Alera decided it was time to start practicing her fighting techniques. Putting her other thoughts away, Alera loosened up with an energy meditation to increase her focus while thinking of the different techniques she wanted to practice. On the Planet of Untouched Ones she had to be careful about practicing her technique. She didn't want to use her energy in such a way as to create any bright flashes of light for them to see from far off, so she made sure to use short bursts with low energy.

Alera finished her meditation, took a deep breath, and started flying around the area, altering her speed as she went. Every now and then, she'd let off random bursts of energy, which to her had no visible color. Instead, when she saw energy, it had a faint, outlined, light gray glow that would soon vanish after passing by an area.

She continued her basic warmups for a few more minutes before stopping. She had started practice arena classes one yelding ago after convincing her parents to let her do so. However, she knew from talking with her friend, Tewa, that she would have to work for many serays to even become a halfway decent fighter in their sector. Even that was difficult though since most people's energy level, including hers, was too low to overcome the better fighter's skills.

Alera was now floating still and remembering what her teacher in practice arena classes had taught her. She spoke to herself, repeating all of the lessons she had learned.

"Your energy is a part of you. You must control it with both your eyes and your mind," she said aloud.

She closed her eyes. She remembered her teacher telling her that even though their eyes were adapted in ways that they could see everything at high speeds and far off distances, the key to being a fighter was sensing the energy around you with your mind.

She took a deep breath. Alera was disappointed that there was no way for her to practice sensing others' energy while on the Planet of Untouched Ones. Practice was the only way she would get better at sensing with her mind. She carried on repeating her teachings despite the lack of people with energy around her.

"Expand your senses. Feel the energy of the people around you. The more space you try to sense, the harder it will be to distinguish the energy sources you are feeling."

Alera expanded her senses, feeling only her own energy until she had reached a point where she could feel the yellow diamond's small energy as well. Then, she opened her eyes and sighed. It was natural for everyone to be able to sense energy, and yet, some were born with incredible energy levels and sensing abilities. Why couldn't she have been one of those people?

Shaking her head, she started practicing her fighting with a few right-handed, quick burst moves on the vast waters below. Using her eyes and her senses, she released small amounts of energy with her right hand facing the water at an angle while turning her body. The release of energy in combination with her slight turns caused her body to rotate in the opposite direction and twist upwards. As she twisted and turned like an ice skater in midair, the water below would splash up as if someone was throwing small boulders into it. The more right hand bursts she let off, the higher she would rise from the twisting of her movements. Once she reached the clouds above, she stopped and flew back down towards the waters again to repeat the technique several times.

Soon, she started on a different technique she had made up herself. Right hand straight down with a quick burst of energy to start her moving upwards and then left hand out with another quick burst to move her to the right. Then, with her right hand up at a diagonal to her right, she let off another burst of energy causing her to twist away and avoid an imaginary attack. She finished by releasing energy with both hands out downward in an arch to stop her from moving down.

After about twenty more minutes, Alera stopped practicing so that she didn't become too tired and instead of going back to the ship, she flew around the planet some more wanting to watch the Untouched Ones. She made sure to fly on the side of the planet that was dark so that she wouldn't be spotted by anyone looking up into the sky.

Alera had learned from classes on the ship that the Untouched Ones had different standards for time and didn't stay out much when it was dark. Instead they based the durations for time off the light their only star shone on their planet. She had spent some time working out the equivalents. Their days were twenty-four hours long instead of the Sanize standard thirty hours per day. They also had just seven days per week instead of the standard ten days. As if their days and weeks weren't weird enough to Alera, they used different names in place of serays and yeldings. A seray was equivalent to one and a fifth of their years and instead of using ten yeldings per seray, they used twelve months per year.

Alera found the names they had given to their days of the week to be quite quirky as well. Who would call a day Wednesday she first thought, when she saw it in one of her classes about them.

Sensing that the yellow diamond was nearby, she went to see what he was doing. Alera always made sure she never got too close to the yellow diamond. She didn't want to do anything that would unlock him. Alera remembered Tewa telling her the reason the Clierns made sure that living yellow diamonds remained locked was because unlocking them or killing them would release black energy into the Universe. She had said that this black energy was powerful, but difficult to find and harness. Only when a yellow diamond died by natural causes or was killed by its own people would it be safe to unlock it because the energy remaining could be let go without any release of black energy.

Alera passed by the ocean, flying in helical patterns to keep herself from getting bored. Within a few minutes she reached the large mass of land that the boy lived on and began to ascend to avoid any large buildings that she might pass. Alera was always fascinated by her visits to their population centers. She never understood how the people on the planet lived with such primitive technology. When she had been in history classes in school they had learned about civilizations on other planets in the galaxy that didn't possess energy either, yet even still, they always had high speed ships for travel and much sleeker, elegant buildings.

Alera was now a short distance away from the yellow diamond. She sought out her favorite tree where she could lie on a branch and relax. She could see the whole neighborhood at the top of the tall, leafy tree and she would observe the Untouched Ones as they went about their nights. Alera descended down to a branch that was strong and sturdy and lay down on it.

After reaching the branch, she spotted the yellow diamond lying down on a large rock, with his eyes closed. This was different than usual since he was never outside this late. Whenever Alera came before, the boy's mother had always come to call him in when the time changed to 8:00. From what she had seen on one of their time devices that flashed on the buildings during her journey to the boy, it was past that time.

Alera took a look at the rest of the small town from her branch in the tree. She could see two brothers, one a few years older than the other, kicking a ball in their backyard. About a block away an animal was barking at a couple who was walking around the neighborhood. In the southern part of town, a family was cooking on their patio, wisps of smoke billowing up from their cooking machine. A few houses down, someone had their sprinklers on, watering the grass. The town was well lit and there were vehicles driving in and out of the shopping area near the center of town.

On the outside of this small town were a large number of forests. From what Alera could see from her branch, the next closest town to the place where the boy lived was a long distance away.

Alera turned her attention back to the shopping area at the center of town. A large vehicle was pulling into a store getting ready to unload its packages and a man in a uniform with a bright badge was standing on a rolling vehicle that moved towards the park near the lake. Alera's eyes soon drifted away from the amusing vehicle and man as he neared closer to the lake and she stared out into the vast horizon, relaxing on the branch.

After a while, the wind began to pick up and it grew colder. Alera had not seen the boy move from his spot in over an hour. She was curious what he was doing outside for so long. Surely he was not sleeping on the rock outside. He had his own sleeping quarters inside his home.

Alera had developed a liking for the boy after seeing him a few times. He was not big and was of average height, but he had smooth, light beige skin and well-toned muscles. His face was symmetric with soft, blue eyes and smooth, brown hair. The boy always smiled, acting with kindness whenever Alera would see him interact with the other people in the town.

Wanting to get a clear look at the boy to make sure he was okay, Alera got up from the branch, careful not to make any noise. As she lost contact with the branch, Alera floated down towards a lower branch. She noticed that there were other people around the area at the lake nearby. She had sometimes seen other kids who would go swimming in the lake at night before and assumed that the same people were there again.

After another fifteen minutes of waiting for the boy to do something, Alera became worried that something was wrong with him. He had been lying still on this rock for a little under two hours. As she looked at him, she noticed that he appeared to be sleeping. Perhaps she should wake him up, but how could she do so without touching him? She would drop a small, green leaf on his face, she thought.

From the new branch she lay on, she used a very small amount of energy to tear a leaf from the tree and guided it a few inches over the boy's face. Then, in an instant, Alera released her hold on the leaf and watched it fall. It fell on the boy's left cheek and slid off onto the rock where he was sleeping. Still, the boy did not move from his position.

Alera was determined to wake him up and decided that since the leaf was too light, a small twig would wake him. Alera had trouble finding one small enough, but found one after a minute. With her energy, she broke it off the tree and began floating it towards the boy.

The twig was about halfway down the tree when a loud scream coming from the lake echoed through the night. The boy woke up, and startled, he slipped on a rock on the ground and began falling face first. Alera forgot her teachings for a split second, released her hold on the twig, and helped the boy from falling by using her energy. Then a quick, silent burst of white light, followed by wisps of silver smoke, originated around the boy. Alera's eyes opened wide and a terrified look appeared her face as she realized what she had just done.

♦

Elias awoke startled and unaware of what was going on around him. As he got up, his right foot slipped on a rock on the ground. He started to fall, but as he was going to the ground, his body stopped and lifted upwards. He felt a weird sensation of a fluid-like substance all around him and yet as Elias looked all around his body, he saw nothing pulling him up.

Without warning, Elias' eyes closed and he saw through his closed eyelids what looked like a bar of light scanning him, moving from his head to toe in a short burst and dissipating into the ground. After the short burst of light had passed, his body began hovering a few inches above the ground. Then, his eyes opened and he saw a cloudy substance originate as a circle on the ground around him. The substance wafted in the air moving towards the sky while still surrounding him.

As Elias looked up towards where the substance was headed, he saw a girl in the trees watching him with her eyes wide open. He wondered who this girl was and if she was doing this to him. In the darkness of the trees, Elias could not see what she was doing. He tried to speak, but his mouth would not open and other than his head, his body stayed in a floating position unable to move. He saw her slip from the branch and she fell out of the tree. She was flailing her hands and legs and looked with wide eyes at him as she fell. As she neared the cloudy substance which was moving towards the top of the tree, she began to slow down. The girl was now floating downwards looking back and forth at him and the cloudy substance.

Elias watched the girl move towards the ground as his body began moving and twisting in the air, doing spins while the cloudy substance around him began to take shape. He tried to stop his body from moving, but to no avail. His hands and feet were also moving on their own and appeared to be directing the cloudy substance into shape. When his body stopped moving, the cloudy substance had formed into a sphere enclosed around him. The sphere contained a series of symbols cut into it that looked similar to English, but with many different symbols. Elias didn't recognize what was in front of him and as he looked at the girl, he noticed that she looked just as confused and frightened.

The girl landed on the ground and looked up at him. Just then, Elias heard a voice from behind that he recognized call out, "Elias."

Elias turned around and saw his mother running towards him. As he looked back around at the girl, he saw her take flight with great speed. She disappeared into the sky, but for some reason Elias could still sense her presence as she flew away.

♦

After realizing what she had done, Alera tried to fly away from the tree and back to the ship as fast as she could. She knew if she got caught she would be in serious trouble this time. As she tried to leave the branch though, she lost her ability to use energy and fell from high up in the tree. Alera tried using energy with her hands to stop the fall, but nothing happened. She tried using energy with her feet and still nothing happened. She panicked as she was falling ever faster to the ground and watched the boy floating in the same spot as the silvery substance glowed all around him. Alera was scared. She couldn't feel any energy in her body. How this was possible?

As Alera reached the silvery substance coming from the boy, her body began to slow down, and she was being guided to the ground. She still felt no energy in her and now she could no longer move her own body either. Alera looked at the boy, who began to move. His body spun around with his hands and feet making odd motions in the air directing the substance around him. Alera looked above her at the substance floating around and noticed that it was coming back towards the boy.

About ten feet from the ground, Alera figured out what the boy was doing. He was using the silvery substance to create symbols in a sphere around him. She was frightened and confused since she could not recognize what the symbols meant. In the distance, near the boy's house, she saw a figure approaching them. Alera knew who it was. It was the boy's mother.

Alera landed on the ground with a light touch, and felt her energy rushing back to her. She knew she needed to escape as soon as possible.

As she prepared to fly back to the ship, she heard the boy's mother scream, "Elias."

After the boy turned around and looked away from Alera, she flew up with great speed towards the ship. Alera knew that her only chance to avoid getting caught was to be on board the ship before anyone found out that she had unlocked the yellow diamond, whom she had just learned was named Elias.

Chapter 3: Shockwave

Elias turned back towards his mother, who was looking at him in awe. The white substance faded away and he felt a gaseous substance become a part of his body. This invisible substance felt similar to what lifted him up when he had fallen from the rock. It was a strange feeling, but he felt like he could control it. Elias wondered if this was a power that the girl had transferred to him.

His mother had come up to him, her eyes wide, yet she spoke in a normal tone of voice.

"Don't worry, son. You'll be fine. Who was that girl?" she asked.

"I don't know," said Elias trying to catch his breath. "She was watching me from up in the tree and then…then all this weird stuff happened. Once I turned around, she just flew away."

"Can you still sense her?" asked his mother.

"How did you know that?" he asked.

"I'll explain what's happening to you later, Elias. Answer the question. Can you still sense her?" his mother asked again.

"Um, yeah, but…but it's getting fainter," he said. He waited a few seconds, but his mom said nothing. "Mom, how do you know what's happening to me?" asked Elias as he looked at his hands. "My body, it feels…weird."

"Elias, you must follow her. Go find her. Find out where she came from," said his mother.

Then, she looked towards the night sky at all the stars, her eyes getting bigger. Elias was beginning to worry about her. After a brief pause she looked back at him, staring into his eyes.

"Elias, come back after you find them and figure out what they are doing here. I promise I'll explain everything when you come back," she said.

"Mom, are you alright?" asked Elias waving his hands in front of her eyes. "You...you know I can't fly, right? How am I supposed to follow her?" asked Elias.

"Yes you can," pleaded Elias' mother, as she pushed him towards the direction of where the girl had gone. "Use the energy within your body and you'll be able to do it. You have it in you, Elias."

How could she think that he'd be able to fly? As he looked at his mom, he saw her eyes look like they were about to water but she continued staring at him.

"Please, Elias," she said again as a tear began to fall down her cheek.

Elias didn't know why she was acting so strange, but he decided to at least try to do what she had asked. Unsure of what to do, he decided he would need to move this newfound substance like a jetpack. Elias put his hands down to the ground and as he did so, he could feel the substance releasing from his hands causing him to shoot off like a rocket, high into the night sky. In mere seconds, his mom was a speck on the ground and he was flying. Elias looked at his body, stunned at what he was doing.

How did his mother know what was happening to him? As he looked down, his mother was no longer visible. Instead, he glanced upon the Earth as he flew further away. He was on the edge of Earth's atmosphere and he could see all the blue oceans and gray clouds swirling around with the huge chunks of land underneath. A few satellites were floating around in space nearby, but he was able to navigate around them.

Elias was worried that he wouldn't be able to breathe out in space, but as he had moved further from the Earth, he experienced no difficulties breathing. Elias did not know why, but flying was not a problem for him either and the substance flowing with his body no longer felt unusual, but natural. It surrounded his body like a suit and gave off just enough light for him to see the area around him.

The longer Elias flew, the more in tune he became with this newfound power giving him the confidence to relax his body. He saw Mars and it wasn't far from where he was flying now. He sensed something faint coming from that direction, but it wasn't the girl. However, he could also sense the girl, and he was getting closer to her. Elias sped up so he could find her and figure out what she was doing here as his mother had asked of him.

◆

Kabec watched the transports as they moved in and out of the area while Haireg was on his break. Kabec was on his first of two shifts and he was quite pleased with himself. He had been moving people and goods to and from the transports and the ship without much delay. On top of that, the ship guardsman Charl had not scolded him once, which was a first for Kabec.

It was a big day for the Lighthouse Sector since the new stadium equipment would be sent out to a multitude of sectors for upcoming exhibition matches later in the week. Also, new galactic maps would be sent out to the newfound sectors in the third octant and to the Clierns' Data Loggers for archiving. Haireg would be back to oversee the process of moving out these important exports as they would be the main source of income for the Lighthouse Sector this yelding.

During a lull in the transport activity, Kabec realized that he had been so busy with the transports that he forgot to make his last two checks on the Underground Settlers and the yellow diamond. Charl was at the shipping bay overseeing the ships that the Lighthouse Sector's exports would be sent out on, so Kabec turned on the Energon Sensor Machine, which was used during low transport traffic to help control the traffic in the area outside of the ring of transports.

The Energon Sensor Machine was a new device with advanced technology that had been created by the sparsely populated Rose Petal Sector. The machine tracked and directed all energy sources moving in and out of the area. It also detected anomalies or dangers that could cause trouble and alert the necessary guardsmen HoloTeles and station commands.

With the machine on, Kabec began his survey of the space near the Underground Settlers. Their goods had already been moved on transports during the beginning of his shift and the transports that they used for travel between their planet and the ship were all grounded on the two moons of their planet, so Kabec expected no transport activity during his check. As he observed the area, he saw and felt nothing out of the ordinary. The energy coming from the Underground Settlers direction was at their usual levels and Kabec recorded this in his log.

Kabec's ability to sense energy fluctuations in detail was far off from Haireg and Charl's ability to do so. He had been training to become a guardsman for about the past two yeldings and so far he hadn't done well on the sensing tests he had taken at the end of each yelding.

He continued his survey of the area and began his check on the yellow diamond. He expected a faint and steady signal, but for some reason Kabec couldn't sense anything when he focused on the Planet of Untouched Ones. He had always felt some small energy coming from the planet before.

Kabec expanded the area he was sensing around the planet until finally he sensed some energy coming from there. He was relieved and began writing in his log before he realized that the energy coming from the area around the planet was much larger than what he should have sensed. Kabec stopped writing and moved his guard station to get a good glimpse of the Planet of Untouched Ones.

As the guard station began to move, he saw an unidentified transport moving towards the ship, coming from the direction of the planet where the Underground Settlers resided. Upon seeing the unidentified transport, Kabec panicked and hit the emergency alert signal. Then, he contacted Charl's HoloTele. As he waited for Charl to come on the screen, he glanced back at the situation and saw something else that worried him. Someone was moving fast and getting closer to the ship from the direction of the Planet of Untouched Ones without a transport at all.

Charl came onto Kabec's HoloTele.

"Why did you sound the emergency alert, Kabec?" asked Charl.

"There's an unidentified entity moving at high speeds without a transport coming towards the ship from the Planet of Untouched Ones. There is also an unidentified transport coming from the Planet of Underground Settlers," responded Kabec.

"Are you sure there isn't a transport cleared for transit to our ship? And an unidentified person without a transport in this area seems highly unlikely," said Charl.

Kabec could tell that Charl did not look too worried about the situation. Charl was used to new trainees panicking from time to time after many serays as a guardsman. However, Kabec was sure of what he had seen.

"I know it's unlikely sir, but I'm positive. There's definitely someone illegally out there. And I haven't been asked for any transport clearance from the Underground Settlers during my entire shift." Kabec looked away from the HoloTele towards the guard station updates as a message came across the screen. "I just received a message from the Underground Settlers saying they sense strange activity occurring nearby as well. Charl, something's definitely wrong out here," he added.

Kabec could see Charl look worried when he told him the Underground Settlers also sensed something awry. Kabec could see him working away on his HoloTele. If the Underground Settlers sensed strange activity as well, then something had to be wrong. What could possibly be happening out there?

"I will alert Captain Renalt, Raina, Kerlan, and Haireg to the situation," Charl said finally. "In the meantime find out as much as you can about it and compile a report for the Standards. You've already turned on the Energon Sensor Machine so if either the unidentified person or transport moves outside the ship's area, we'll know. Tell all incoming transports to immediately fly to the ship's emergency bay and tell those that are too far away that they need to go back to the guard station on the spaceway transit. After doing that, fly back to the ship immediately."

"Yes, sir."

Kabec moved to the other side of the guard station and pulled up several hologram display screens. He switched the mode of the alert systems on the space transit warning panels to a crimson and black checker to stop all transports before giving them the orders Charl had given to him.

He turned on the hologram messaging feature to broadcast his presence to the incoming transports and spoke in a monotone voice, staring into the center of the display screens.

"We are now under emergency alert. All incoming transports within the brown zone move immediately to the emergency bay on the Shockwave. Everyone outside the brown zone fly back to the spaceway transit guard station Zelnar 649-21 and wait until you are told it is safe to resume your transit to the Shockwave," he said.

After giving the message, Kabec moved his guard station back into its usual position around the ring of transports and put the station in lockdown mode. Now, only the guardsmen, ship's hierarchy, and the Standards would be able to gain access to the guard station. Kabec flew back towards the ship at a moderate speed with a transport as he stayed on alert for the two unidentified people while compiling his report for the Standards. He was close to the shipping bay where Charl would be awaiting him, and from the corner of his eyes, he saw something at the other end of the ship. Near the "o" in the Shockwave nameplate, Kabec saw the unidentified transport fly towards the lower deck and slip underneath the ship, heading towards the emergency bay on the other side.

Kabec disobeyed his orders and followed the transport, knowing that he would be able to reach the emergency bay in time to confront the unidentified transport. He darted underneath the ship and headed towards the direction where the transport had gone. They were too close to the ship for Kabec's mediocre sensing to determine the transport's exact position with energy fluctuations so he flew out past the ship to get a better view of the area.

As Kabec passed the emergency bay, he glanced inside, noting that all the incoming transports were entering the bay, which was preparing to close its gateway. Looking back out at the space near the other end of the ship, he saw the unidentified transport moving fast towards the bay opening. Kabec was not too far from the transport to get in its way, but he was not an adept fighter. He knew his only option to divert the transport would a simple beam of energy directed at it to break it apart.

He flipped on his special visor, which would predict the flight locations of nearby moving objects. Guardsmen used the visors for sending out random transports to divert the Untouched Ones, but Kabec learned to use it to aim his energy beams from time to time. Locked on to his target's predicted location, he fired his energy beam and darted towards the emergency bay gateway.

Kabec flipped his visor off as he flew back and saw his beam hit the transport dead on, shattering it into a myriad of pieces, causing whoever had been controlling it to stop. The person behind it was now in clear sight and Kabec recognized who had been controlling the transport.

It was Alera. Kabec was furious. He changed course and flew towards her. He made sure he got to her before she could try to fly into the emergency bay. He had moved close enough for her to hear him.

"Alera. The emergency alert has been sounded and now the Standards and Captain Renalt have to come out to inspect everything all because you decided to break the rules. Come with me," he yelled.

Kabec had never been so mad before and he saw that Alera was frightened. She followed Kabec to the shipping bay looking distraught. Now pleased with himself for having stopped Alera, Kabec had forgotten all about the other unidentified person. As they reached the shipping bay, there was a host of people there looking about. On the shipping bay were all the members of the ship's hierarchy except Haireg, who Kabec assumed had taken up his position at the transport guard station.

Alera's parents were also on the platform, their faces filled with concern. Once they saw Alera with Kabec though, their expressions turned to relief.

Alera cried once she saw all the people waiting for them on the shipping bay and even though he was upset at her, Kabec could not help but feel sorry for her. He knew that this time she would be in much more trouble than the simple probationary punishment she usually received when breaking the rules.

◆

Elias was closing in on the girl, but as he neared Mars, he sensed many more people around. Had there been people living on Mars all along? He slowed down a little, unable to discern the girl's signal from the other signals around him. He could also sense an even larger signal coming from up ahead near where the asteroid belt would be, but at the moment he could not see anything past Mars, which was blocking his view. Elias flew over Mars and as he made his way toward the asteroid belt, he could see what he was sensing.

It was incredibly large. Elias slowed down even more, amazed at what he was looking at. How had nobody on Earth ever seen this before? In front of his eyes was a spaceship large enough to be able to fit one-fourth of Mars inside of it. On the front of the huge vessel appeared the name *Shockwave* with a metallic shine reflecting off the gray matte letters on the dark black ship. There were lights on in different regions of the ship, and of the few openings Elias could see that gave entry to the ship, only one appeared to be open. This was near the end of the ship and Elias assumed this was where the girl must have gone to enter the ship.

Elias was unsure about whether he should try to enter the ship or not. It was just floating there with little activity going on around it, but what was odd was the nametag on the ship was in English. His first thought was that this could be some sort of government secret he had stumbled upon, but put that notion to rest after realizing just how bizarre this night had been so far.

Slowing down to a gliding pace, Elias began to inspect the ship from a safe distance to see if he could find out anything else about these people. He saw three figures heading toward him from the opening on the ship. Elias wasn't sure what to do, but rather than fly away he waited for them to approach him.

As the three figures approached him, Elias noticed they were wearing spacesuits, but different from those he had seen on Earth. These were like fitted jumpsuits, but appeared much more advanced than the ones on Earth, with slithering lines of light on them flashing throughout. There was also a small beam of sky blue light coming from their suits that projected out into a sphere the size of a baseball, and a pocket in the suit for what appeared to be a small tablet.

Having approached Elias, the three figures floated in space in defensive poses while keeping their distance from him. The middle figure began to speak in a rather serious tone.

"I am Ramses Winsat, assistant to Captain Renalt of the Shockwave, main special institution of the Lighthouse Sector. With me is Vardun Uruas, a fighter from our sector and Raina Ensar, a Standard. State your name and the business you have here in our sector," said the middle figure.

Elias could see the three people in front of him in detail now that they were close enough to him. The middle figure, who had called himself Ramses, was a large man, a few inches taller than Elias, who felt like a towering figure. Ramses' white skin contrasted with his light brown eyes and made his spiked black hair stand out. To the right of Ramses was Raina, who was several inches shorter than Elias. She looked beautiful with glistening tan skin, but at the same time there was something fierce about her dark brown eyes and long, flowing dark brown hair. On the other side of Ramses, Vardun was about the same height as Elias and somewhat lean.

He had pale white skin, but his endless, dark green eyes and short, dark red hair made Elias think he was not as weak as he appeared.

"My name is Elias Rayhan from the planet Earth. I wish you no harm. I believe one of your people was on my planet and she did something to me. I followed her here to find out who she was," responded Elias despite his growing nerves.

"From Earth?" said Ramses, looking confused and shocked. There was silence for a moment before he blurted out, "You're the yellow diamond."

After a brief pause, Raina looked at Ramses.

"Yes. I sense nothing from the planet. He must be the yellow diamond," she said.

Vardun nodded at Ramses.

"He must have great control of his mind to make it all the way out here," said Vardun. He paused as he stared at Elias some more. "I find it strange that he seems to have more energy than the readings indicated before he had been unlocked."

"I agree, Vardun. We will discuss this back on the ship," said Ramses, looking at the other two in succession. He then turned his attention to Elias and said in a calm voice, "Elias Rayhan, we will escort you to our ship now. Is this understood?"

Elias didn't know what was happening, but thought it best to agree to go with them to the ship. This way he'd at least be able to find out whom they were and what they were doing so close to Earth.

"Yes, I understand," responded Elias.

"We will guide you to our shipping bay now. Please refrain from using your own energy," said Ramses.

Vardun moved to Elias' left, Raina to Elias' right, and Ramses behind Elias. The three of them guided Elias with their energy towards the opening on the Shockwave. Elias, now unsure of what would happen to him, waited for what they would do with him once aboard the ship.

Chapter 4: A Different Universe

Ramses, Vardun, and Raina set Elias down on the shipping bay platform and then Ramses walked over to a man waiting on the platform. The man was also wearing a spacesuit but it looked like his suit was too small for him because his rotund features stretched it out making it appear as though it would tear at any second. Despite this man's ill-fitting suit, this tall man still had an official air about him, with a clean shaven face, wise blue eyes, and short, brown hair.

"Captain Renalt," Ramses said to him, "this boy named Elias Rayhan is the yellow diamond from the Planet of Untouched Ones. From what I can discern, Alera must have unlocked him during her journey to the planet and he followed her here."

Ramses looked sternly at the girl Elias had been chasing. Alera had a sad look on her face and seemed as though she had been crying. She was taller than Raina and had smooth, long black hair. Looking into her pale blue eyes, there was something about her that Elias couldn't pinpoint that made her quite attractive to him. She stood next to two people far back on the platform, well away from Captain Renalt and the others. Elias assumed they were her parents. They were both taller than her and both looked rather worried as they stood next to their daughter. Her mother was holding Alera in her arms and Alera's father had his left arm across her mother's shoulders.

Captain Renalt looked out towards space, lost in thought. While waiting for him to say something, Elias looked towards three other people on the platform with them, who had all stayed silent.

The one closest to him was a tall, lean man with toned muscles and dark black hair. He sported a rugged goatee and his sharp brown eyes seemed as though they never blinked. Behind him was a man of moderate proportions with clenched teeth and narrowed eyes. He was angry and an electronic visor was up on his head, covering most of his light brown hair. The last of the three was a short man, just an inch taller than Raina, with a square face and black hair in the style of a buzz cut. He also had a black visor on that shielded his eyes, but this man looked like he did not belong with the rest of the group since he stood there looking unconcerned, unlike everyone else.

"It was an accident. He was going to fall and I helped him without realizing what I was doing. I didn't mean to do it!" blurted Alera.

"Quiet, Alera. You are already in enough trouble. Do not interrupt them," said Alera's father in a deep, quiet voice.

Ramses and the angry man with the visor on his head both looked over towards Alera, but Captain Renalt seemed to ignore her comments as he continued looking out into space. He seemed to be in no hurry and took his time before speaking.

Eventually, he said, "Thank you, Ramses. Please disable the emergency alert." He then turned to the angry man and said, "Charl, would you please get an Orbital Series 6 and bring it to us."

Charl went to do what had been requested of him. Captain Renalt turned to the others.

"Kerlan, Raina, Ramses, and Subedai, we will discuss the situation in my ship deck. Selnius, you and your family will wait in the Gondi conference room until we are finished with our meeting." Then Captain Renalt turned to Elias. "Elias, please come with me and Vardun when Charl arrives with the Orbital Series 6."

Elias nodded his head in agreement, but he was confused. He had no idea what an Orbital Series 6 was and he was still surprised that they spoke perfect English. He had many questions to ask, but waited, feeling that now was not the right time.

After Captain Renalt's orders had been given, everyone flew in their own separate directions into a hallway that led into the ship. Elias could see the hallway was filled with people. It was wide enough to fit his house inside of it from side to side and as tall as a seven story building. The floor was made of large, dark black rectangular tiles that resembled oversized television screens. On the tiles, Elias could see writing in many different colors and all of the tiles appeared to have something different on them. The sides of the walls were made of the same material Elias had seen on the outside of the ship, and the walls were filled with hologram screens which some people where using. Elias also noticed what looked like street vendors with booths spread apart along the left side of the wall for as far as he could see into the hallway. The ceilings were made with a material that was clear in color. Above the clear material were square stones with intricate patterns etched into them and the stones changed colors as people glided past them down below.

Elias turned his attention to an incoming gray vehicle. Charl had come back controlling what looked like a cross between a car and a hovercraft. The front had a hood similar to an SUV and a windshield like a convertible. There were also tinted panels up on the sides of the vehicle, but there was no roof or wheels to be seen.

As the vehicle came closer, he saw that the inside contained six seats made of a material that Elias had never seen before. The seats were in rows of two with the floor of the back row being raised a good three feet above the floor for the front two rows. The back was finished out by a tall sheet of black metal curved around the back row that declined in height as it approached the middle row.

An attached side compartment was on the left side of the vehicle that reminded Elias of lifts utility people used to fix traffic lights. Charl was in the attached side compartment and he controlled two hologram screens that didn't appear to have many options to control. He drifted near them and came to a halt near Vardun.

Charl left the side compartment as Vardun took over the vehicle's main drive controls.

"Thank you, Charl. You will come with me and Vardun to my ship deck to discuss the situation at hand. Please notify Haireg of your absence. Have Atecka and Ighun take your place as ship guardsmen for oversight of the exports until you come back and tell Kabec to find his way to my ship deck as well. His accounts of what occurred today need to be heard and recorded," said Captain Renalt.

"Right away, Captain Renalt," Charl snapped.

Captain Renalt used his energy to guide Elias into the seat on the right side of the back row of the Orbital Series 6. Startled, Elias wondered why these people kept using their energy to move him everywhere. They must've known he could fly on his own. Perhaps he was being given special treatment. He had heard Captain Renalt and Ramses calling him a yellow diamond.

Elias watched Charl fly into the seat on the left side in the front row while doing something with his small tablet of sorts projecting out a hologram. Captain Renalt flew into the seat next to Elias and then Vardun moved the vehicle forward out of the shipping bay and into the vast hallway.

There, Vardun directed the ship upward away from the people flying around at lower heights and soon they were near the ceiling moving along at a brisk pace. The vendors that Elias had seen earlier were moving by like lane lines on a highway. Soon, there were no vendors or hologram screens on the walls to be seen. Now, the side walls were made of large panels the size of movie theater screens, each showing images of different people or different places. As they flew by, Elias thought he had seen a map of the Milky Way Galaxy on one of the many panels.

As Elias watched the people passing by below, he heard Captain Renalt cough to get his attention before speaking.

"I apologize for the manner in which you have arrived to the Shockwave. It was a necessary precaution due to the regulations that have been set up in this sector. I'm sure you have many questions to ask of us," said Captain Renalt with a smile on his face.

"Oh, ummm, yeah. Uhhh, where do your people come from?" asked Elias, saying the first of many questions that had come to his mind.

Captain Renalt looked at Elias and chuckled.

"We have been living in this sector of space for ten serays now, which would be twelve of your years. Before we arrived, this area had actually been unused for an extremely long period of time. You see, a large battle amongst our people took place a few million serays ago. In that battle a much larger ship was destroyed from the fighting and this sector eventually became a ghost sector so to speak. That is until we arrived," he said smiling.

"Oh, okay," said Elias, although he was still confused. "How do you know our English language so well?"

"Your English language. Interesting. Well, we were the ones that created it," said Captain Renalt.

"What?" asked Elias.

"You see, investigations into the battle I mentioned showed that a rather large chunk of that ship got ripped apart and landed on your planet, wiping out multiple species in the process. About one thousand serays ago, an excavation crew found out that most of the large chunk had reached your planet undamaged and it was taken back to the Clierns. However, inside of it was a small part of a library that was scattered about the planet which included hologram recordings and books of our language, which you now call your English language. As a result of the ship's destruction, your people learned our language, although you have changed it slightly."

Elias couldn't believe what he was hearing.

"Who are the Clierns?" asked Elias.

"The Clierns are a group of people who make up the government for our entire Universe," said Captain Renalt.

He looked away from Elias and watched Vardun controlling the hologram screens. Elias had not been paying attention to where Vardun had taken them while he was talking with Captain Renalt. The Orbital Series 6 slowed down to a stop and they were inside a smaller hallway than before.

There were three rooms in this hallway, two on their right near the entrance to the hallway and one at the end. The doors were at least two stories tall and wide enough to fit three cars from end to end. Despite being much smaller than the doors that were on the outside of the ship, Elias still found them impressive.

The floor in this hallway was made of a dark green grass unlike the black rectangular screens Elias had seen in the other hallway. A line of blue lights spread every ten feet apart ran along the entire hallway about three-fourths of the way up each of the side walls. However, the one thing Elias noticed that had not changed from the hallway before was the ceiling.

Captain Renalt flew out of the Orbital Series 6 and landed on the floor below. Elias followed suit and flew out of the Orbital Series 6 on his own. It seemed strange that a floor inside would be made of grass, but it did feel soft under Elias' shoes.

"Hmm, he does it so naturally," whispered Captain Renalt to no one in particular after Elias had flown out.

Charl got out of the Orbital Series 6 and Vardun took off with it out of the hallway. Captain Renalt turned around and walked toward the room at the end of the hallway. Charl and Elias followed Captain Renalt. As they entered the room, Elias noticed the walls of this room were all made of a shiny silver metal except for the ceiling, which was still the same as the ceilings Elias had seen before. A large bookshelf with books was located near the right side of the entrance to the deck and set into the wall. Elias was able to read a few of the titles as he walked by which included, *Catastrophes of the Ancient Days*, *Cliern Laws and Regulations: Sector Managament*, *Dyoman: Tales of an Elite Ilay Member*, and *Past History: What is Known About the Lighthouse Sector*.

A light flashed in the corner of Elias' eye and he looked towards the left side of the entrance. On the corner of the wall was the same shining beam of light that formed into a sphere Elias had seen coming from the spacesuits that Ramses, Raina, and Vardun had been wearing when they approached him in space. Also on the left wall near the light was a door near the entrance, which was ajar. Elias glanced inside and saw what appeared to be an advanced sink. There was no faucet that he could see, but the bowl-shaped sink was there along with a strip of light formed into a ring surrounding the top edge of the sink.

Walking past the bathroom, Elias focused on a table in the center of the room. Raina and the man with the black visor over his eyes named Subedai were sitting by the table conversing in whispers, but Elias was more intrigued by a hologram of the solar system projected above the table. Everything on the solar system was labeled, albeit not with the names used on Earth. Elias saw the ship they were on, which had been labeled *Shockwave*, and the asteroid belt was labeled *Decoy Transports*. As he looked towards Mars, he noticed the label for it was *Planet of Underground Settlers* and Earth had been labeled, *Planet of Untouched Ones*. Elias continued to look around in awe at everything he was seeing on the ship for the first time.

"Where are Ramses and Kerlan?" asked Captain Renalt.

Before Raina could answer, two people came walking through the entrance to the room.

"I apologize for our lateness," said Ramses as he and Kerlan, the man with the goatee, walked past Elias toward the hologram projecting table.

"The spaceway transit guards at Zelnar station 649-21 have been given the go ahead to continue normal activities, Captain Renalt," said Kerlan.

"Good. Subedai, please send a message out to everyone on board the ship letting them know that the emergency alert was a false alarm caused by one of the youths venturing outside the ship without permission. Do not mention the yellow diamond yet," said Captain Renalt.

Subedai pulled out his small tablet hologram device.

"Yes, Captain Renalt," he responded.

Elias had still been standing nearby the entrance unsure of what he should do. Everyone had taken their seat in round chairs that were hovering in midair near the table with the solar system hologram except for Captain Renalt. Subedai was busy sending out the message Captain Renalt had given him and Raina was manipulating the map of the solar system with her hands. Suddenly, everyone turned their heads looking his way and Elias thought they were all staring at him waiting for him to do something. Before he openen his mouth to saying something, Elias sensed someone approaching from behind him.

"Sorry I'm late, Captain Renalt. I was using the lavatory and didn't read Charl's message until afterwards," said the person.

Elias turned and saw a young man walk past him towards the others. He was taller than Elias and had a similar build to Vardun. His smooth white skin contrasted with his clean cut black beard and his blue eyes stood out under the lights in the room. This young man went to sit down on one of the hovering chairs with the rest of the people waiting. Elias wondered if he too should take a seat and looked towards Captain Renalt for guidance.

As if reading his mind, Captain Renalt smiled and spoke to him. "Elias, you may sit at the table over by the window for now."

Captain Renalt had pointed to a different table at the far end of the room. Elias walked towards the table that Captain Renalt had pointed to, moving past everyone else at the table with the hologram map of the solar system. As he walked by, Elias noticed several screens around the room that kept showing all sorts of code on them, but not with the typical zeros and ones he had seen on Earth. These codes were in symbols he had never seen before. Elias also took note of a few shelves high up on the wall that contained strange gadgets.

Elias passed over the step up to the floor the table stood on. On either side of the step that separated the table area from the rest of the room were multiple horizontal railings reminding Elias of the ropes in a boxing ring. The table Elias went to was rather large, semi-circular, and made of a mahogany-colored metal that eerily reminded him of the doors in his home. The tabletop was made of a large black screen that was similar to those that Elias had seen in the hallway leading to the shipping bay. Around the table were six round hover chairs with small circular stands next to each chair.

Just beyond the table was a large curved window. Elias looked through it and saw the vastness of the universe with the multitude of stars scattered about. He looked for Earth, but realized the window was positioned away from his home planet. He looked away from the window and sat down on a hover chair rather cautiously, expecting it to fall as he sat on it. To his surprise, it did not move at all and it felt as though he was sitting on a pile of soft feathers.

Looking back towards the group around the table with the hologram map of the solar system, Elias saw Captain Renalt use his energy to close the door to the room. Captain Renalt then moved to an empty chair, sat down, and began conversing with the others.

Elias put his hands down on the tabletop and a small square of the black screen, about the size of a poster, lit up. On it was a welcome screen that displayed the title, *Captain's Ship Deck*. He looked back up to see if any of the others had noticed what he was doing, but they were too busy talking to each other. A three-dimensional map of the room appeared on the screen and showed his position on the captain's ship deck. He tapped the table on the map that the others were sitting at and a side note popped up to the side of table on the map labeled, *Hologram Projector*. He tapped on the side note and the screen changed to show the details of the hologram projector while the three-dimensional map shrunk to a smaller size and moved to the top right of the screen.

Elias began reading the details of the hologram projector, but soon became distracted by the conversation happening by the actual hologram projector table which had gotten much louder.

"You disobeyed my orders, Kabec. You flew out to confront an unidentified transport and you're lucky it happened to be Alera!" Charl screamed at the young man, presumably Kabec.

"Charl, please do not interrupt again. There will be plenty of time for comments afterwards. Might I remind you, it was on your and Kabec's watch that she was able to leave the ship in the first place," said Captain Renalt. He turned to Kabec. "Kabec, you will be placed on probation for disobeying Charl's orders. Now, please continue with your accounts of what happened."

"Yes, sir. After shattering the transport and discovering Alera was behind it, I confronted her. I told her to follow me. I didn't notice the yellow diamond, nor did Alera mention anything about him," said Kabec. "That's all."

"What have you done with the report you filed for Raina and Kerlan?" Captain Renalt asked.

"I have it ready for them on my HoloTele. Would you like me to transfer it to them?" asked Kabec.

"No. I'll decide what to do with the report. You may go now, Kabec. Please be sure to send me the report and delete it from the archives," said Captain Renalt.

Kabec got up from his chair and opened the door with his energy. He flew out and closed the door behind him.

"We will need the report. If you wish not to tell the people aboard about the incident, that is your decision, but we are obligated, as workers of the Clierns, to notify them of the situation and give them the proper facts. I know we are good friends, but there is nothing I can do about this," said Kerlan.

Captain Renalt exhaled.

"I understand, Kerlan. I will send the report to you and Raina after the meeting," he said. "We must determine what punishment Alera will be given. By Cliern law, as a person under twenty-five serays of age, she will have to go to the academy for at least six yeldings for this crime. Does anyone insist on a harsher punishment for Alera?"

There was a long pause as nobody seemed to want to be the first to say anything. Charl shifted in his seat and he seemed to have calmed down some since yelling at Kabec.

"Alera has broken the rules too many times before. She doesn't respect our authority and she crossed the line this time by unlocking the yellow diamond. The Clierns will certainly not be pleased with our sector if we were to give a punishment of only six yeldings at the academy. I do not wish to further punish one of our own, but I think nine yeldings at the academy is the least that is necessary to keep the Clierns from interfering," said Charl.

Subedai, Ramses, and Raina nodded their heads in agreement with what Charl had said, but they did not seem happy. Once again, there was a long silence as everyone sat around the hologram projector table. It seemed as though these people were punishing the girl for going to Earth and giving Elias these powers. He didn't understand what was so bad about what she had done.

The silence lasted for quite a while so Elias thought it would be okay to ask them a question as they sat there.

"You keep referring to me as a yellow diamond. What is a yellow diamond?" asked Elias.

All of them looked over to Elias as if they had forgotten he was still there.

"A yellow diamond is a person who has energy within them but cannot use it until they are unlocked by another with energy," Ramses said.

"So what's wrong with that?" Elias asked.

"To unlock a yellow diamond means that black energy is also released into the universe, which is illegal. You were unlocked by Alera. Now you are no longer a yellow diamond. In fact, your energy is less than ordinary."

After a brief pause, Captain Renalt spoke to Elias.

"Now that you have gained the ability to use energy, you will have two options. You may either live with us aboard this ship or stay on your planet. However, if you choose to stay on your planet, you cannot use your energy in front of anyone other than your immediate family as we do not wish for your people to know of us," he said. "If you do use your energy improperly on your planet, we will be forced to rectify the situation and then make you come live with us aboard our ship. As proper protocol dictates, we will give you up to a month on your planet to make your decision. Kabec will take you back to your planet and stay with you until you make your decision. He will be there to help answer any questions you may have about us. Please wait for him here until he arrives." Turning to everyone else, he continued. "This meeting is adjourned. I will give Alera and her parents the news on her punishment. Charl, please inform Kabec of his new responsibilities."

Everyone got up from their chairs and filed out of the room. Elias tried to take in everything he had just heard. There were so many things he still didn't know, but he also had so much to think about now. All alone with his thoughts, Elias waited in the captain's ship deck for Kabec to arrive.

◆

Selnius was deep in thought as he waited for Captain Renalt to come to the Gondi conference room. How could Alera have done this? What would be her punishment? Would she serve her punishment in the Lighthouse Sector?

The room was silent. Alera was over by the other end of the conference room with her face lying on the table just staring at the wall. She hadn't said a word since they entered the conference room. Luna, his wife, was sitting in the chair next to him, a look of great sadness on her face. She too must've known they would not see their daughter again for some time. The minimum punishment for Alera's offense, even accidental, was at least six yeldings in an academy.

The academy was a place people were sent to teach them obedience to authority and understanding of their crimes, and it was run by the

Clierns' Dasunes for people who broke Cliern law. It was not the worst punishment one could receive as the people who committed major crimes were sent to the Clierns' main sector, Sanize, to be dealt with by the Falhul, the head group of the Clierns. However, the conditions were not pleasant inside an academy either. Selnius shook his head, no longer wanting to think about the fate that awaited his daughter.

The gateway to the room opened and Alera sat up. Captain Renalt walked into the room and Selnius saw the frown on his face. Selnius and Luna had seen Captain Renalt many times before when Alera had gotten in trouble as a child, but this time Selnius' heart was beating faster than ever, knowing this was no ordinary visit. Captain Renalt sat down on a chair across the table from Luna.

"Alera, please come over by your parents," said Captain Renalt.

Alera got up and sat down in the chair next to her mother.

"Please don't take Alera away from us, Captain Renalt. She is only a child and what she did was an accident," pleaded Selnius.

"Selnius, you know I have no choice. She broke one of the Clierns' laws and she was not forced to do so. Accident or not, she has to be punished," said Captain Renalt.

He paused and looked toward Alera. "Alera, you broke Cliern law by unlocking the yellow diamond named Elias Rayhan. Not only that, but you did so while illegally leaving the ship, taking a transport with you to the Planet of Untouched Ones, and then stealing a transport from the

Underground Settlers to get back to the ship. For this reason, we have decided that your proper punishment will be nine yeldings in the academy in our sector. Your family will not be able to visit you other than for emergency reasons for the next three yeldings. Your punishment will begin in two days after the details of the incident and your determined punishment have been sent to the Clierns later today by Raina."

Alera dropped her head after hearing the news and Luna put her arms around her daughter. Selnius was both distraught and surprised by the news. He had expected a much harsher punishment. He had seen many cases on the news of people that were given sentences of three or four serays and sometimes even moved to a different sector's academy.

"Is there nothing that can be done to shorten the punishment?" asked Selnius.

"No, Selnius. The punishment we have determined is the best that can be done. If it were any shorter, the Clierns would not be happy and would likely sanction our sector," said Captain Renalt, who paused and then sighed. "This punishment is the first of this magnitude for our sector and we all do not wish this upon Alera, but it must be done."

"I understand, Captain Renalt," said Selnius. Then he looked at his wife and daughter sitting next to him with sadness.

"Alera, we will be coming to your living quarters in two days to bring you to the academy after you have had your breakfast. Please pack what you need beforehand," said Captain Renalt. The room was silent for a short while. Then, Captain Renalt got up from his chair. "I must go now.

Luna and Selnius, if you need anything or have any questions, please let me know."

Luna and Selnius nodded in acknowledgement and then Captain Renalt left the Gondi conference room.

♦

Elias and Kabec had landed on Earth a few hours after the meeting in the captain's ship deck had ended. They had flown back to the wooded area behind Elias' house and were now walking on the forest floor. The leaves swishing underneath their feet and branches crunching with every step could be heard in the silence. It was three o'clock in the morning and dark outside, but in the distance Elias could see lights on inside his home. His mother must have stayed awake, waiting for him to come back.

"That's your home up ahead?" asked Kabec.

"Yeah. My mom is waiting for me. She'll want to know what happened," said Elias as he rubbed his eyes.

Despite the adventurous night he was having, Elias was still tired and wanted nothing but to sleep on his own comfortable bed for hours. He knew he wouldn't be getting sleep for a while though since he'd have to explain to his mother what had happened.

Elias looked over to his left at Kabec, who had been looking everywhere around him as they walked towards the house. He seemed quite uncomfortable on Earth as if he was expecting someone to jump out at them. Elias could not help but smile and although he had only been with

Kabec for a few hours, there already seemed to be a budding friendship between the two.

Soon, they had reached the house.

"Should I wait outside?" asked Kabec.

"No, it's alright. You can come inside," said Elias.

Elias opened the back door giving way to a slow creaking sound. Both he and Kabec walked into the kitchen and Kabec placed his belongings onto an old dirty mat lying on the tiled floor. The lights were on in the kitchen and his mother sat on a stool by the island watching television. She turned around as soon as she heard the door open and got up from her chair staring at Elias with a smile on her face. She came up to him and gave him a hug. Then, she took a step back, still smiling at him.

"And who is this?" Elias' mother asked him as she looked towards Kabec.

"You should sit down," said Elias as he took a seat at the kitchen table unsure of how exactly to let his mother know what had just happened in the last few hours.

His mom sat down and Kabec did the same on the opposite side of the table.

"Mom, this is Kabec Hiknal," said Elias.

"Hello, Kabec. It's a pleasure to meet you," said Elias' mother.

"Hello, ma'am," replied Kabec.

His mother did not sound nervous or worried at all. Elias was puzzled.

"So, uh, apparently I can fly," said Elias not able to conceal disbelief in his voice.

His mother continued to smile at him in silence.

"Um, okay, I was expecting a different response," said Elias trying to gather his thoughts. He didn't understand why his mother was acting so strangely. "Anyways, I followed that girl like you told me and—"

"Elias, you've been gone for hours now and you look exhausted. Get some rest for now. We'll discuss everything in the morning," said Elias' mother getting up from her chair.

"What?" asked Elias sounding shocked. Why wasn't his mom more worried or curious?

"Come on now. Up the stairs. Both of you," she said waving her arms in the direction of the stairs.

Elias tried asking his mom what was going on, but she kept shushing him every time he spoke, leading them out of the kitchen and up the stairs. They arrived at the second floor and stood in the hallway. There were four bedrooms on the second floor of the house and two bathrooms, one in the master bedroom and one in the hallway for the remaining three bedrooms.

"Kabec, you may sleep in that room over there," Elias' mom said. She pointed to the guest bedroom that was adjacent to Elias' room. "Go to sleep you two. We'll talk more about this in the morning."

"Thank you, ma'am," said Kabec, taking his things and going over to the room.

"What's going on? I just flew into sp—" said Elias eyes wide looking confused and shocked before his mother interjected.

"It's past three in the morning. We're all tired. This is not the time to discuss these things, Elias. Now go to bed. I won't say it again. Good night to you all," commanded Elias' mother.

Kabec was standing in front of the room Elias' mom had told him to go to and he was running his fingers across the artwork on the mahogany-colored door to the room.

"The patterns on this gateway seem eerily familiar. Where did you get this gateway?" asked Kabec.

"That door was built by Elias' father when he built this house," said Elias' mom with a smile on her face. "Now please, go to bed you two."

Then, she went into her room and closed the door behind her. Kabec had gone into his room and Elias looked back towards his mother's room. She was acting so strange and Elias didn't understand it at all. After standing alone in the hallway for some time, Elias realized he was not going to be able to do anything about it tonight and he went into his room.

When he walked in, he saw his queen-size bed with dark green sheets and soft fluffy black pillows. Then he remembered how exhausted he was and didn't even bother changing into his pajamas. He plopped down onto his bed, with his head resting on a pillow and closed his eyes. Within seconds he was off to sleep, dreaming about flying around in space.

Chapter 5: The Amazon Jungle

Elias woke up with the sun shining through the windows. He felt well rested and got up from the bed stretching his arms to the ceiling while exhaling. He remembered having a nice dream, but couldn't remember what it was about. Looking at the clock on the wall, he saw it was three minutes after ten o'clock.

Elias wondered if anyone else was awake now and opened the door to his room. He walked into the hallway and saw that both the doors to his mom's and Kabec's rooms were closed. He couldn't hear anything coming from the kitchen downstairs either. He went to the bathroom to take a shower and brush his teeth. After a refreshing shower he went back to his room to change into new clothes before heading downstairs for breakfast.

As he put his clothes on Elias remembered Kabec looking at the doors to the bedrooms the night before and wondered what was so intriguing about them. He had never paid much attention to the patterns on the doors before, but now he stared at them, grazing his fingers over them. Elias thought he recognized some of them – they looked similar to some of the symbols he had seen the day before when he was inside the sphere the cloudy substance had formed, but he assumed it was just his mind playing tricks on him.

Elias heard a sharp click from a door opening out in the hallway. He stopped looking at the door to his room and went out into the hallway to find Kabec standing there.

"Good morning, Kabec," said Elias.

"Good morning. May I use the lavatory?" asked Kabec.

"Yeah, the bathroom is right there," said Elias, pointing to it.

Kabec went to the bathroom and Elias went downstairs to make breakfast. A few minutes later, he heard footsteps coming down the stairs and Kabec walked into the kitchen wearing a different suit than he had on the night before. His hair was wet and he looked around the room as he sat down at the kitchen table.

"Do you want anything to eat?" asked Elias, scrambling some eggs with a spatula.

"Yes, that would be nice," said Kabec. "The lavatory you have wastes a lot of water. On our ship we have devices that wash and dry us and they use a lot less water than your devices do here."

"Oh, yeah. Well, from what I saw on your ship, your technologies are a lot more advanced than ours," said Elias.

Elias took bread out of the toaster and put the slices onto a plate along with the scrambled eggs he had just cooked. He set the plate on the kitchen table in front of Kabec and went to get a glass.

"Thank you," said Kabec.

"Hold on. I'll get you some orange juice as well," said Elias.

"What is this?" asked Kabec, using his energy to lift a piece of toast in the air.

Elias chuckled. "I take it you don't get this kind of food on the ship. It's toast with salted scrambled eggs," said Elias. He poured some juice into Kabec's glass. "Hopefully you'll like it."

Elias went back to the stove as he continued to cook. He heard a door opening upstairs and he knew his mother must be awake.

"Huh, well, it's edible. Rather plain, but edible nonetheless," said Kabec while eating his food.

"Yeah, sorry about that," said Elias as he put more bread into the toaster. "Some of the food we eat can sometimes be plain, but it's quick and easy to make so we don't complain too much."

Kabec ate while Elias continued cooking. Once Elias finished his cooking, he sat at the table to eat his breakfast with Kabec. A few minutes later, he heard footsteps coming down the stairs and his mother walked into the kitchen. His mother, Hannah, was a short, quiet woman in her early forties. Her long brown hair was put into a bun and glasses covered her soft blue eyes. She went to the coffee maker and started making her coffee before acknowledging them.

"Good morning," she said.

"Good morning," responded Kabec.

Elias closed his eyes for a few seconds before opening them again and taking a deep breath. He stared at his mom making coffee for a few seconds before speaking.

"Um, aren't you the least bit curious what happened last night?" asked Elias, befuddled by his mom's nonchalant attitude.

He couldn't take it anymore. He didn't understand why his mother acted like everything was normal. His mother turned and looked at him. Then her eyes shifted towards the floor in front of her, as she appeared to be thinking about something. She looked back up and sighed.

"I'm sorry, Elias. Let me get my breakfast first and then I'll explain everything I know."

She put some scrambled eggs and two pieces of toast onto her plate. Then she prepared her coffee and sat down at the kitchen table.

She took a bite from a piece of toast and said while chewing, "Now, where should I begin?" His mom paused. "Hmm, I guess I should start, by telling you about your dad," she said looking up at Elias.

Despite the excitement of the last twenty four hours, Elias' eyes dilated as he heard this. He was on the edge of his seat now as his mother had almost never talked about his father.

"Uh, so when I got out of college I started out as a journalist in New York City. Actually, I lived in an apartment in New Jersey, but anyways, I frequently went to this coffee shop in New York. The first time I ever went to that coffee shop was the first time I ever saw your dad. I was sitting on the second floor just doing some work and I saw him sitting alone by the window just looking outside."

She shook her head.

"I'm sorry. You probably don't want to hear any of this gooey romantic stuff do you," she said.

"Mom, you've never told me anything about dad before. I want to hear anything about him," said Elias.

She smiled at him.

"Okay," she said.

Elias' mom had never even shown him a picture of his dad before and only after Elias whined for days on end when he was younger had she told him his dad's name. Whenever Elias would ask her about his dad after that, all she would say that he was an amazing man who loved them very much and that Elias would have to wait until he was older to learn about his father. His mother took a sip of her coffee and kept telling the story.

"So I saw your dad and he was sitting there. He was there alone and he didn't have anything on his table, but I was still too shy to go talk to him at that point so after a while I just left," she said. "Your dad, well, he was really good looking and well, I'll show you a picture of him later today, okay."

Elias nodded. His mom took another long sip of her coffee. Then, she bit into her piece of toast again. Elias waited for her to continue.

"Then one Friday night, I had just written a great article that people had loved so I was in a really good mood. I went to the coffee shop again and your dad happened to be there again. I hadn't seen him in there since the first time, but this time I went up to him and introduced myself," his mom said. "I was so nervous, but he just…I don't know, there was something about him. I ended up asking him out."

"Obviously he said yes," said Elias.

Kabec had finished eating his food, but Elias' food was just sitting there since he was too focused on the story about his father to eat anything. Elias' mom looked at Kabec.

"We must be boring you with this story," Elias' mom said. "You don't have to stay here if you don't want to. I can take your dishes and put them away."

"Oh, no, don't worry about me. I don't mind hearing the story. It's actually quite interesting to hear about Earth stuff," said Kabec.

"Okay. I'll continue the story once you're done eating, Elias," his mom said. "And yes, he obviously did say yes."

She finished the rest of the food on her plate while Elias gulped down his breakfast. He wanted to hear more about his father.

"Let's sit in the living room. It's more comfortable there," Elias said showing Kabec where to go.

Elias put his dishes away and dried his hands on a towel. He walked into the living room and took a seat in a chair facing the front of the house. Kabec was sitting opposite of him, next to the window, and his mother sat down on the couch facing the all-in-one system.

"The next night, we went on our date. Your dad was a very charming person and a gentleman to say the least. The date went great, but afterwards I could tell that something seemed to be bothering him," said his mother. "He wouldn't say what it was though, but I really liked him so I didn't press him about it or anything. Eventually, we ended up at the docks by the river. We were sitting there, just talking, and he pointed out this shabby little houseboat on the water."

His mom closed her eyes and appeared to be laughing inside. Then she shook her head while smiling.

"Stupid old me didn't realize that it was actually his boat and I may have made fun of it a lot. Like a whole lot. It looked so sad. He told me it was his and I felt awful. Not only did he say it was his, but he told me he built it himself," said Elias' mom. "I think that kind of stuck with him a little because as you know your dad built this house and he certainly made sure I wouldn't be able to make fun of it."

She took a deep breath and stared at Elias for a few seconds. Her eyes seemed to be watering and she seemed to be having trouble getting out what she wanted to say next.

"The next part is, uh, well," she said taking another deep breath. "Your dad he wanted to impress me after the whole houseboat debacle. He started moving his hands around the air and I had no idea what he was doing, but then he produced this, this thing. It was…it was so beautiful. There were rainbow-colored ribbons of light just swimming around each other forming a globe." His mom started moving her hands in front of her. "I thought he was trying to do some magic trick. It didn't seem real."

Kabec started moving his hands over and under each other outlining a sphere. Elias and his mom watched Kabec start to form streaks of light that were red and orange. It seemed like he was struggling and soon he gave up what he was doing.

"That's one of the hardest things to do. You said it was a full rainbow?" asked Kabec.

"Mmhmm," responded Elias' mother.

She looked back to Elias. "Your dad was one of them." She paused. "So yeah, that was your father."

The room stayed silent for a little while as Elias tried to take everything in that he had just heard. Then, a soft noise came from Kabec's small hologram projecting tablet in his suit.

"I'm sorry," said Kabec pulling out the tablet. "I need to take this. Is there anywhere I can talk in private?"

"There's an office room just over there," said Elias' mom.

She pointed to the room and Kabec went inside and closed the door. Then, she looked back at Elias.

"So that's why you never told me about dad," said Elias.

"Yep. It's kinda hard to explain to your son that his dad was an alien with special powers and everything," his mom said.

"What happened to him? I know you said he died when I was young, but how?" asked Elias.

His mother stared at him, and she bit her bottom lip like she wasn't sure she wanted to tell him. Elias saw a tear fall from her eyes.

"I was nine months pregnant with you and we were driving to the hospital," she said. "Back then, our house was pretty far away from the closest city. We...we didn't make it to the hospital before I started going into labor. We pulled over on the side of the road."

"Why didn't dad just fly you to the hospital?" asked Elias.

"I told him not to. Flying isn't exactly normal so people would realize he wasn't, you know, human," said his mom. "In hindsight, I'm sure there was a way he could've done so without being spotted, but I wasn't thinking straight."

"Why didn't dad just not listen to you?" asked Elias.

She sighed.

"Your dad always listened to me," she said. "Anyways, I gave birth to you on the side of the road and everything turned out fine. That is, until after you were born. I was lying down in the back seat and I had just closed my eyes ready to go to sleep because I was so exhausted. Your dad, he was holding you. He started talking to you while we waited for an ambulance to come, but soon he wasn't speaking English anymore. I have no idea what he was saying to you, but when I tried to open my eyes for a split second, his eyes seemed glossy. I was worried, but I was so tired I just laid there." She paused for a second while taking a breath. "I heard him say, 'I love you, Elias.' Then, he came over to me, kissed me and said, 'I love you. I'm sorry.' I passed out shortly after that and I don't know what happened, but I woke up the next morning in the hospital with my family there. Your dad wasn't there and they said he hadn't been there when the ambulance had arrived to take both of us."

"Dad left us?" asked Elias.

"No, definitely not. Your dad would never do that. He was an amazing person," she said. She sighed. "When I finally went home with you, I went up to our room and there was a note on the bed. All that was written on it, in a special language that he had once taught me was, *'My life must come to an unexpected end. I love you both.'* I don't know exactly what happened to him and that note was the only thing I found."

They sat in silence for a few minutes.

"Okay. Enough sitting here. You still have finals to study for next week." she said.

"Are you serious?" asked Elias as he laughed.

She stared at him without wavering from her expression. Elias smiled and laughed again. He loved his mom no matter how quirky she acted at times. Not wanting to keep getting that look, Elias went to his room to go study.

♦

Maraye had drugged the guardsman maintaining the space near the portal. This was the only guardsman on duty to make sure that the portal extension wasn't destroyed or damaged by anything out of the ordinary and now, with the guardsman fast asleep, no one would be alerted to anything amiss. Maraye headed to the portal extension platform that resided on the outskirts of the Orbital Sector, opposite where the yellow diamond had been unlocked a few days ago.

He moved through space focusing on his mission. Maraye was following orders to hack into the Cliern data center to obtain classified information and with the device he was given, he would be able to do so without anyone noticing something was wrong. He knew it had been done many times before by other members of the Nagen, but this was the first time he would hack into the system himself.

He reached the portal extension and saw an alert coming from his HoloTele. He ignored the HoloTele for the time being and followed his duties as he placed the device above the portal's energy scanner. Once the device was turned on, it began producing small energy patterns into the scanner in a detailed and complex manner. Waiting for the hacking device to finish its process, Maraye pulled out his HoloTele and saw that there had been an emergency alert on the Shockwave because a child had gotten outside the ship. Maraye chuckled to himself since he was wise enough to know that emergency alerts were never activated just because of misbehaving children. He put his HoloTele away and the hacking device had completed its process with the energy scanner to open the portal extension. He decided that on top of the classified information he would also obtain all recent reports regarding the Shockwave, inputting the necessary commands into hacking device.

After a few minutes, the device had obtained all the information asked of it and disconnected itself from the portal extension. Maraye took the device, connecting it to his HoloTele and looked into the files on the Shockwave. A recent one had been submitted by Raina and he retrieved it. As he read the report he was surprised. The yellow diamond in the Lighthouse Sector had been unlocked. He put the device away and went to his small ship just outside the boundaries of the Orbital Sector pleased with the success of the mission.

◆

It was Thursday afternoon and almost two weeks had passed since Elias' adventurous night. The day after learning about his father, he asked Kabec if what had happened to his dad was normal among Kabec's people, but Kabec said he had never heard of such an occurrence. That same day, Elias' mother had learned of the decision Elias would have to make, and she told him that he needed to go to the ship. She didn't want him to leave, but she knew that he needed to learn more about his powers.

School had ended the week before on Tuesday, but Elias was still busy. He started the process of packing his belongings and he and his mom also spent time fabricating a story to tell everyone they knew to explain his upcoming disappearance.

The sun beamed high in the sky and Elias was tossing a baseball around with his best friend Isaiah.

"I'm going on a trip to the Amazon jungle for about two years," Elias told him as he threw the baseball to Isaiah.

Isaiah caught the ball and held on to it. He just stared at Elias for a few seconds before throwing the ball back to him.

"The Amazon jungle? Where did you even find out about something like this?" asked Isaiah.

"I was reading some guy's blog on the internet about him going there a few years ago and it seemed pretty interesting so I looked it up online. I'd be part of a group of students that live in the Amazon and we'd get taught by a couple teachers while we're living there. But since I found out about the program rather late, I had to make a decision pretty quickly," said Elias as he threw the ball up high like a fly ball.

"When are you leaving for this Amazon jungle trip?" asked Isaiah after he caught the ball.

Then he threw a grounder to Elias. Elias snatched it with his glove.

"Early Saturday morning after the summer celebration tomorrow night. Like I said, I had to make a decision really quickly," said Elias.

"Saturday morning. We've been friends for nine years and you tell me you're leaving the country for two years only two days before you have to go?" asked Isaiah

"You were on a cruise ship for a week. How was I supposed to tell you?" asked Elias.

Isaiah shook his head and they continued tossing around the ball for a few minutes.

"Let's go inside. It's getting hot out here," said Isaiah.

"Alright," said Elias.

He and Isaiah headed into Isaiah's home. Once inside, they got snacks from the pantry and went to Isaiah's room. Elias felt bad about lying to Isaiah, but he knew he couldn't tell him the truth. No matter how good a friend he was, he knew he couldn't ask him to keep such a huge secret. Elias had said goodbye to all his other friends earlier in the week. Each time he told them he would be leaving for the Amazon jungle, the fact that he was leaving Earth for the Shockwave dawned on him more and more.

Elias sat down on Isaiah's bed while taking off his glove and then he put the baseball inside the glove. He set the glove down on the floor and looked around the room, realizing that this was the last time he would be inside it. He had hung out with Isaiah in here so many times, but he never got used to all the crazy things Isaiah had. On top of his dresser was his prized chewing gum collection. Isaiah had kept chewing gum from every single time he ever bought a new pack. He even dated the time and place he bought it from. Elias remembered asking him why, but Isaiah never gave him a good reason. On the wall, to the left of the dresser, hung an old St. Louis football jersey from the year 2000, with the number 81 and the name Hakim on the back. He remembered Isaiah telling him that his grandfather Ashok had given it to him. Nobody had any idea who the player was or why his grandpa had given him that jersey so everyone in the family just assumed that his grandpa had gone crazy by then. Underneath the jersey on the wall was a television that was so old that it didn't work with cable. It had a slot in it for these things called VHS tapes that were like big square books that played grainy, old films.

"C'mon, Elias. You're not seriously going to the Amazon jungle. You're just making that up. I've known you for nine years. There's no way you would just decide to go to the Amazon jungle," said Isaiah, who was sitting in his computer chair.

"I don't know what else to say. If you don't believe me, there's nothing I can do about it," said Elias.

There was a long pause during which they looked at each other in awkward silence. Isaiah sighed.

"Well, whatever it is that you're actually doing that you can't tell me about, good luck."

"Thanks, Isaiah," said Elias.

There was another long period of awkward silence.

"Your mom making her apple pies for the summer celebration tomorrow?" asked Isaiah changing the subject.

"Yeah. She started making them before I left," said Elias.

"I'm telling you, she could open up her own shop selling those things. They're amazing," said Isaiah as he took the baseball from Elias' glove and began spinning in up into the air. "You hear that they're opening up an RBR store in town?"

"Where at?" asked Elias.

"Next to the movie theater on Pine Street," said an excited Isaiah.

Elias and Isaiah kept talking and Elias updated Isaiah on what had happened in the past week while he was gone on the cruise. Elias hung out with Isaiah for the rest of the night enjoying his time with his best friend and forgetting all about having to leave for the Shockwave in a few days.

Chapter 6: A Day's Work

An alarm sounding like orchestra music rang out, breaking the silence in the cabin. Elias' opened his eyes, but he was still tired as he turned over on his bed and put the covers over his head trying to block out the sound. It was his second morning aboard the Shockwave and he hadn't gotten much sleep since coming on board.

"Fifteen more minutes. Just shut up for fifteen more minutes," said Elias to the noise echoing throughout his cabin.

A pleasant female voice spoke out throughout the cabin.

"I am sorry, Elias, but I have been programmed to wake you at this time and I am not allowed to turn off the alarm until I have sensed that you are awake," the voice said.

"I wouldn't be talking to you if I weren't awake," exclaimed Elias, as he put a pillow over his head.

The orchestral music kept playing, and after a few minutes, the gateway to Elias' cabin opened with a swishing sound. Kabec walked in and sat down on a chair near Elias' bed. Next to the bed was a device which Kabec began to manipulate using the energy scanner on it. The orchestral music turned off and Elias lifted his head from under the covers.

"Why does the alarm have to be on every morning?" asked Elias.

"The ship's hierarchy want you to get used to our times standards. That's why they put the adjustment device in your room. It'll help you get used to our customs," said Kabec, shifting his chair.

"Well, that thing should at least have a snooze command," said Elias as he got up from the bed rubbing his eyes.

"Your breakfast has been prepared for you, Elias," said the female voice.

"Thanks," said Elias.

He used his energy to take a tray that appeared from a compartment in the wall near the entrance of his cabin and set it down on a small dining table.

"So when do I start learning how to make my own food?" asked Elias.

"Hopefully later today. We can go buy food for you once you're processed. Then, Tasich is going to teach you the nuances of the foods we have in the Universe and show you how to cook them properly," said Kabec. "Also, if I'm on guard duty at the transports, Siara will be able to help you with anything you need. She's more knowledgeable than I am on most questions you might have. I'll give you her contact information later when you receive your new clothes and HoloTele."

"Oh right. You said yesterday that you'd tell me what you did on board the ship. So, what are these transports and why are you guarding them?" asked Elias.

Elias took a sip of a strange greenish-brown liquid that was on his breakfast tray. Despite the look, the drink was quite good and had a taste similar to that of a fruit smoothie.

"Transports are the large rocks that your people call asteroids. We use them to disguise our movements. Not that it's a big deal if you guys found out about us, but that often proves to be bothersome rather than helpful," said Kabec. "My job is to guard them so that our ship knows who's coming in and out of the area. I also have to make sure that there isn't any illegal usage of them, like when you were unlocked."

Elias continued eating his breakfast as Kabec checked his HoloTele. There were five small, purple balls, the size of marbles, and two white cubes of some flaky food, the size of Elias' palms, next to the drink on his tray. Elias picked up one of the purple balls, put it in his mouth, and bit down. He was pleased to find that it had a soft texture and sweet juices started spreading inside his mouth.

"So what's on my plate today?" asked Elias.

Kabec looked up from his HoloTele and surveyed the tray.

"The drink is called elifran. It's made of walio plant and juice from the rivers of the Conservatory Sector. The purple fruit is called nadu and it comes from the Spiral Sector. Those white cubes are called orteya. They're a local delicacy from the Sunset Sector," said Kabec, looking back to his HoloTele.

Elias cut up a quarter of an orteya. He put it into his mouth and it dissolved as it hit his tongue, tasting like a vanilla milkshake with almonds, only better. Elias closed his eyes as he enjoyed the scrumptious flavor of the orteya. After finishing the first bite, he gulped down the remaining orteya that was left on his plate before consuming the remaining nadu.

"So I've looked at the schedules and planned out what we'll do today," said Kabec. "First, we'll finish the tour of the other parts of the ship we were unable to see yesterday. Then, we'll eat and get you processed before going back to the teaching arena to have you signed up for private beginner's lessons. Afterwards, we'll go buy the books for your classes and buy your food as well. That should conclude the setup for your adjustment phase. After that, you'll be free to do whatever you want for the rest of the day."

Elias nodded and finished his breakfast, drinking the last sip of elifran. Then, he guided his tray back to the compartment in the wall, which closed afterwards. Kabec manipulated the energy scanner on the adjustment device and then moved towards the entrance to the cabin. Elias got up and went to the bathroom, which was similar to the one he had seen in the captain's ship deck. He went to brush his teeth with the new toothbrush he was given the day before. The toothbrush was connected to the sink and it worked using a high rate of vibrations, but felt soft to the touch. He had been told that with this toothbrush, toothpaste wasn't necessary, but there would be small amounts of enhanced water sprayed on his teeth every five seconds from the toothbrush. As he spit out the water from his mouth, the light strip that ran around the edge of the sink lit up and four sprayers opened up from the sink to release small amounts of water into the bowl. Then, the middle of the sink opened and the spit and water went down the drain. As soon as all the spit was down the drain, the sprayers stopped releasing more water and the sink closed as Elias finished brushing. He had already learned the day before that the sink was programmed to determine what was needed by the user allowing it to conserve water for when it was needed.

He pushed a button next to the mirror that lay on top of the sink and from the wall came a device. He put his hands inside for about eight seconds as it misted a cleaning fluid over his hands and dried them. The device then went back into the wall and Elias left the bathroom.

Elias walked back into the bedroom and saw Kabec at the entrance with the gateway open.

"You ready to leave?" asked Kabec.

"Almost. Just let me get my shoes on," said Elias as he moved towards the bed.

He put on his shoes and walked out of his cabin into the hallway. Kabec closed the gateway behind them and swiped a card on the gateway's scanner to lock the cabin before flying off. Elias and Kabec flew side-by-side with each other near the top of the cabin hallway as they went, passing by multitudes of people below them, some of whom were walking on the floor. As Elias had learned the day before, some people preferred to walk from time to time, especially in the cabin hallways where there was an abundance of children flying sporadically about. Elias had also noticed on the previous day's tour that most of the hallways aboard the Shockwave looked similar to the one that led to the captain's ship deck. The few exceptions were the hallways that led to the outside of the ship which looked similar to the hallway connected to the shipping bay.

The Shockwave was a large ship, but the ship's core operating system and storage space made up about half of the ship's size. On a daily basis, the ship held around one million people, most of whom were human. Elias had yet to see someone that wasn't human, but Kabec said last night that they would meet one today.

"Our first stop is the manufacturing room where they make stadium equipment and maps. Those are our two biggest exports," said Kabec, gliding through the hallway towards an intersection.

"Stadium equipment?" asked Elias.

"Yeah, for Orace Petrans matches. Oh, I forgot. You haven't heard of the Orace Petrans yet," Kabec said, moving lower in the hallway with Elias following him.

"No. What is it?" Elias asked.

They made a right turn into a new hallway and began heading towards the lower parts of the ship.

"Well, it's a fighting competition and it dates back so far in history that even the Clierns' historians don't know much about how it started. The name itself supposedly comes from the names of the final two contestants from the very first one. Anyways, like I said, it's a fighting competition and it cycles only once every three and a half serays so each one is really important. Anyone from anywhere in the Universe can take part in it if they want to," said Kabec.

They continued weaving in and out of hallways and the traffic was beginning to die down. As they flew, Kabec continued telling Elias about the Orace Petrans.

"The competition cycle starts off with local matches to determine who'll compete in the league matches. That usually takes about one yelding. Then, they have a three yelding break before the league matches begin. There's about eight yeldings worth of round robin league matches and then a four yelding break. At the end of the league matches, twenty four of the top fighters move on to the Orace Petrans championship rounds, which take place over the next eight yeldings. The top eight seeded competitors get a pass in the first round and they battle single elimination all the way through the championship match," explained Kabec. "The champion of the Orace Petrans is then declared an Elite Ilay Force member and is put in charge of security for a whole galaxy of their choosing."

"Sounds intense. So who's the Elite Ilay Force member in the Milky Way?" asked Elias.

"There isn't one. Nobody's chosen our galaxy, which is why that guy Jaru that you heard about yesterday can do whatever he wants," said Kabec slowing down outside a large clear gateway.

Elias looked through the gateway and he saw masses of people inside split into numerous large, transparent workstations with an array of objects in their grasps, guiding huge chunks of materials into machines, and spraying fluids.

"Here we are. This is our money maker. The stadium objects are being cranked out in there. The maps are also being made in here, but it's blocked off by that wall over there. They ship everything out on the right side of the room, which is connected to shipping bay. Follow me," said Kabec, waving his card past the scanner on the gateway and flying into the room after it opened.

They flew up towards the ceiling of the room and Elias watched the ceiling tiles change colors. He was amazed by the advanced technology he learned about the day before. The tiles on the ceiling detected traffic and sent the data back to a portal on the ship where people's jobs dealt with analyzing it and creating efficient solutions for any traffic issues before problems arose.

Elias looked away from the ceiling, which was a few feet above them now, and out over the room they were in. It was much bigger than it seemed from outside and he could see the far end of the room a few miles away from where they were, but only on the right side, where there was no wall blocking his view. The noise inside the room was immense, and people had on odd headsets that were connected to their suits. From the corner of his eye he saw a flash of green and turned his eyes thinking that he'd seen someone that wasn't human. To his dismay, it was just a human wearing a green spacesuit and Elias looked back towards Kabec, who began gliding along further into the room, signaling for Elias to follow him.

Kabec moved towards the floor, careful to avoid the people whizzing by, and Elias did the same as he followed. When they reached the floor, they had landed inside a rectangular cubicle with a long desk that spanned the width of the cubicle. Behind the desk was a woman with long, curly, black hair, who looked like she was in her late thirties. Kabec made gestures towards his ears at the woman, who glared back at Kabec. She did not seem like a person Elias would want to have on his bad side. She flew from behind the desk with two of the odd headsets and placed them on Kabec and Elias, connecting the one she put on Kabec to the spacesuit he wore.

A voice, which Elias assumed to be the woman's, began speaking.

"Kabec, you were supposed to signal me to give you the headsets before you came into the room. I assume this is Elias?" asked the woman.

"Sorry, Sredia. I forgot. I don't usually come in here," said Kabec. "Elias, this is Sredia Phenper. She's head of manufacturing and in charge of this entire room."

"Hello," said Elias.

"Hi, dear," said Sredia with a smile. She turned to Kabec and asked, "How long will you two be in here?"

"Probably just an hour," responded Kabec.

"Okay. Be sure to check out with me when you leave," said Sredia, as she moved back to her position behind the desk.

"Yes, ma'am," Kabec replied. Then he said, "Alright. Let's go, Elias."

He flew back up towards the ceiling. Elias followed him and Kabec continued to talk.

"So this is where you'll be working in about three yeldings. You'll probably be helping Sredia with small stuff until we can find you a more permanent job," he said.

Elias nodded as he kept flying behind Kabec. He saw another person in a green suit and remembered that Kabec said he would see a non-human today.

"Are there any non-humans in here?" Elias asked.

"No. I already told you, there aren't that many of them aboard our ship. You should see one when we go to the training arena though," he replied.

They kept flying near the top of the room while Kabec pointed out the variety of stadium tiles that were being built. There were large, square tiles with octagons of varying sizes etched on them; large, rectangular tiles with a kite shape logo painted onto one of the corners; shiny, circular tiles of different sizes placed into square tiles with a hole in them;, plain, square tiles of varying sizes; and many other sorts.

"A dozen people usually work in a group for each different type of tile. The more important tiles over there have about sixteen to twenty people working on them though," said Kabec, pointing to an area where several groups were making more complex looking tiles.

They slowed to a halt when they neared the center of the vast stadium equipment making region of the room. Kabec looked out over the many people working.

"They make thousands of tiles every week, but most of our customers only need them for training purposes. It makes the job for these guys a whole lot easier though because they don't inspect the training quality tiles. They only inspect the tiles for actual matches, but that's only about nine weeks of extra work every seray," said Kabec.

"How many hours do people usually work in a day?" Elias asked.

"Usually four hours a day, but it can vary based on the tile group you're in. I know a few of them work two hours a day and some others spend six hours a day. The more complex the tile, the longer it takes to finish the work. Thing is, they obviously pay more to the people working longer," said Kabec, as he waved a hand at Elias signaling them to keep moving.

Elias continued looking at the different groups making the stadium tiles. There were so many different processes going on at once. He saw one man using his energy through a tool to etch patterns into a polished, square tile while another was placing circular tiles into a machine that enclosed them and spit them out looking the same as when they had entered. People were flying around the room with bags of materials in a variety of colors that they would drop off to groups that were working and other people were packing finished tiles into metal boxes. Elias noticed the boxes weren't ordinary though as they would adjust sizes for each layer of tile that was placed in them or change shape on their own based on the tiles being added.

"Why are they using so many different colors for making the same tile?" asked Elias, pointing to one group making red, blue, green, and black tiles.

"Each sector orders different sets of colors than the other sectors in their local galaxy group. They want to show that they're different from everyone else. Some sectors even order tiles in uncommon colors to try and make them stand out. That group over there is making tiles in indigo, cerulean, viridian, and saffron," said Kabec, pointing to the group making those colored tiles.

Next to the group that Kabec had pointed out, was another group that contained about forty people, much more than any Elias had seen throughout the entire manufacturing floor. They were making gigantic clear tiles the size of gateways and there were no modifications that Elias could see being added to them. Every now and then, a worker would hold up a tile while another worker would blast it with their own energy.

"What are those guys in the corner over there doing?" asked Elias.

"Oh, they're making different tiles than everyone else. Those are the stadium shield tiles that protect the people attending the matches from the actual fighting that goes on. Those tiles have to go through rigorous testing because if one of them breaks someone usually ends up getting seriously hurt. Oh, and it also stops the fight because new tiles have to be put in place of the broken ones."

"Do they break often?" asked Elias.

"No. If they break, the manufacturers are the ones who have to pay to fix the problems, not to mention the manufacturers lose any reputation they had for making stadium quality tiles," replied Kabec. "I've only heard of those tiles breaking twice before. The last time one broke was around one hundred twelve serays ago and the time before that was around three hundred ninety-six serays ago, when four of them broke from the same blast."

"Must've been some fight," said Elias.

"I imagine so," said Kabec.

They were drifting to the end of the stadium tile section of the room and approaching the wall that separated the map making region of the room. They glided along the wall moving to the right and Elias looked ahead towards the shipping region of the room. He could see the large corridor Kabec mentioned earlier that led to the shipping bay. The vehicles in the corridor moved like clockwork. Elias stopped looking over at the shipping area as they reached the wall's end and they turned to the left. They had now reached the other side where the maps were being made.

The map making scene was quite different than that of the stadium equipment. For one, there were no enclosed workstations. Instead, there was one continuously long work bench that snaked from one end to the other in a U-shape, reminding Elias of an assembly line. The only tools that people were working with were HoloTeles as each person was adjusting hologram maps that appeared from a device used to display the maps.

"Not much to tell you about here. What you see is pretty much what you get. Each person is assigned to a specific HoloTele, which has a different local galaxy group, and they make sure everything is properly updated and uploaded into the system."

"So everyone has the maps on their HoloTeles?"

"Oh, no. Those HoloTeles don't belong to the workers. They stay here and are locked into the workstation," said Kabec. "They're also not connected to any outside networks so no one could hack into them, although accessing any classified data is near impossible anyways without authorized personnel. Actually, most people don't have maps because they are extremely expensive to make due to all the work that goes into them. There are over ten thousand workers here and there are another one thousand that do quality checks on the completed devices in a room elsewhere on the ship."

"Oh okay."

He and Kabec were floating in the same spot, not having moved any closer to the map makers since they had made the turn past the wall. Kabec scanned the map makers as he was thinking.

"Let's see. What else is there about this place that I can tell you? They make about two hundred maps each week. Most of the maps go out to special institutions, but there are always a handful of people that buy them because they have the money," said Kabec.

Elias interrupted him. "What are special institutions?"

"Sorry, I forget that you don't know these things. Special institutions are the name we give ships of the larger variety like this one that are not for transport, but for everyday living," replied Kabec. "Um, anyways, so the maps usually go to special institutions and the special institutions are then able to send them out through their data system using detailed energy scanning to transport ships." There was a brief pause. "I think that's about it. We should get going anyways. We're running a little behind schedule now."

"Okay," replied Elias.

They flew back towards the entrance of the room on route to Sredia's cubible. When they reached Sredia's cubible, she escorted them out of the room and then took their headsets from them. They both waved goodbye to her and glided off to their next stop, the training arena.

Chapter 7: The Man in the Booth

Elias noticed that the hallways were always bustling with people whom often stopped to talk to others they knew. Black screens were abundant along the walls and vendors selling food, books, and gadgets were spread throughout the ship. Every now and then Kabec would wave to someone he knew, but he didn't stop to chat. Soon, the number of people in the hallways they flew through diminished and Kabec began to fly faster.

"The training arena is up ahead. Fighters are usually the only ones around here at this time of day."

"I'm feeling a surge in energy coming from up there," Elias said.

Kabec looked towards Elias while gliding along the hallway.

"That's normal. The people at the training arena usually have the highest energies on the ship," he said.

Kabec slowed down and looked toward the end of the hallway. Elias could sense someone approaching them. Then, he saw something wobbling on four legs start to come into their hallway from a connected one at the end of their hallway. Elias didn't know what it was, but it was not human. Its teal skin and hairless body reflected under the lights. Although lengthy, the creature was very short, making it look like a mix between a crocodile and dinosaur. Finally. Someone that wasn't human, thought Elias.

Just as the creature began to stand on two of its legs, Kabec shot a large burst of energy at it and then began flying towards it. Why had Kabec attacked the creature?

Elias watched the creature crash hard into the wall at the end of the hallway after being hit by the blast. Its skin slipped off its body a bit and the creature got up and moaned.

"What's the deal, Kabec? Why you gotta hit me like that?" asked the creature.

"Stop whining like you're actually hurt. What are you doing here anyways, Quincey?" asked Kabec.

Quincey popped up and the skin he wore had come off, revealing that it was a complex costume. Quincey was a human just like Elias and Kabec and his bright blue eyes stared at Elias, observing him like a museum exhibit.

With enthusiasm, Quincey responded. "Well, when I heard Siara say that you were showing the new guy around, I had to come see you guys," he said. He turned back to Elias and shook his hands. "Name's Quincey. Quincey with an e. And you are?"

Quincey stopped shaking his hands and took out something similar to a pair of glasses. He blew on them, wiped them clean and put them back in his spacesuit rather than putting them on. Then, he looked back at Elias with a smile.

Elias responded looking rather befuddled.

"My name's Elias – Elias Rayhan. It's, uh, nice to meet you, Quincey," he said.

"Nice to meet you too, Elias," responded Quincey. He turned to Kabec. "Hey, Kabec. Not only do I get to see you guys, but it's also the perfect excuse to watch the training arena. Vardun is preparing for his match and he's putting on quite a show."

Quincey looked at Kabec, who seemed to have no reaction to the news. After a short pause, Kabec smiled.

"Interesting. Is he practicing with Samara?" asked Kabec.

"Yep," said Quincey smiling. "I wonder if she could get me into a practice with him. You know, when he's not busy."

Kabec shook his head.

"Go back to work, Quincey. I'm busy and the sooner we move along, the sooner I'll be free today. I'll see you later," Kabec said.

"Later," said Quincey.

He flew around them once before swooping down to pick up his costume. Then, he sped off down the hallway.

Elias looked on, baffled at how Quincey had acted. He turned to Kabec, who chuckled.

"Quincey's not like that most of the time. He acts goofy every now and then. Once you get to know him though, it's hard not to become friends with him," he said.

"I see," said Elias. "Who's Samara?"

"She's a friend of ours," Kabec answered. "Her family and Vardun's family have known each other for a while so they've trained together ever since she started fighting herself."

"Oh, okay," said Elias.

"The training arena is just down the hall here," Kabec said flying up ahead towards a clear window.

Elias followed him the short distance before they reached the window, which Elias recognized to be a multitude of stadium shield tiles they had seen in the manufacturing room. He looked through the tiles and his mouth opened in shock because there below them lay an enormous, picturesque training arena with bright lights and numerous booths layered about for people to watch.

Kabec must have seen the expression on Elias' face.

"I know. It's pretty cool," said Kabec.

"I feel like I'd be like a gladiator if I was in there," Elias replied.

Inside the vastness of the training arena he noticed two people with illuminated spacesuits floating in the air spread about a half mile apart near the center of the training arena.

"Is that Vardun and Samara?" asked Elias.

"Yeah. I assume they're taking a break for a bit," said Kabec while he started using a small black screen that was by the window. "I'm going to check when they're scheduled to finish. Since I'm showing you around for the first time, I've been given permission for us to watch from one of the booths. Normally those are reserved for people that buy them out."

Elias nodded and Kabec continued using the small black screen. Elias looked back out to the arena and waited for something to happen. After a couple minutes had passed, he saw Vardun and Samara move further away from each other landing on two separate platforms that were hovering in the air.

A few seconds later Elias sensed an uptick in energy coming from Vardun as he jettisoned himself down towards the floor with blistering speed leaving a long, grayish-white streak in his wake. Elias sensed Samara moving as well, but her energy was lower than that of Vardun's, who flew faster than she did. However, she did not follow Vardun. Instead, she flew towards one of the many square stadium tiles floating around the arena, one that had a circular tile placed within it. By the time she had reached the tile, Elias sensed Vardun was already coming back up from the floor at her with two smaller square tiles that were glowing and had archer's targets etched into them. He sensed Samara use her energy to dislodge the circular tile and take the disc with her as she retreated higher with her back facing the ceiling.

Elias was focused on the battle at hand, but looked over to Kabec as he spoke.

"I got everything worked out," he said. He paused and looked to the arena. "It looks like they finished their break, but they're almost out of time with their session so they'll be done soon. Let's quickly go sit down and watch what we can."

Elias saw that a lighted hallway had opened up to their left. He followed Kabec, who flew through the hallway, before turning right and unlocking the gateway into a booth. Kabec waited for Elias to go in first before closing the gateway behind them.

Inside the booth were many chairs with tall backs, and on the left was an unattended station for food. The chairs were spread about on three different levels with tables in front of each chair. The booth was rather dark inside as one dim light lit up the room.

"Where do I sit?" asked Elias sensing that someone else was in the booth with them.

A gruff voice emanated from the lowest level of the booth. "Down here," it said.

Kabec flew to the lowest tier of seats in the booth. Elias followed behind, curious as to who was in the booth with them. There were four chairs on the lowest level and whoever was in the booth with them was sitting in the chair second from the left. Elias couldn't see who it was as Kabec blocked his view while greeting him with a handshake and talking in soft whispers. Once Kabec had finished shaking hands, he moved past the person and sat in the chair to the far left.

After Kabec had moved, Elias saw the person and stared at him, rather dumbfounded. In front of Elias was a man with pitch black skin, a pure white face, and a patch of bright yellow hair on top of his head. Even his eyeballs were solid black and Elias realized the man was not wearing a spacesuit, but a pair of tight black trunks that Elias could see because of the reflections the trunks gave off from the dim light. The man had no nipples and his muscles were uniform throughout his body beneath his smooth skin. He had hands the same as those of a human, but no toes on his feet, which looked similar to scuba fins, only thicker.

The man scanned Elias up and down.

"Yes, you must be Elias. Even the young humans on the ship don't look at me like that," he said. He let out a deep sigh. Then, he spoke in a thick voice. "Well, sit down now. You don't want to miss Vardun's training. That is what you two came here to see, isn't it?"

Elias nodded and sat down in the chair to the man's right. Elias was quite stunned by his first encounter with a non-human. He tried to relax as he sat on the chair, the blue cushions conforming to his body. His eyes were now back on the training arena as he watched the battle rage on inside.

Despite being unable to watch the battle during their quick move to the booth, he had still been able to sense what had happened between Vardun and Samara. Vardun was a stronger fighter than Samara, but her tactics would sometimes help her overcome her shortcomings in power and speed.

Samara used many of the tiles as defense mechanisms and she had five small, oblong spherical tiles with her while Vardun was floating near the middle of the arena. Vardun fired off streaks of energy around her before moving closer and taking a large square tile with stripes etched on it. Samara fended off the energy attacks with two of her tiles and aimed another two in the direction where Vardun went to after having taken his striped tile. The two tiles exploded to dust as they neared Vardun, but missed him as he avoided them and fired off his striped tile at Samara. She moved the remaining tile she had behind her before curling up into a ball. She spun and was rolling in place, firing off energy to deflect the energy coming from the striped tile which had shattered and released six long horizontal lines of energy at her. After deflecting the attack, she fired off the last tile she had at Vardun as she came out of her spin.

Instead of avoiding the blast as he had done before, Vardun grasped the tile with his energy before the tile had a chance to release its energy. He swung it in a circle around him before redirecting it back at Samara, who had sped off towards the other end of the arena after throwing her tile. Elias sensed Vardun swing the tile back to Samara while he conjured up a separate energy blast, which he directed at where Samara would go to avoid being hit by her own tile.

"Watch out. Don't go to the corner," blurted Elias, so focused on the battle that he forgot that they couldn't hear him inside the training arena.

It was too late. Samara had indeed avoided being hit by her own tile coming back, but was leveled by the second blast from Vardun that sent her smashing into the wall.

Elias looked over to his left to see the man and Kabec's reactions, but they were both just staring at him.

"I'm sorry. Was it bad that I yelled out what was happening?" asked Elias, unsure of what was wrong.

They both kept staring at him for a few awkward seconds.

"No, it's not bad. It's actually quite remarkable for someone like you. You were able to sense that coming?" the man asked.

"Yes," Elias replied. "Is something wrong about that? You guys were able to sense it too, right?"

The man smiled and laughed. "Well, of course I was able to sense it. I've been sensing for well over a hundred serays now," he said.

"I wasn't able to," said Kabec, looking at Elias from his chair on the far left.

"Oh. I thought everyone could sense energy? I mean, I've been sensing like that since I've been on this ship," Elias said.

The man got up from his chair and flew over to the food station.

"Well, yes, everyone can sense energy, but most people don't sense that well. For the most part, a person's ability to sense is reflected in their energy level," said Kabec still looking puzzled. "It usually takes someone serays of practice to sense like that…and yet you say you've been sensing like that this whole time. Interesting."

Kabec shook his head after his last statement, grabbed his HoloTele from his suit, and began fidgeting with it. After a minute, Kabec looked up from his HoloTele.

"I'll be back in a bit," he said to Elias.

Elias watched Kabec leave the booth. He looked to the training arena, but he had already known from his senses that the battle had ended and both Vardun and Samara had left. Sitting in his chair, Elias wondered if he should have just kept his mouth shut. The other man came back to his seat from the food station.

"You look tense. Lighten up. You should be happy that you have such extraordinary gifts," the man said. He put his tray of food down on the table in front of his chair. "I don't believe I had the chance to introduce myself to you, Elias. My name is Jeeho Lavidaus."

Elias shook hands with Jeeho, who had a firm grip.

"Hello. Um, just curious, but, what exactly are you?" asked Elias. "I don't mean to be rude. It's just that, I've only seen humans before."

"Yes, yes. I know all about you. Don't worry about it," Jeeho said while smiling. He brought a glass of elifran from his plate to his mouth and took a sip before leaving the glass floating next to him. "I am an ivorian. My species originated on the planet Light Shadows, but I was born and raised on the planet Silicate, where most of the people on this ship used to live."

Jeeho took another sip from his glass before eating a bright orange puree on his plate.

"I'm sorry, but I haven't been taught much about the geography here so I don't know anything about either of those two planets. Are they close by here?" asked Elias.

Jeeho had been eating the puree using his energy to suck it into his mouth like it was spaghetti. He stopped the steady stream of puree coming from the plate and licked his lips.

"Hmm, well for you, I'd say probably not. However, to us, it is somewhat close by," he replied. "Silicate is on the other side of the center of this galaxy from where we are now and Light Shadows is a small obscure planet about one star away from Silicate. I imagine your people, having stayed only on one planet, believe these distances to be quite far though, do they not?"

"Yes, that's definitely far for where I come from," said Elias.

Jeeho continued to eat the food on his plate and the room was silent for several minutes. Elias stared into the empty training arena wondering when Kabec would be back and what it was that he was doing. Elias looked over at Jeeho, who had finished eating.

"So what do you do on the ship?" Elias asked.

"I give help to the map makers from time to time. Many serays ago, I was an explorer though, searching the undiscovered areas of space," said Jeeho.

"An explorer. Did you ever come across anything interesting?" asked Elias.

"Only once," said Jeeho in a low voice. "I visited a planet not far from the outskirts of this sector. It was full of human life, but none of them possessed energy. Back then, I was always fascinated by those who lived without energy, but I kept to myself since they wouldn't have seen anything like me before. I observed them from a distance, but I could have sworn I was being followed by someone because I kept sensing an extremely faint energy source somewhere near me. Then one day, I stumbled upon some old boulders by a canyon near the town I was observing and ancient symbols of our people's past were etched into them. It didn't make sense to me how the ancient symbols were carved into the boulders. They were almost impossible to reach without energy so it must've been there for quite some time. I tried getting a closer look at the boulders and I flew over to them. I was floating over them, scanning the symbols hoping to recognize what they meant, but then I heard feet stomping on the ground not too far from me, coming in my direction."

Jeeho sighed and took a deep breath.

"Unfortunately for me, a man from the town had been riding by on his animal and saw me flying over the boulders. As you now know, those of us with energy are taught by our elders not to show ourselves to those without so I knew I had to leave the planet immediately. I'm sure after a while the man that saw me will think I was simply an illusion, but I never got the chance to look at those ancient symbols ever again."

The gateway to the booth opened and Kabec had come back in looking calm now.

"Sorry about that. We need to get going though, Elias. We have to make a stop by the captain's ship deck now before we go to the processing room," said Kabec.

"Oh, right. Okay," Elias answered. He turned to Jeeho. "It was nice to meet you, Jeeho."

"Yes. I'm sure we'll talk again someday," Jeeho said.

Elias got up from his seat and flew out of the booth following Kabec, who moved at a quick pace.

"Why are we going to the captain's ship deck?" asked Elias.

"You'll find out when we get there, but the sooner we do the better. Captain Renalt is taking time from his check of the ship to see us," said Kabec, picking up the pace.

They weaved through the hallways and away from the training arena. As they flew towards the captain's ship deck, Elias thought this unscheduled visit to Captain Renalt must be related to his unusual sensing during Vardun's training session. After a short period of time, they arrived outside the gateway of the captain's ship deck. Kabec swiped a card in the front of the energy scanner on the gateway, which then opened.

They both flew into the room, where waiting for them, at the far table that Elias had sat at a few weeks earlier, were Captain Renalt, Raina,

Kerlan, and Ramses. They all looked up from the lighted tabletop screen when Kabec and Elias had flown into the room. The two middle chairs at the table were left empty for Elias and Kabec.

Captain Renalt smiled. "Hello, you two. Elias, it's good to see you chose to stay aboard the Shockwave. Could you please stand over here in front of the table? And Kabec, have a seat by me please."

Kabec glided into a chair at the table while Elias floated over to the spot which Captain Renalt had pointed at.

"Is there something wrong?" asked Elias.

"Wrong? No. Out of the ordinary? Yes. But there's nothing for you to worry about. Raina, if you will please proceed," said Captain Renalt.

"Yes, Captain Renalt," Raina said.

She looked to the upper shelves where the many gadgets lay. She retrieved a large, cone-shaped, metallic one. The device turned on a lighted hologram screen with numerous options at the tip of the cone once she placed the device several feet from Elias. Raina then went up to the hologram screen.

She smiled at Elias. "This device measures the energy of an individual. All it does is scan a directed area and then give a reading which is accurate enough to determine what tier energy level someone possesses," she said. "Normally, this is illegal to use since it can supposedly measure the average energy potential that a child will have when they grow older. However, this device is also used to measure the potential of yellow diamonds, like you once were." She paused for a second. "Based on the story of your feats at the training arena that has been told to us by Kabec, we wish to measure your readings once more as our previous measurement for you would seem to be quite far off. The device takes approximately twenty seconds to work, but it requires that there be absolutely no release of energy throughout the process from the person being scanned. So, whenever you are ready to begin the test please say so."

Elias gulped before taking a deep breath and then letting out the air. He looked at all the faces staring at him from the table. He looked back to Raina, who was still smiling, waiting for him to give her the signal.

"Ready," said Elias.

When he saw Raina activate a button on the hologram screen, he closed his eyes, not knowing what to expect. He stood there, waiting for something to happen, but nothing did.

"You didn't need to close your eyes, dear," said Raina.

Elias opened his eyes and she was using the hologram display screen. She saw him open his eyes.

"The test is over. Thank you. You may have a seat at the table now," she said.

Relieved, Elias flew into the empty chair next to Kabec. Kabec smiled at him as he sat down. He heard Raina sigh while reading the hologram screen on the device. Then, she turned to the group at the table.

"Well, Captain Renalt, it reads the same as it did before," she said.

"Hmm. The energy predictor was never tested on yellow diamonds. It could simply be a flaw in its detection. I definitely sense more energy in him than what the readings tell us, but nothing so great that he should have been able to sense Vardun's movements," said a puzzled Captain Renalt.

"This is unusual, but there have been several cases in Cliern history of people with similar types of abilities," said Kerlan. "Zelake, an Elite Ilay of the Twilight Galaxy, was one that I can remember from my younger days. He had much more energy than Elias does, but still, Zelake was able to sense much more than his energy levels suggested."

"Yes, I remember reading articles about him. Captain, this is indeed an unusual phenomenon to most of us, but it is nothing new to the Clierns. Though there is no change in the readings from before, we will amend our earlier report to the Clierns to include a footnote about this new bit of information," said Raina.

Captain Renalt took a deep breath.

"Well then. It appears as though you are quite the unique person, Elias. I sincerely hope you use your gifts wisely," he said.

"Yes, Captain Renalt," replied Elias, happy that the tension in the room had dissipated.

"You two may leave now," said Captain Renalt as he looked to Elias and Kabec.

Kabec and Elias got up from their chairs and flew out of the room. After Kabec had closed the gateway behind him, he turned to Elias.

"Sorry I freaked out about it," he said. "It's just... well you heard them in there. This isn't something usual, especially to those of us that are younger. I mean I had never even heard of it before. I was—"

"It's okay, Kabec. I get it. I would have done the same thing," Elias said.

Having spent so much time together over the past few weeks, he had become good friends with Kabec. Elias knew Kabec was just trying to make sure he didn't screw up with any of his responsibilities involved in Elias' transition aboard the ship.

"Thanks," said Kabec. "Let's go eat and then we'll get you processed into the system."

They flew out of the captain's hallway and back into the bustling main hallways of the ship as Elias enlightened Kabec with the tale that Jeeho had told him in the booth.

Chapter 8: New Friends

"Here you go. The book on food basics. It has everything you need to know about our food in there," said Tasich, handing the book over to Elias. "I don't use it much anymore so you can keep it for now."

Elias had been introduced to Tasich by Kabec a few minutes ago. Tasich was a young, tall guy with dark brown skin, short black hair, and green eyes. He came off as someone who looked relaxed and pleasant to be around.

"Thanks. I'll be sure to make good use of it," said Elias.

He placed the book on a shelf with his other books and the new clothes he had gotten earlier in the day.

"Kabec said that you also need to learn how to use the cooking machines," Tasich said.

"Um, yeah. He said you'd show me how to cook, actually," replied Elias. "I haven't learned anything about the food here and I've been getting my food made for me the past two days."

"Right. I see the adjustment device in your cabin," said Tasich looking at the device. "I'm assuming you haven't been able to buy your own food then either?"

"No, not really. Well, after I got processed, we went to go buy some snacks from a vendor, but that's all we had time for before Kabec's shift started," answered Elias.

"We should go out and buy some food then. Can't make a meal without any ingredients," chuckled Tasich. "This works out quite well, actually. I'll be able to show you the different selection of food available at the stores."

They headed out of the cabin and Elias locked the gateway using the energy technique he had been taught when he was processed. He had a card that he could use just in case, but he wanted to get used to doing things the proper way.

After closing the gateway to his cabin, he and Tasich walked down the hallway. Kids flying in the hallway were abundant during this time of day since they were no longer in classes or getting training lessons. One of the kids came up next to Tasich and started walking with them.

"Hey, Tasich. How's it going? Who's the new guy? Aren't you gonna introduce me?" asked the kid.

Tasich laughed. "Whoa, calm down there, Cufri. I'll introduce you to him. This is Elias Rayhan. He was the yellow diamond on the Planet of Untouched Ones." Tasich turned to Elias. "Elias, this is Cufri Nytre."

"Cool. I've never seen a yellow diamond before," said Cufri.

"Uh, thanks," said Elias, who couldn't help but smile. "So, how old are you?"

"I'm six and a half serays old. How old are you?" asked Cufri.

"Um, hmm," said Elias realizing he had never actually calculated how many serays old he was before. "Let's see." He paused for a few seconds. "I'm twelve and a half serays old."

"He's two whole serays younger than you are, Tasich," said Cufri sounding surprised.

"Yeah," replied Tasich.

One of the other kids called out Cufri's name and Cufri looked over to her. She was waving for him to come over to a group of kids. Cufri flew off towards the group and waved goodbye to Elias and Tasich.

"See you guys later," Cufri said to the two.

"You know, you have a great cabin for someone living on their own. It's huge. They even gave you a lounge area and a small teletron too," said Tasich as they continued walking.

"Oh. Most people don't have teletrons?" asked Elias.

"Well, most families will usually have a teletron, but it's rare to see a single person have one because they're just so expensive," replied Tasich.

"Why's that?" asked Elias.

"I've never really thought about it much before. I guess it's because they don't make that many," said Tasich shrugging. "I mean teletrons are fun for watching Orace Petrans matches, cooking shows, and a few entertainment shows every once in a while. Otherwise there's really only the news and historical documentaries on most of the time. It's kind of a luxury since most businesses on the ship have communal teletrons for customers to watch. Besides, most of the time people would rather be out and about, socializing, training, or going on vacations."

They had reached the intersection outside Elias' cabin hallway, which connected to six other hallways. Elias looked at Tasich, waiting for him to pick one to go to.

"Okay, so before we go, you should know that there are nine grocery stores on this ship. You can find their locations on any of the black screens they have on the walls. They're pretty easy to use, so I'll let you figure them out later," Tasich said. He paused for a second. "The stores are all owned by different people and they all have the basic food supplies, but each one has their own unique supply of more exotic foods. For the most part, the quality of the basic foods don't vary that much from store to store. However, some of the items are better at different stores, but they usually charge extra for them. You got everything so far?"

Elias nodded. "I think so," he said.

"Great. I think we're ready to go then. We'll fly off into that hallway and go to Emium's grocery store. Follow me," said Tasich, as he flew up and over to one of the hallways Elias hadn't been down before. Tasich looked back at Elias. "Oh, right. I forgot. If you're ever looking for a snack, or a meal that's already made, you should go to a vendor. They're all different, but they all have decent food."

They flew through the trafficked hallway passing a few shops, some with shelves of books and others with several gadgets by the windows.

After a few minutes, they were floating by the entrance to a grocery store. The gateway was wide open and there was a small sign on the floor that read "Emium's grocery" just as they entered.

"Here we are," said Tasich.

Elias was confused. The place did not look like a typical grocery store. There were machines ten feet apart from each other on all sides that looked similar to mall directory maps. They spanned the width of the store, about an entire soccer field long and were stacked in five vertical rows. Behind the machines was a large, clear wall.

"What are those machines?" asked Elias. He could not see food anywhere.

"Those are the tellers. That's where we buy our food from. Let's go to one further up," said Tasich flying up to a machine on the right side of the second row from the top.

Once they reached the screen, Tasich tapped on it and it lighted up, showing a white background with a dark blue word *Austine* appearing in the center. Then, the screen switched to a menu of only two options.

"Austin with an e. Interesting," whispered Elias.

"Huh? Oh yeah. Austine is a group of famous energy coders from the Nocturnal Sector here in our galaxy. They made the programs for this grocery store, so their name appears on the screen every time you shop at a teller. After a while you get used to seeing it show up," said Tasich.

"Oh, okay," Elias said.

He started reading the different menu options that had come onto the screen. Tasich spoke to Elias while he read the screen.

"So the two options you see are either, *shop now*, or *schedule groceries to be delivered to your cabin*," he said. "Most families usually have their food delivered to them. You create a list of the things you need using the tellers and then the store continually sends them to your cabin about once every week. You can always change what food you get and how much food you receive by going to a teller at the store." Tasich paused. "You'll be choosing the *shop now* option though, since you still need to figure out what you'll usually get each week."

"Okay," said Elias, pushing the *shop now* menu button.

After pushing the button, an energy scanner came out from the right side of the machine.

"What do I do now?" asked Elias.

"So, the energy scanner comes out for you to input your specific energy code that you learned when you were processed. That energy code contains all the information about you. Once you put it into a scanner, the device is linked to the information it needs," said Tasich. "In this case, this scanner obtains your finances and cabin location, if you have one. This allows it to receive your payment for the groceries and also organize delivery for your food. Once you put your energy code in, a new menu of food will come up to let you shop."

Elias input his energy code into the scanner. Then, the scanner went back into the machine and a menu with hundreds of different food options appeared on the large screen.

"Wow, that's a lot of food," said a stunned Elias.

Tasich chuckled.

"I suppose. This is actually an average size grocery store. I've been to a few stores in larger sectors that have at least five times as many options as we do." He paused. "Okay. So this is actually simpler than it looks. Everything you see is placed into groups based on what type of food it is. For instance, here, you have your juices, *Bloodshot Pmelu*, *Conservatory River*, *Neural Berafe*, *Airglow Haeli*, and so on. The juices are always named by the sector they come from and the source from that sector."

Tasich pushed the menu option for *Conservatory River*. The large screen expanded the option and displayed numerous details about it along with a picture of the juice in a bowl.

"Okay, so here's one that a lot of people aboard the ship buy," said Tasich. "It's called Conservatory River, meaning it comes from the rivers of the Conservatory Sector."

"Oh, yeah. I remember that," interrupted Elias. "Kabec said that was in the elifran I drank for breakfast this morning."

"Yeah. Conservatory River juice is relatively inexpensive, so you'll see a lot of people drinking elifran. Um, okay, where was I?" Tasich asked aloud. Then, he quickly remembered. "So if you look at the screen here, you'll see details come up on the food you selected. This tells you the price, size, and shelf life of the food most importantly, but there's also some background on taste, smell, appearance, and uses for the food."

Elias read the details on the screen for the Conservatory River juice. The price, size, and shelf life showed only numbers, *23*, *8*, and *2*, respectively and the descriptions for taste, smell, and appearance were *slightly sweet*, *none*, and *clear*, respectively. Under uses was a list of items, including elifran and Elias assumed the rest of the items were also foods that could be made using the juice.

"Hello, Tasich," said a woman's voice from their left.

Both Tasich and Elias looked over to their left. Elias saw an elderly woman at the machine next to them.

"Oh, hello, Wexyne," said Tasich.

"What have you been doing since we last talked?" she asked.

"Let's see. I went to the Aden Experimental School for Cooking in the Pearl Sector about three yeldings ago. I was there for about five weeks learning how to become a professional chef."

"I'll have to come over sometime to try some of your food then," Wexyne said.

"It'd be my pleasure," said Tasich. Then, Tasich introduced Elias. "Wexyne, this is Elias Rayhan. He's the yellow diamond from the Planet of Untouched Ones. Elias, this is Wexyne Kirchodd."

"Hello," Elias said.

"Well, it sure is a pleasure to meet you, Elias. In all my serays, I have never actually met a yellow diamond face-to-face before. What do you think of our ship so far?" asked Wexyne smiling.

"Um, it's quite interesting. I'm just trying to get used to everything here. This is only my second day so I'm learning a lot still," responded Elias.

"I see. Well, make sure you treat him nicely, Tasich," said Wexyne.

"I will," said Tasich.

"It was nice talking to you two, but I have to be going now. I just came by to quickly change our delivery schedule. Me and Lemrus are going on vacation to the Rainbow Sector soon."

"I hope you have a good time," said Tasich.

"Thank you, dear," said Wexyne.

Then, she left Emium's grocery store. Tasich and Elias looked back to the large screen on their teller.

"So, back to the groceries," said Tasich. "I was thinking that we could make palemta. It's relatively quick and easy to make and doesn't require many ingredients. The recipe for palemta serves three regular plates, but I figure we should make more in case you like it and want more."

"Alright. What's palemta and what do you need to make it?" asked Elias.

"Palemta is a patty made from a mixture of taryium, which is a type of fish, esinse sauce, pieces of kadryeaum, which is a type of bread, and your choice of vegetables," answered Tasich. "I usually use walio plant and qualem as the vegetables."

"Okay," said Elias collapsing the Conservatory River juice option and looking at the hundreds of options on the screen. "So, where is--the seafood section? Hmm."

"Actually, if you just push that button in the corner there, it'll allow you to search for what you're trying to find," said Tasich.

"That's useful," said Elias.

He pushed the search button and typed in *taryium*. After he finished typing, the menu narrowed down to one button that read *Oceanic Taryium*, which Elias pushed. He looked at the price, size, and shelf life and saw *34*, *4*, and *1*, respectively.

"Oh right. I was going to ask before Wexyne started talking to us, what the units were for all these numbers," said Elias.

"Well, those three details are all standardized. Price has units of credits, size is in boxes per package, and the shelf life number refers to weeks after opening before it has to be thrown out," said Tasich.

"Boxes per package?" asked Elias.

"Yeah. The food is placed into standard sealed boxes and then the boxes are placed into packages. So when you get a package of the taryium, there are four boxes of it inside," replied Tasich.

"Okay, that makes sense," said Elias.

Elias read the details on the screen for the taryium, which also showed a picture of a normal looking fish. Then, he noticed an option on the expanded detail screen for the taryium that read *purchase*. He pushed it and a quantity field popped up, which read *1*.

"You'll want to change that to two," said Tasich watching Elias use the teller.

Elias changed the quantity to two and then hit the button to confirm. Afterwards, another screen popped up on the bottom right with a list that was similar to what would be seen when buying something on the internet on Earth.

"Here, let me help you find the rest of the stuff," said Tasich.

While Tasich helped Elias, he could not help but feel like he was shopping online, except it was strange since he was shopping for groceries. After a few minutes, they had added all the items to his purchase list that was needed to make palemta.

"You'll probably want something to drink as well," said Tasich. "I usually like to drink milk with my dinner, but it depends on how much you're willing to spend. Milk is a little more expensive than some drinks."

"Let's go with milk, then. I've got sixty thousand credits for the next three yeldings until I start working in the manufacturing room. The people who processed me told me it was above average for three yeldings of work, but they said I was given extra to try different things since I'm new," said Elias. "This counts, right? Or is it too expensive?"

"No, no. Milk definitely fits into that category. Wow. Sixty thousand credits and you have an awesome cabin," said Tasich. "They must really want you to like the ship so you stay on and don't go back to the Planet of Untouched Ones."

Elias bought a package of milk, which contained ten boxes and cost him one hundred forty credits. The shopping list on the screen displayed his final total as two hundred thirty-eight credits. An option on the shopping list read pay and Elias pressed it. He noticed a robot behind the clear wall come up to his teller, pause, and then go back down. Afterwards, right underneath the teller, a compartment opened with a metal box that had Elias' name etched on it. The energy scanner also popped out again.

"There's your stuff," said Tasich pointing to the box in the compartment. "You can take it and then you need to input your energy code again to confirm your purchase."

Elias took the box out with his energy.

"Where'd the robot come from?" he asked.

Then, Elias put his code into the energy scanner and it went back into the teller. Tasich answered as he and Elias left Emium's grocery store.

"They come from the warehouse down below. If you stood close to the wall you could see some of it. They made the wall clear so that kids can watch what goes on down there and not bother their parents while they shop," he said.

They were back in the hallway and Tasich led them in the direction back to Elias' cabin. They were going through the intersection just outside Elias' cabin hallway when Quincey came up from behind them and starting flying backwards in front of them.

"Hey. It's my best buds," exclaimed Quincey. "Is that food? What are you guys making?"

Tasich shook his head.

"Quincey, fly forwards. You're going to fly into someone," said Tasich. "And I'm teaching Elias how to cook palemta."

"I'm starving. Any chance I could join you guys?" asked Quincey with his eyebrows raised.

"You mean you want to mooch some food," Tasich said. "Well, it's not up to me. That's Elias' decision."

They had gone into Elias' cabin hallway and were now walking on the floor. Elias was amused by Quincey. He seemed to always be in a good mood and joking around.

"So, what do ya say, Elias? Can I join you guys for dinner?" asked Quincey, looking at Elias with a big smile on his face.

Elias chuckled. "Sure, why not."

"Thanks!" said Quincey.

A noise came from Quincey's HoloTele and he took it out to look at it.

"It's Samara. She and Siara want to know if we're free to hang out. Can they come and eat too?" asked Quincey.

"I don't know how much food I have. If I have extra, they're more than welcome to join us," said Elias.

"You have more than enough food. You'll just end up having to buy more sooner though," said Tasich.

"Excellent. What's your cabin number?" Quincey asked Elias.

"Eight forty-two," replied Elias.

Quincey fiddled with his HoloTele, sending a message to the two girls. Elias, Quincey, and Tasich arrived outside Elias' cabin, he opened the gateway, and they walked in.

"Whoa. This is sweet," said a surprised Quincey, whose eyes were big as he looked around the cabin.

Elias closed the gateway once they were all inside. He and Tasich went to the kitchen and Elias put his grocery box down on the counter.

Quincey took a seat on one of the chairs in the lounge area and pulled up another chair to rest his feet on.

"They gave you a teletron in here and you have a lounge area in your cabin. Boy, do you have it good," said Quincey, who closed his eyes and continued to relax on the chair.

Elias chuckled and Tasich just smiled and shook his head. Tasich showed Elias how to open his box of groceries by unlocking the four sides with energy and then they took the packages of food inside the box and placed them on the shelves above the counter next to the wall.

"Where do I put the box?" asked Elias, holding the now empty box.

"The compartment by the gateway where your meals came from before," answered Tasich. "That's called a shuttle compartment. That's where you receive and send items to and from your cabin. You just have to specify on the panel next to it what you wish to do."

Elias took the box over to the compartment and chose the *waste* option before putting the box inside. Once inside, the compartment closed and the box was gone. Then, a pleasant sound rang once throughout the room.

After hearing the sound, Quincey opened his eyes.

"That's probably Samara and Siara outside," Quincey said.

Elias opened the gateway and Kabec was standing there.

"Oh, hey. Come in," said Elias.

"Hey," said Kabec, who came into the cabin and took a seat on one of the chairs in the lounge. He looked at Quincey. "How did you get here?"

"Elias and Tasich bumped into me in the hallway and Elias, being the gracious person that he is, invited me to dinner," said Quincey.

Kabec looked confused. Then Tasich spoke from the kitchen.

"He found us in the hallway and now he's mooching off of Elias."

"That makes more sense," said Kabec.

"It's not mooching. Me and Elias will be hanging out together so often since you guys are all going to be too busy most of the days that I'm sure he'll come over and eat my food too," said Quincey. Then, he shook his head and mumbled. "Ha, mooching."

"It's fine guys. I don't mind," said Elias.

As he was about to close the gateway, two girls who looked older than him walked up to the cabin. The girl on the left walked gracefully and had bright blonde hair and soft brown eyes, reminding Elias of women from the 1920s he'd seen in history books and movies. Elias sensed a familiar energy signal from the girl on the right, and realized that this was Samara, whom he had seen training with Vardun. Now that he saw her up close, he was stunned. She was gorgeous. Her hazelnut eyes and her long, black hair brushed off her shoulders contrasting with her milky-white skin.

"Hello. I'm Siara," said the girl on the left in a pleasant voice.

"I'm Samara. You must be Elias," said Samara also introducing herself.

"Yes, I am," said Elias. "It's nice to meet you two. Please, come in."

After they walked in, Elias closed the gateway. Samara walked over to Quincey, took the chair he was resting his legs on from under him, and sat down on it.

"Wow. This is a really nice cabin," said Siara, standing in the lounge area and looking around. She turned to Elias. "Thanks for having us over for dinner by the way."

"Yeah, it's nice not having to cook sometimes. We'll pay for our share of the food though," said Samara.

"No, it's fine. You're guests. I couldn't allow you to do that," said Elias smiling.

They all conversed for a while in the lounge area, telling Elias what they did on board the ship and asking him questions about Earth.

"Really. What's it like having an animal in your house?" asked Quincey after learning that Elias had a dog.

"It's nice. Fuzzy's like one of my friends," said Elias.

"It is pretty cool. I mean, I only got to spend several days with the dog, but still, I know what you mean," said Kabec.

"We should start making dinner, Elias. Teaching you how to use the cooking machines might take some time," said Tasich.

"Okay," said Elias.

He and Tasich got up from the lounge area and went to the kitchen.

"What are you teaching him to make, Tasich?" asked Siara.

"Palemta," Tasich replied.

"If you want, I can go get some talleyk for us to drink. I have some in my cabin," said Samara

"Thanks, but I bought Rainbow Uthenve milk for us to drink," replied Elias.

"Rainbow Sector milk," said Siara sounding quite surprised. "That's expensive. Why didn't you tell him to buy cheaper milk, Tasich?"

"I did, but he wanted to try the milk from the Rainbow Sector," Tasich said. "We met Wexyne at the store and she told us that she and Lemrus were going there on vacation."

"Really. I've always wanted to go there. That's where the artist Sonali and her band lives. They perform a light and music show every two weeks and it's supposedly one of the best groups around the local galaxy group," said Samara.

"Isn't it expensive though? Atecka told me it was something like eight thousand credits per ticket just to see them play. And that was without meals included," said Siara.

"Yeah, it is," said Samara.

"I'm going to close off the kitchen for now. I'm not going to be able to teach Elias anything about cooking if we're distracted," said Tasich pushing a button to bring a wall down from the ceiling.

The wall separated the two areas of the cabin and now it was silent inside the kitchen where Tasich and Elias stood. Inside the kitchen were two long counters, separated by an aisle. On the counter adjacent to the wall, there were the shelves for putting groceries, a few machines, and some empty counter space. On the other counter lay a stove and more empty counter space.

Tasich began to explain the devices on the counter next to the wall.

"So, there are typically four different machines in the kitchen. First one is the box manager," he said. He put his hands on a device that had four small, box-sized, vertical shelves in it with trays and a gateway that closed it. "The name speaks for itself. If you want to open a box of food, simply place the box inside the machine, close it, and it'll break the seal, open it, and add the expiration date to the display on the box. If there's anything left over in the box when you're done cooking, you just place it back in the box manager, and it'll cover it with a film and be ready to put away."

Tasich went on to the next machine, which was just to the left of the box manager.

"This is the food manager. It measures your food for you and places them into small bowls," he said.

The food manager also had four box-sized shelves, but they were set horizontally in a row in this machine. There was also another layer of horizontal shelves on top of the bottom layer, except they were recessed.

"You put the box in the compartments and specify the amount using the displays. Then, bowls with the desired amount come out of here and your food box also comes back out here," said Tasich pointing to the top and bottom rows to show where the bowls and boxes came out, respectively.

"So far, everything seems relatively simple," said Elias. "There's the box manager for opening and closing the food boxes and a food manager for measuring out the food."

"Yeah. I guess it's really not that hard to learn to use the machines," said Tasich.

He went over to another machine on the left, which looked like a small soda dispenser. Next to it were also four large, clear, cylindrical containers that had a small, off-center hole on the top of them.

"This is where you can get water from if you need it. There's the display here on top for you to set the temperature. Then you simply lock one of these cylindrical containers into the device's mechanism and hit dispense," Tasich said.

"Got it. What's next?" asked Elias.

"On this counter, you have some extra space to prepare the food. Then you flip on over to the other counter, and the stove is there for you to cook the food in," said Tasich.

"That I know how to use. We have stoves on Earth as well," said Elias.

"Oh right. It uses basically the same principle as the ones on Earth except it has a different method of heating and cooling. I would explain it to you, but it's rather boring so I'll save that for when you take your classes," said Tasich. "Anyways, let's go about making this palemta shall we."

Tasich started taking down some of the food boxes from the shelves.

"Sounds good," said Elias.

He and Tasich went about preparing the palemta together. Elias was enjoying his time on the ship so far. The company of new friends made it easy to transition to his new life on the Shockwave which he knew had only just begun.

Chapter 9: Beginner's Lessons

"How are your classes going?" asked Kabec.

"They're not," said Elias.

"What do you mean?" asked Kabec.

"Well, since I don't know anything around here the teachers gave me a set of books and videos to go over for a test. Once I'm able to pass that, they'll put me into the actual classes," said Elias. "Apparently it shouldn't take more than five or six weeks though."

"Well, at least you finally got our time standards down, so that's one less thing for you to study," said Quincey as he smirked.

Elias shook his head.

"Stupid adjustment device. Keeps waking me up every morning. I couldn't wait for it to be gone after a week, only to remember that a week here is ten days and not seven," said Elias.

Elias, Kabec, and Quincey were flying to the teaching arena where Elias would be able to take his first private beginner's lessons. Over the past eight days, Elias had been doing so much, including learning how to cook, studying his materials, getting used to the ship's technology, and most of all, finding his way around the ship. During that time he had spent a lot of time with Quincey, who helped Elias learn his way around. It seemed like Quincey was never busy, but Elias knew he worked four hours a day at the news station and despite the silliness that Quincey displayed when they first met, Elias found out that Quincey acted normal most of the time.

Quincey chuckled.

"You do know that they programmed that thing just for you, right? I mean, I don't know about you, but most people would love to have their meals prepared for them every day and have their cabin cleaned for them," said Quincey.

Elias sighed and then smiled.

"I guess everything has its ups and downs. At least I finally know the days of the week: Aria, Kejaerd, Vertur, Neivol, Catair, Masderen, Xal, Oorag, Biwu, and Thayke," he said.

They had slowed to a halt once they had reached the teaching arena. There was a gateway there similar to the one for the manufacturing room. Through it, Elias saw a woman inside working with a child, whom looked to be no older than five serays old.

"That's Kassy Velletts. She's been teaching novice and intermediate classes for over twenty-eight serays. She'll be teaching you," said Quincey.

"She's a fun teacher and almost everyone on the ship knows her," said Kabec. "She teaches the kids and gets to know all the parents that way too."

Elias was shocked.

"Everyone on the ship," said Elias. "That's almost a million people. That's crazy."

"No, not really," said Quincey. "We talk to each other a lot, and after twenty-five serays on board, you're gonna know a lot of people."

There was a digital schedule with a bright orange background showing on a small portion of the gateway. A clock at the top of the schedule read *06:27 - Kejaerd*. Elias saw his name appear on the schedule for the next slot with the words *private lesson* appearing after it. Below his slot were five more slots for other classes. After looking at the schedule, Elias looked back into the room and continued watching Kassy and the girl whom she was training.

"Hmm, I didn't know Jinea took private lessons. This explains why she beat me in our little battle the last time we met," Quincey said.

Kabec smiled.

"Yeah, that's why she beat you. It has nothing to do with the fact that she's so much better than you," said Kabec.

Elias laughed.

"She beat you in a fight? She's a small little kid," he said sounding surprised.

"Size and age don't matter. She's very strong. And apparently she gets her very own private lessons," mumbled Quincey, trying to defend himself. "Look, I'm just glad that Samara didn't see it."

"No, but she did hear about it. All of us did," said Kabec smiling. "There's nothing to be ashamed of, Quincey. She'd be able to do the same against all of us. We're just smart enough not to challenge her."

Quincey shook his head.

"She egged me on. I couldn't say no," he said.

The gateway to the teaching arena opened and Jinea was leaving. The time was 06:31 now and the schedule changed to a light blue background.

"Hello," said Jinea.

"Hey, Jinea," said Kabec. "You know, I really wish you would've told me you were fighting Quincey last yelding. I would've loved to watch that."

"Oh, I'm sorry. We could fight again now if you want," said Jinea while smirking at Quincey.

Quincey answered.

"Ha, no thank you. I think one fight is good enough. Besides, I don't get to take private lessons like you do," he said.

"Uh huh," said Jinea smiling.

She went and hugged Quincey, who hugged her back.

"Jinea, I don't believe you've met our friend, Elias Rayhan. He used to be the yellow diamond on the Planet of Untouched Ones," said Kabec.

"Hello, Elias," exclaimed Jinea shaking his hand.

Elias smiled.

"Hi there," he said.

"So what was it like living on the Planet of Untouched Ones?" asked Jinea, letting his hand go.

"Um, it's a little different. We don't have all this technology and nobody has any energy there, but otherwise it's pretty much the same," said Elias.

"I can't imagine what it's like to live without energy," said Jinea shaking her head.

"It's not all that bad if you don't know anything else," answered Elias.

A voice from the training arena interrupted them.

"Ahem. Elias, I believe you're supposed to start your session now," the voice said.

Elias turned around and Kassy was staring at them. He looked at the clock on the schedule and saw it was 06:34.

"Sorry about that. I was talking to Jinea," said Elias.

"It's alright. We should get started though," said Kassy.

"Bye everybody," said Jinea as she flew off.

"We came by to watch Elias, if that's okay?" asked Kabec.

"Yes, that's fine. It might actually be helpful. I can use you two for examples," said Kassy.

They all flew into the teaching arena and the gateway was closed behind them. The four of them gathered in the middle and Elias looked around. The teaching arena was small in comparison to the training arena.

"Welcome to the teaching arena, Elias," said Kassy. "My name is Kassy Velletts. Some logistics about this place. This arena is ten miles long on each side with the corners angled inward. The arena is used only to gain a mastery of flying, teach simple finesse techniques, and of course simple fighting techniques. Lastly, the gateway there is reinforced with a clear stadium panel on the inside that opens and closes with the gateway so don't worry about it being damaged during training." She took a deep breath. "Now, the first thing we will do is a quick diagnostic of your skills. Do you have any questions?"

"Um, just one. Well, not a question, but—I know you mentioned on the message you sent to me that the first lesson is free, but I have the necessary credits to pay you," said Elias.

"Nonsense. I never charge anyone for their first private lesson with me. You should be allowed to decide whether you continue with them or not. And besides, you can only learn so much from one lesson. Shall we begin then?" asked Kassy smiling.

"Okay," responded Elias.

"Excellent," Kassy said. "First part of the diagnostic is going to be to test your ability to fly. This is rather simple. I have set up the tiles you see around the arena to light a path for you to move through. I'd like you to fly around the tiles as fast as you can, like an obstacle course. If you are unable to complete a maneuver, then we'll start from there. No pressure. Just do the best you can." She pulled up a small timer around her right arm on her suit. Then she looked at him. "I'll only be timing you for my own observational purposes so don't worry about how fast you complete the lap. Whenever you're ready, you can start over there and fly until you complete a full lap."

He moved forward a little and looked back as the other three watched him. This seemed rather simple to Elias. He went through the course moving straight, moving up, turning right, left, and then left again. He continued throughout the course making diagonal turns and ending the course with some helical flying followed by quick starting and stopping until he came out at the end. He had completed the course with no missteps in less than ten seconds.

Kassy looked at her timer on her suit.

"That's the fastest time I've ever had going through the course by about six seconds," she said. "Then again, you are the oldest person by at least ten serays to ever go through it so I suppose that could explain it."

She retrieved a number of tiles and placed eight of them in outlines of two squares on each side of him. Of the remaining tiles, she placed two of them above him and two below him at different heights.

"Second part of the diagnostic is to see how well you can control your energy. For this test, you need to hit as close as you can to the center of each tile with your energy. These tiles are special because they light up to show where you've hit them, so you'll know how you did. After you hit the tiles, move them over there to form a line for us to observe your results," said Kassy smiling at him.

Elias went around hitting each of the tiles as Kassy directed him to do and moved them into a line. At the end, the four of them looked at the line of tiles. Elias had hit every one of them dead center.

Kassy looked over to Kabec.

"I thought you said he was a beginner," she said.

"Well, I thought he was. He's never done any of this before," replied Kabec.

"He's a natural," whispered Quincey, staring at the tiles Elias had hit.

Kassy shook her head in disbelief.

"He hit all of them dead center. That's amazing for a beginner. From what I've seen so far, he's up to speed with anything I would teach him," she said.

She opened up a compartment near the entrance and brought a black visor over to them. Then, she gave it to Elias.

"Put this on now. The last part is to determine your sensing abilities, although at this point you've already made a mockery out of my beginner's diagnostic," said Kassy. "Kabec told me that you have special abilities when it comes to sensing. Apparently despite your lower energy level, your sensing abilities are spectacular, similar to the condition of the Elite Ilay back in the day named Zelake. If that's the case, this should be really easy for you."

"Wait, what?" asked Quincey sounding shocked.

"Oh, yeah. I forgot to tell you about that. I'll tell you about it later," Kabec said to Quincey.

Elias put on the visor and everything went dark. He couldn't see anything around him, but he sensed Quincey, Kabec, and Kassy where they were floating.

"Don't panic now. It's supposed to be dark," Elias heard Kassy say. "What I'm going to do next is move the tiles around you, some of them will be coming towards you, others moving to your right and left, and so on. What I want you to do is the same as the previous test, hit as close to the center of the tiles, except this time, I'll move the tiles after you've hit them, okay."

"Okay," replied Elias.

Kassy's voice was loud.

"First tile will be coming from me and I'm going to have Quincey and Kabec move two other tiles," she said. "We'll cycle like that for about three or four times. Once you sense a tile start to move, just hit it."

Elias waited while Kassy gave her instructions to Quincey and Kabec. Once they had finished, there was silence. Elias sensed Kassy reach for a tile to move at him and he hit the tile. There was a long pause, and then Kabec reached for a tile. Elias hit that one and as he did so, he also sensed Quincey getting another tile from the opposite portion of the teaching arena. Elias used his energy to hit the tile Quincey had grabbed and another long pause followed.

"Alright. Take your visor off and leave it by the gateway. Let's go. All of you. Now," said Kassy.

Elias took off his visor and saw her flying out of the teaching arena. She floated by the entrance waiting for the three of them. Elias looked to Kabec and Quincey, both of whom shrugged and then flew off following Kassy. Elias left the visor by the gateway and followed them out. Kassy closed the gateway and flew off.

Elias, Quincey, and Kabec followed her as she weaved throughout the hallways. Elias recognized the hallways and they seemed to be going towards the area of the ship where most of the school classes were taught. They came upon the practice class arena, which Kassy opened the gateway to and flew inside.

Inside the practice class arena were about a hundred kids that looked like they were around ten or eleven serays old. They were all watching an older woman, who was floating in front of them, but they turned around to see what was going on at the entrance.

"Hello, Eneray. I'm very sorry to bother you at the beginning of your class, but I needed to talk with you for a few minutes. It's somewhat urgent, if you don't mind," said Kassy to the older woman.

"It must be for you to interrupt my class," Eneray replied.

Kassy and Eneray went to an empty part of the practice arena to talk. The students, on the other hand, were still paying attention to Elias, Quincey, and Kabec.

After a short period of chatter, a girl in the class spoke up.

"Hey, Quincey. Did you do something wrong?" she asked.

"No. I didn't do anything. I don't know what's going on," answered Quincey.

"Yeah, this is odd. I've never seen or heard of Kassy doing anything like this before," Kabec told Elias.

"Oh. By the way, how did I do with the sensing diagnostic?" asked Elias.

"How'd you do? How'd you do? You were sensational. We didn't even get to move the tiles before you hit them," exclaimed Quincey.

Kassy and Eneray had finished talking and were coming back. The class stopped chattering.

"Alright, class. We have a newcomer with us today," said Eneray. She pointed to Elias. "Kassy tells me that this here is Elias Rayhan. He was the yellow diamond that lived on the Planet of Untouched Ones. Apparently, despite his low energy level, he has quite the ability to sense at a much higher level. So we're going to have a little fun to start today's class. I need a volunteer who would like to match up against him for ten minutes."

A girl, who looked a little younger than Elias, flew up out of the class.

"I'll do it," she said.

Eneray looked over to the girl and hesitated.

"This will not be a typical fight though. Elias will be wearing a black visor so he cannot see. All he will be allowed to do is deflect your attacks or evade you," said Eneray. "He will not be permitted to attack you back and he will not be allowed to use any of the tiles around the arena for defensive purposes. To defeat him, you must directly hit him twice in the ten minute period, meaning it won't count if he parries your attack, even if yours is stronger."

Eneray looked over at Kassy with a slight look of concern. Then, she looked back at the girl who had volunteered.

"Thank you for volunteering, Tewa. Kassy and I have agreed that for this matchup, you should go easy on him with the strength of your attacks since he is not as strong as the rest of us. Is that understood?" asked Eneray.

"Yes, Eneray," said Tewa.

"Class, please make your way to the spectator area," said Eneray. Then she turned to Kassy. "Make sure to go over the rules with him again."

Kabec and Quincey looked at each other with grins on their faces.

"Good luck," said Quincey.

Kabec and Quincey headed to the spectator area with the rest of the class. Kassy began going over the rules of the match that Eneray had just told them to make sure Elias understood. Elias had never been in a fight before.

"There's nothing to worry about, Elias," Kassy said. "This is just a better test of your sensing abilities. You did so amazing on my basic diagnostic that I just have to see how well you can actually sense. Now, go on out to the platform opposite of Tewa. The time usually starts when a multicolored ball of light dissipates at the center of the arena, but you'll be able to sense it as well."

Elias looked at her.

"Oh, okay," he said.

He ventured out into the practice arena towards his platform. Elias estimated that the practice arena was about one-fourth as large as the training arena and yet it was hundreds of times larger than the teaching arena. Eneray came up to him and gave him a black visor. Then, she flew off to the spectator area, where everyone else was sitting.

Elias looked over to the other platform at Tewa, whose serious facial expression had not changed at all. He landed in the middle of his platform, positioned himself to face Tewa, and put on the visor. Just like in the teaching arena, everything became pitch black around him.

Elias sensed Tewa at the other end and waited for the starting ball. He took deep breaths thinking to himself that ten minutes wasn't all too long. And besides, this wasn't a real fight. They were just testing his sensing abilities.

He sensed something moving from the spectator area towards the center of the arena. This must be the starting ball. When the object reached the center, there was a short pause. Then the ball burst and Elias knew the match started.

Tewa wasted no time after the starting ball burst, as she moved towards a section of tiles near her. Elias waited on the platform, not sure where to move. Then, Tewa sent two tiles towards him, but to his right and left. Why did she want to miss him? The tiles shattered a short distance before reaching Elias and the energy released from them were arcing inwards right at him. Now he knew. She wasn't avoiding hitting him. She was using his lack of knowledge to her advantage.

Elias was just able to block both attacks by putting his hands out to deflect the attacks away from him with small bursts. Having realized it would be better not to be a still target, Elias moved from the platform, and flew erratically around the arena while still facing Tewa.

She was not at all fazed by his tactics as she already had three more tiles in her grasps and hurtled them right at him this time. After she threw them, she launched herself towards the bottom of the arena and fired a burst aimed at the floor.

Elias was confused again by her strange tactic, but he focused on the three tiles coming hot at him. He recognized the tiles. They were like the ones Samara threw at Vardun that caused small spherical blasts. Elias dodged them by moving to his left, avoiding the full brunt of the three tiles and aimed a short burst towards the one closest to him to deflect its blast.

Then, he sensed it, something coming from underneath him. The burst Tewa had aimed at the floor was close by. It must've deflected off the floor and come back towards him. He just spun out of the way of the attack, but Tewa was blazing right towards him with another tile from below.

Elias retreated upwards and knew she would corner him if he kept going up much longer. She must've thought the same thing because she fired her tile to his right and unloaded a separate duo of bursts herself. Elias sensed the tile to be a horizontal striped one and knew he couldn't deflect both attacks at the same time with her bearing down so close to him ready to continue her attack.

Thinking fast, Elias decided to outpace the horizontal striped tile before it shattered and hit the ceiling. Elias launched upwards with amazing speed, but he could tell he still wasn't going to be able to avoid all of the tile's energy. Not knowing what else to do, he balled himself up and started spinning off energy as he continued moving upwards. Then, he bounced off the ceiling at an angle, deflecting and avoiding the attack from the horizontal striped bars of energy that had come from the tile. Not wanting to be in the corner any longer, Elias zoomed towards the other end of the arena and was floating near Tewa's starting platform.

Expecting Tewa to be close behind him, Elias was surprised when he sensed that she was still in the corner, not moving at all while her two bursts had deflected off the ceiling and dissipated as they neared the floor. She floated in the corner for what seemed like an eternity to Elias. Well on alert, he was sure there were no surprise attacks coming at him. What was she waiting for? The ten minutes were not up. It felt like a minute had passed at most.

Then she flew at him, but she had no tiles with her. She fired out multitudes of bursts in quick succession at him while still coming after him. She was moving a lot faster than before and these bursts were stronger than the previous ones. Elias flew away from her and evaded the bursts she sent at him, but she fired more and more at him with a furor she hadn't had during the first minute of the match.

Elias avoided Tewa's attacks while flying away from her, but soon her attacks started to also include random tiles, which he found himself needing to deflect with his own bursts every so often. Tewa now moved so fast and made moves from one place to another like lightning that it was becoming more difficult to sense where she and her attacks were coming from all the time, but it was still more than manageable for Elias.

Tewa's next attack that Elias sensed coming towards him was extraordinary. There were at least eight different tiles and three of her bursts headed in his direction. A tile leading the way was a very small, but powerful square one headed straight at him while two more were the spherical blasts coming in on his right. There was also a large, star-shaped tile coming at him at an angle to his right behind the small square one and three more circular tiles would be deflecting off the wall and coming at his back at different heights. The last tile was a large, spinning, checkered, circular one coming slowly at him from below and Tewa's three bursts were heading from her direction above him at a diagonal.

Elias reacted with blistering speed to the attack, blasting away the first small, square tile. Then he spun rapidly in an air cartwheel to his right, sending off bursts from his body to mitigate the spherical blasts, before unloading a small, powerful burst, pushing himself away from the star-shaped tile and toward the wall, which fended off the energy that it had sent launching at him. Now worried about the three circular tiles that were coming at his back, he did a turnabout flip and in a downwards sweeping motion, blasted the three circular tiles' energy to smithereens, when he sensed the spinning, checkered tile below him releasing its energy. He spun like a skater and let off a huge circular swath of energy at the checkered squares of energy coming at him from below and then swung his feet upwards to send a large burst deflecting Tewa's three rounds of energy before shooting off down below and launching himself off the floor away from her.

Despite the numerous maneuvers and heavy thought put into that last sequence of attacks, the time that passed during all of it was mere seconds. In time, Elias became aware that Tewa would not have been able to have such aggressive attacks in a real match because she would be left vulnerable too often if she did. However, Tewa was taking full advantage of Elias not being allowed to attack her back and she became more aggressive the more and more Elias eluded her attacks.

Elias felt like he had been out there for an hour having performed so many different moves and avoided so many attacks, each one stronger than the next. The battle continued to rage on for some time and Elias began to wonder if the ten minutes was going to pass soon. Kassy had forgotten to mention when he would know when the time had passed. Would there be another time ball to signal the end of the match?

After a few more volleys of attacks from Tewa, Elias sensed something coming from the spectator area again and recognized Eneray coming out to the arena.

"Time is up," yelled Eneray.

After Eneray had called time, Elias relaxed, thinking the match was over. But then, he sensed more attacks coming from Tewa. What was she doing? Eneray was in the arena with them and had called time. Elias stopped relaxing and began to avoid the attacks again, which were still growing stronger and faster than before.

"Tewa. Time is up," yelled Eneray again.

However, Tewa still didn't stop her attacks. Eneray flew over and stopped in front of Elias, blocking him from Tewa. Tewa stopped and just floated there as did Eneray.

Elias wasn't too tired from the frenzy of attacks he had seen and he took off his visor. Tewa was breathing much harder than he was and she just stared at him.

Eneray just looked at Tewa for a while before speaking.

"Very nice job, Elias," she said.

Elias looked over to the spectator area where Quincey and Kabec sat and saw that not only did they look in shock, but so did Kassy and the entire class.

"This wasn't a fair matchup. You said go easy on him, but he's obviously stronger than I am," said Tewa, taking deep breaths while she spoke.

"Yes, we know that now. That's why I didn't stop the match when you started attacking him with your full strength," said Eneray.

"You should've added another minute," said Tewa, having caught her breath. She still stared at Elias even though she was talking to Eneray.

"Tewa, this was only a test to help Kassy with her diagnosis of Elias. The ten minutes accomplished that and that's what matters," replied

Eneray. "Come now, Tewa. Class will start at the spectator area with a presentation on tactics."

Eneray left for the spectator area and Tewa followed her. Kassy, Quincey, and Kabec had left the spectator area and were coming towards him now. As Eneray and Kassy passed each other, they had a short conversation that ended with Kassy nodding.

"Elias, we'll go back to the teaching arena to discuss things," said Kassy.

Then, the four of them left the practice arena and went on their way back to the teaching arena. Quincey and Kabec had both been quiet while they went back. What was wrong? Why had Tewa been so mad and why had everyone looked so shocked?

They entered the teaching arena and Kassy closed the gateway behind them. The three of them stared at Elias for a little while before he grew impatient.

"What?" asked Elias.

"Sorry. It's just--well, your energy level is phenomenal, which makes absolutely no sense. We can't sense it coming from you and yet we all saw it at the practice arena," said Kassy.

"Oh, well I'm sure that happens to some people, right?" asked Elias.

"No. It's unheard of for a person's energy level to be that much higher than what others can sense," answered Quincey.

"That's not entirely true, but it is ridiculously rare. There are two people in history that I can think of with abilities like his, but both of them went on to become Elite Ilays. I'm not sure if Elias is quite there, but he could certainly give Vardun a hard time for his top spot in our sector right now. With some proper training and practice, I'd dare say Elias could actually beat him," said Kassy shaking her head.

"Anyone with the knowledge to train him already has a fighter they're busy with. It'll be near impossible to find someone now, just before the Orace Petrans cycle begins, unless you'd be able to," said Kabec.

"No, I wouldn't be able to. I only teach beginner's level skills, but there is someone that would be able to train him on fighting," said Kassy looking at Quincey and Kabec as if hinting at something.

There was a brief period of silence while Kassy continued to stare at Quincey and Kabec, both of whom stared back at her.

"There's no way Tewa would to agree to do it. Not even if he paid her a ridiculous amount of credits," said Quincey breaking the silence.

"It's either that, or have ordinary people like yourselves just teaching him the basics and hoping he can learn the rest on his own," responded Kassy.

Kabec was looking down at his feet and thinking before he looked back up and sighed.

"Thanks, Kassy," he said. "Let's go guys. We'll have to figure out a way to convince Tewa to help him."

Quincey and Kabec left the teaching arena and Elias followed them. Why would Tewa not want to help him? Was it because he beat her in their match?

Chapter 10: Ancient History

Alera had gotten used to the daily grind by now, but she was pleased to be on break after making storage containers. She had spent the past two yeldings at the Lighthouse Sector's academy and still had seven more yeldings to serve out her punishment. The academy was a dreadful place for anyone who was used to the freedoms of living without restrictions.

The people placed in the academy received three meals a day instead of the usual four meals people enjoyed. The meals, which were cheap and often lacking flavor, consisted of a grain, a meat or fish product, and a drink. Today, they were having kaydreaum, pletom, and shalbak for their lunch. Each person also had to take one chewable tablet a day to give them the remaining nutrients they needed to stay healthy so the Dasunes, who watched over them, need not worry about anyone becoming ill.

Alera was weary from the long hours at the beginning of her day. She and everyone else at the academy had a routine schedule that never changed. They started the day with breakfast and everyone ate it in their own rooms. After eating, they went to the classroom for an hour to learn the Cliern law. Then, each person would be assigned to six intense hours of work creating spaceway guard stations, planetary platforms, or storage containers. On occasion, they would be assigned to six hours of work reading and filing crime reports instead. The six hours of work was followed by the break Alera was on which she tried to enjoy as best as she could.

She chewed on a piece of pletom she had put in her mouth. The fish was sprinkled with some flavored powder that had been added to it, but it still tasted bland. While she ate she watched the dining hall teletron, which was showing an old documentary about Oolabe, a former member of the Falhul and one-time explorer, who ventured into the now well-known Mahogany Sector in octant three.

There were five people at the Lighthouse Sector academy and only one of them was in the dining hall with her. Talking to others was not encouraged so the other three people went to their own rooms where they could read and eat during the break.

"Forty-five minutes remaining," said a voice coming from the speakers throughout the academy.

Alera sighed and consumed some of her shalbak drink, which had enough of a fruit flavor to make it satisfying in comparison with the rest of her meal. She often thought about what it'd be like to eat on the Shockwave again, but then she became sad that she had been punished and put into the academy.

In time, she had grown frustrated at herself for being so naïve to get into the situation she was in, but she also felt that the yellow diamond, Elias, whom she had unlocked, was also to blame. Why did he have to be so clumsy? If he had just gotten up from that rock without falling, she would've never done anything and she'd be sitting at home right now eating fresh screlan candy or her mom's tasty ziote snacks instead of this terrible academy food.

Alera closed her eyes and shook her head. She stopped thinking about what could have been. She did not want to be in a bad mood for the rest of her day so she focused her attention back to the teletron once again.

Once the break ended, she would be sent off again for an hour of assembling lights followed by an hour of cleaning the academy. After all that, she would be free from work for the day. People showered in their own rooms after finishing all their work and then the third and final meal of the day would be given to them in their rooms.

Alera, on the other hand, did not shower after work . Instead, every day she chose to use the academy's training facilities to better her fighting skills despite being tired from her work. She was the only one at the Lighthouse Sector's academy who used the facilities.

"Thirty minutes left," said the voice again from the speakers in the academy.

Alera took a bite of her kaydreaum and continued learning about Oolabe's adventures. Only seven more yeldings she thought. Seven more yeldings and she'd be free.

◆

Elias was sitting at the table in his cabin, reading a chapter on early Cliern formation and the choosing of Sanize as the capital city.

Sanize was named the capital of the Clierns in the first official seray and it has remained the capital since then. Reasons for choosing Sanize to be the capital included its variety of cultures and people along with its central location in the Universe at the time. Today, Sanize is still filled with an abundance of cultures and people, but due to explorers that have ventured out into the unknown, mostly from the 2nd, 3rd, and 7th octants, Sanize is no longer located at the center of the Universe.

Elias ran his finger over the *2nd, 3rd, and 7th octants* phrase, which was highlighted. A three-dimensional map popped out from the book to show Sanize, signified by a small, spherical, red dot and the eight octants of the Universe were shown around it.

Elias looked at the different colors in each octant which showed the expansion of each one throughout time. Octants one and eight had almost no expansion until the last five hundred serays and even so, in the past one hundred serays it looked like the unknown areas next to them showed little exploration.

The pleasant sound of the gateway signal, which Elias had learned was a specific energy strumming on a set of bells, rang throughout his cabin. Elias looked over at the monitor by his cabin gateway and saw Quincey and Kabec waiting outside.

Elias opened the gateway and let them in.

"What are you doing?" asked Quincey, sitting down in one of the lounge chairs.

"Reading for tomorrow's ancient history class. What's up?" said Elias looking up from his book.

"We just finished work so we thought we'd stop by," said Kabec as he sat on a chair next to Quincey.

Elias pushed a button at the bottom of the page he was reading and the page lit up a bright orange color. Then, he closed the book and went over to the lounge to sit by Kabec and Quincey.

"You're finally off probation at the guard station right?" Elias asked Kabec.

"Yeah and that means that my pay finally goes back to normal too," replied Kabec.

"I still feel bad about that. You sure you won't take any credits from me? It was my fault that it happened," said Elias.

"Nope. I'm not taking anything from you," said Kabec. "Did you and Quincey have any luck yesterday in finding someone to help train you?"

"No. We did find someone in the Airglow Sector advertising her services, but it's way too expensive for me to have her come here all the time," said Elias. "Why can't I just ask Tewa if she'd help me? I didn't do anything to purposely get Alera in trouble."

It had been over a yelding since they left Kassy's teaching arena after his first private lesson, but they had not yet asked Tewa to help him train to fight. Kabec and Quincey said it wasn't a good idea to approach her so soon after their matchup because they thought it would be best to give her some time to cool down.

They had also told Elias why Tewa would not be willing to help him. She was best friends with Alera, who got sent to the academy because of Elias. Kabec also pointed out that he was the one that caught Alera so Tewa was mad at him too, which wouldn't help matters.

"He might as well. What's the worst that could happen?" said Quincey.

"Yeah, I guess you really don't have any choice now, but to ask her," replied Kabec.

"I'll go do it now then. The sooner the better. Any idea where she'd be right now?" asked Elias getting up from his chair.

Kabec shook his head.

"I don't know either," said Quincey. "But, Samara might know. She hangs out with Tewa sometimes during local matches or group training sessions."

Elias had walked over to his cabin's gateway and opened it.

"You want us to go with you?" asked Kabec getting up from his chair.

"No, I think I should do this alone," said Elias heading out of his cabin.

"Wait, you're just leaving us here? You know we can't lock your cabin, right?" asked Quincey.

"Yeah. That way I know you'll be here when I get back," said Elias smiling as he flew off into the hallway. Quincey's head popped out of Elias' cabin.

"Can we at least eat your food?" yelled Quincey, but Elias ignored him and continued flying.

Elias headed to a cabin directory station while he got out his HoloTele to ask Samara if she knew where Tewa might be. Otherwise, Elias would just have to hope that Tewa would be in her cabin.

He navigated through the hallways until he had come to a screen where he could access the cabin directory. He activated the screen and then input his energy signal into a scanner. Elias looked up Tewa's name in the directory and the number *614* showed up as a bolded title with the members living in the cabin underneath in a list and Tewa's name was highlighted in green. Elias clicked the button on the screen to show the location of the cabin on the ship and saw where it was. Samara hadn't answered his message on the HoloTele yet, so Elias signed off of the screen with his energy signal and flew off to Tewa's cabin.

Halfway to Tewa's cabin, Elias' HoloTele made a sound and Elias looked at it. Samara had answered back.

I talked to her today when I was going to the training arena. She said she was going to the Jeeho Fighting Library to study some videos. Good luck trying to convince her to train you.

Elias headed in the opposite direction and made his way to the Jeeho Fighting Library. He had been there once before when he had taken the tour of the ship with Kabec and only one person was in there when they had gone. Elias walked in through the opening to the library, which didn't have a gateway, and saw that Tewa was the only one there. She was sitting at a table at the far end of the room watching a hologram video.

She looked up at him as soon as he had come in and continued to glare at him as he walked up to the table she was sitting at. Elias smiled and sat down opposite her. The video she was watching had been paused and was suspended there between the two of them.

"Hi," said Elias.

Tewa pushed a button on the table and the video shrunk down and out of sight. She crossed her arms on the table, took a deep breath, and continued to glare at Elias.

"Hello," said Tewa in a toneless voice. Then, she paused. "Is there something you want from me?"

Elias hesitated.

"Yes," he said. "I, um--I heard you know a lot about fighting. Um, more specifically, um, I heard that you're a master on techniques and strategies and uh, some other stuff. So, I was, um, wondering—"

"You want me to train you," Tewa interrupted.

"Yeah. How'd you know?" ask Elias surprised.

"It doesn't take a genius to figure it out. After how you did at the practice arena, everyone could see how good you were. You needed a trainer though, but it's almost impossible to find someone that's not already training a fighter by now so you came to me," explained Tewa.

"Oh," said Elias not having realized how obvious it was. "So, would you be willing to train me?"

He waited for an answer from Tewa, who continued staring at him and showed no emotion. Then, she looked around to her right and appeared to be thinking about something before staring back at him and continuing to stay silent.

"Look, I know you're mad at me for what happened to Alera," Elias said, "but I didn't do anything to purposely get her in trouble. I didn't even know she had gotten sent to the academy until Quincey and Kabec told me four weeks ago and when I found out, I went straight to Captain Renalt to tell him that she shouldn't be punished. I asked him if there was anything I could do, but he said that I couldn't do anything to change the situation because she broke—"

"I talked to her after it happened. I know what she did. She didn't go into detail too much, but she did tell me what happened," said Tewa. "You're the one that slipped on a rock of all things that got her into this mess in the first place."

"I didn't know she was there or anything, I was just trying to get up. On Earth, slipping on a rock isn't...it's not that uncommon. It happens all the time. I know that's hard to believe, but back on my home planet what I did wasn't that unusual. Trust me," pleaded Elias.

"Just because I'm not from your planet, doesn't mean I don't know about your planet. I know it was normal for that to happen to you. It's just," said Tewa shaking her head, "that I'm upset at you because Alera's at the academy and you were involved. And to make things worse, I can't even see her or talk to her for the first three yeldings that she's in there." She sighed. "I wish we could behave like the people on your planet. Then I could just get really mad at you and tell you no, I won't be your trainer." Then she sighed again. "But—"

Elias jumped up from his chair. He looked at her with his eyes wide open and he was smiling.

"Wait, you'll do it. Really?" exclaimed Elias.

She nodded although she still didn't look happy about it.

"Thank you so much," said Elias.

He went over to Tewa and hugged her although she acted somewhat reluctant. Elias could tell that she wasn't mad at him for hugging her though.

"Under certain conditions," said Tewa, once Elias had let go.

"Of course. Whatever you want. I can pay you—"

"I don't want any credits. All I ask is that every time we have a training session, whether to study or to practice, you bring me a meal. I'll let you know what I want beforehand," said Tewa.

"Deal," said Elias with a smile on his face still.

Tewa got up from her chair, took out the video from a slot in the table, and walked to the shelf behind her to put it back.

"Meet me here for our first session at 24:31 on Masderen and I want any meal from Lascady's restaurant that has vesapell in it," said Tewa as she put the video back.

"Right, okay. Got it. Thanks, Tewa," said Elias getting up from his chair.

He started walking towards the entrance to the library.

He kept walking, but then he stopped and looked back at Tewa. She looked like she was going to cry. Elias went over to her and hugged her again. This time, she hugged him back and he could see her eyes were watering and she was sniffling.

"I miss her," whispered Tewa.

"I'm sorry," whispered Elias as he hugged Tewa.

Several seconds had passed before Tewa replied.

"I know," she whispered back.

Chapter 11: Search for the Truth

"The following video will show the most prominent explorers, including the few who went to the Planet of Untouched, um, I mean Earth and their findings in our octant," said Elias' history teacher, Uidena Sinye through the class' linked headsets.

Uidena smiled at the class and started the video. Elias knew Uidena had said Earth instead of the Planet of Untouched Ones because Elias was there. Elias had talked to him after the first class they had and let him know that it wasn't offensive to call it the Planet of Untouched Ones, but Uidena had insisted on calling it Earth now that he knew someone from there.

"Why is there a large gap in the exploration of our zone for so many serays?" asked Wehlal, a tall, skinny, light-skinned boy sitting nine seats to Elias' left.

The video paused once Wehlal had asked the question as it awaited for Uidena to resume it.

"The destruction of the Ketejesuse Tamachristron ship created turmoil around this zone for thousands of serays. It forced people to move to suitable nearby planets and people were angry over the destruction of their homes. They acted irrationally because of their anger and violence became prevalent to the point that it was unsafe to venture through the zone. Over time, more and more people eventually moved out towards safer zones in the octant until the population in this zone became scarce," answered Uidena.

"Why didn't the Clierns do anything about the violence?" asked Elias.

"At the time, the Clierns were not as well organized to oversee every zone in the galaxy with the proper authority and as a result they did not have the necessary resources to send a large enough task force to control the area. However, they did provide refuge to people who went to the borders of our zone that were adjacent to other zones in our octant and octant three," said Uidena.

Uidena resumed the video. Elias watched as the images flashed by on the screen showing different explorers, crew members, their ships, and areas of exploration. The videos felt like short movies to Elias because the graphics and photography were hundreds of times better than anything he had seen on Earth. As he watched the video, Elias wondered if any of the recent explorers that were being shown to him had ever known his father. With him living on Earth, they would have had to run into him at the very least.

Ever since Kabec had told Elias that his dad's name wasn't in the Cliern database, Elias had been going to the Explorer's Library six times a week for two hours a day and reading accounts of recent explorers that ventured near the Earth before the Lighthouse Sector had been founded. So far though, Elias had found nothing in them that would lead to clues about his dad.

"Quick note. The base of an explorer's income comes from the Clierns, established sectors, or a group wanting to develop a sector that will pay them an exploration fee," said Uidena while the class took notes. "If an explorer is able to find useful resources outside a specific zone, the revenue from those resources is split 60-20-20 for the next twenty-five serays between the people that harvest the resources, the nearby sectors of that zone, and the explorer's crew. There are some exceptions to the rule, but those are only applied in unusual circumstances."

"Why do the sectors next to the new areas get any revenue from the resources if they don't harvest them? It seems to me that they should only get the revenue if they are in fact the ones harvesting the resources," said Mahila, a short, teal-haired girl sitting to Elias' right.

"That's logical Mahila, but we must think about this using foresight. When new resources are found, the harvesters will need to transport them to other areas of the Universe. They will ultimately do so using the nearby sectors' transportation systems that are in place. Also, new sectors almost always need the support of their nearby neighbors for various supplies in the first five serays," replied Uidena.

"So the rule is in place to incentivize established sectors to help startup sectors and therefore foster growth and expansion," said Mahila.

"Yes, that is essentially what the rule does," said Uidena. "That's why we have given twenty percent of our resource revenues to the Orbital Sector and the Sunset Sector for the last ten serays and will continue to do so for the next fifteen serays."

They continued watching the video for another fifteen minutes before the end of class. The class took their headsets off and left the room, but Elias stayed over for another fifteen minutes to ask questions and summarize what he learned, as he had done for the last two and a half yeldings. Uidena and all of Elias' other teachers had suggested that he do so to make sure he'd understood everything.

"I've been studying up on recent explorers around our zone and I know there were three different ones in our sector alone. Serpico was the first one to venture out in this area and confirm that it was safe. Then, Jeeho came out here and he found the two planets Itta and Toreal where we get our resources from. And I believe Pulcher also got a commission to do another exploration that would thoroughly check the area and make sure there were no oddities. I'm curious though, who's the one that gets the resource revenue from our sector?" asked Elias.

"Well we're one of the unusual circumstances I was referring to. Since three explorers were needed due to the chaos that was previously in the area, all three of them had some claim to the resource revenue. Eventually, they brokered a deal in which twelve percent goes to Jeeho because he actually found the planets and four percent goes to each of the other two," said Uidena as he powered down the teaching devices.

"What about their crews?" asked Elias.

"Well, each explorer has their own deals with their crew members beforehand. Although Jeeho didn't have a crew. He was a strange one. Still is as a matter of fact," said Uidena chuckling.

"Hmm, okay," said Elias.

"Any luck finding clues about your father in the readings I recommended?" asked Uidena.

"No. I just finished reading Serpico's accounts, but I couldn't find anything that would even resemble another person with energy," said Elias sounding frustrated.

"Well, Serpico came here around thirty serays ago, so it's possible your father may not have been in the area at the time," said Uidena.

"Okay, well, I'm starting on Pulcher's accounts tomorrow. Hopefully something turns up," said Elias. "It's a shame that Jeeho didn't write anything other than what was required to lay claim to his revenue."

"Have you asked him about his explorations here?" asked Uidena.

"Yes, but he said that descriptions and accounts do not tell the whole story. Then, he gave me a map with his exploration path. He said that there are still a good amount of unknown planets to be found along that way and if I really wanted to know what he saw and felt, I should go there myself," said Elias.

"Like I told you, he's a strange one," said Uidena. "Well, good luck with Pulcher's accounts then. Is there anything else related to today's material you need to understand?"

"No. Thank you for your help, Uidena. I look forward to class on Neivol," said Elias.

Elias set the box of food that he had gotten from Shedin's restaurant down on a table in the training arena fighter's lounge.

"Thank you," said Tewa.

She opened the box and placed the food onto a tray she already had ready.

"You know that's the meal that takes the longest to make, right? I was sitting in the restaurant for at least thirty minutes," said Elias.

"I know," smiled Tewa. "Maybe you'll learn not to get smart with me like you did last time."

"I was just using a different technique, and mind you, it worked perfectly fine," said Elias.

Tewa shook her head and sighed.

"Look, I know you can do an assortment of different flashy moves, but at the league levels, you'll need to be more disciplined. I'm just trying to get you ready for the league matches," she said.

"Don't you mean local matches? They're still over a yelding away. We have plenty of time to practice," said Elias.

"No, I meant league matches. And they're only four and a half yeldings away," said Tewa.

"I'm confused," said Elias.

"You're far and away better than anyone around here. There's no way you aren't going to qualify from the local matches. I'm not worried about that," said Tewa.

"Oh," said Elias. "But I've been hearing people talking more and more about Vardun and Jerematrius as the front runners."

"That's because nobody knows about you. I make sure no one sees you train on purpose. The fewer the distractions, the better for you," said Tewa.

"Speaking of seeing me train, Kabec and Quincey wanted to watch me train for once. They said they'd stop by in about twenty minutes, if that's okay?" asked Elias.

"So you're asking me if they can use my family's booth," said Tewa.

"Uh, yeah," said Elias with some hesitating.

She sighed.

"Fine. I'll just have to make sure Quincey doesn't go blabbing all over the ship about you afterwards," said Tewa.

Tewa finished her food and then the two of them started their pre-training lesson. She showed Elias a series of clips from previous league matches and then they discussed tactics and techniques. After going over what she wanted to get done today, they made their way into the arena.

"Are Kabec and Quincey still coming to watch you?" asked Tewa as they floated in the middle of the arena.

"Yeah, they should be here in a minute or two," answered Elias.

"Well, I don't want any interruptions once we start," said Tewa. "I guess we'll wait for them."

After a minute had passed in silence, Quincey, Samara, Siara, and Kabec were all at the training arena viewing window. Tewa looked over at Elias and glared at him.

"You said only Quincey and Kabec were coming to watch you," said Tewa as they both moved to go nearby the viewing panel.

"That's what Quincey said. I guess he must've invited more people," said Elias shrugging.

Siara started using the main screen. Then, her voice rang out over the speakers in the arena.

"Where should we go?" she asked

"Hey, Siara. Hold on a second. I need to say something to everyone first," said Tewa.

"Oh, okay," said Siara.

"It's nice that you want to watch Elias and all, but his training is to be kept private. So no matter how good he is, I ask that you don't talk about it with other people. Is that understood?" asked Tewa.

They all responded with some form of a yes.

"Quincey, this means you especially," said Tewa.

"I won't tell anyone. I promise," said Quincey. "You know, you're a lot nicer when you're not training Elias and we're all just hanging out."

"Samara, you're no longer working with Vardun anymore, right?" asked Tewa.

"Yeah, Jeeho started training with him last week so I'm not working with anyone anymore," said Samara.

"Okay then," said Tewa.

She let them into the training arena outer ring and the four of them made their way to Tewa's booth to watch. Tewa closed a panel by the viewing window panel and then both Elias and Tewa went to the center of the arena again. They started off with their usual energy meditation for a couple of minutes.

"Are you relaxed and ready?" asked Tewa.

"Yes," responded Elias.

They stopped their energy meditation and started the training session. They spent the first fifteen minutes going over old techniques Elias had learned from the previous lesson and he went through them with no trouble.

"Guess you don't want to show off today. A bit surprising since people are actually watching now," said Tewa.

"Yeah, that thirty minute wait at the restaurant did the trick. If I had known I was training with a dictator," said Elias mumbling the last part.

"What did you say?" asked Tewa.

"Nothing. Nothing," said Elias.

"Thought so. We'll start on the new techniques now," said Tewa.

They went through the motions of each of the new techniques until Tewa was certain Elias had mastered them. Then, Tewa cranked up the intensity and the two of them dashed around the arena with Elias using both the new and old techniques to battle with Tewa. After ten minutes, they took a break and Tewa was breathing hard while her energy around her glowed a bright gray. She shook her head in disbelief.

"How are you--how are you not tired?" she asked.

Elias shrugged.

"I don't know. I guess it's just not tiring for me," said Elias.

"I was afraid of this," she said catching her breath. "I can't continue to battle with you at this level."

"Wait, that doesn't mean you're gonna stop being my trainer? I've learned a lot from you and I really don't want to go back to Quincey. It was awful training with him," said Elias.

"No, no. I can still train you, but it's just going to be impossible for me to help you with any defensive training. You'd need to find someone who could push you for that because I'd get too tired for you. We can still work on offensive techniques and other things," said Tewa.

"You know, maybe, I am tired, but, I just can't tell that I'm tired because of all the adrenaline," said Elias.

"Adrenaline?" asked Tewa.

"Yeah, you know. Your body gets a boost of energy and you don't feel anything until after you stop doing whatever it is you're doing," said Elias.

"I assume that's an Untouched Ones thing," said Tewa, "but no, you're definitely not tired. You can tell because once you get tired, your energy will start to look a brighter gray. I've told you that before remember. And eventually, when you get really drained in actual matches, your body will start giving off energy like smoke and it'll get change color from light blue to dark purple and finally to neon green."

"Right. And after that you turn bright yellow followed by bright orange and then you're dangerously close to death," said Elias. "I remember, but I was just kind of hoping that maybe there was something else. It's fun training with you."

"Well thank you, but I think we're done in here for today though," said Tewa.

"We still have an hour and twenty minutes left," said Elias.

"Yeah, I know, but I haven't planned for you to do offensive techniques today. I'll need time to prepare for that," said Tewa. She floated there for a while and appeared to be thinking. "Hmm. I wanted to put this off until next week, but I don't really see any other options. We'll watch an old match from the championships."

"Yes," whispered Elias.

"Why are you so excited?" asked Tewa.

"You haven't let me watch any championship matches this entire time and now I finally get to see one in its entirety and not just some small clip for lessons," said Elias.

"Yes, and I did that for good reasons. I didn't want you copying what you see from other people. I want you to think using your instincts and abilities," said Tewa.

"I see. Well, where are we going to watch the match?" asked Elias.

"I was assuming we'd watch it in your cabin. I still want to keep it a private lesson and you have your own teletron," said Tewa.

"Okay. We should tell them we're done here," said Elias.

The two of them made their way out of the arena and to Tewa's booth. As soon as they entered the booth, Quincey was the first to greet them.

"That was crazy. I thought you were amazing when we saw you destroy Tewa in that battle, but you're at least twenty times better than that now."

"He did not destroy me in that battle," said Tewa.

"Uh, he kinda did," smiled Quincey.

Tewa shook her head.

"Anyways, as you pointed out, Elias has reached a level that's ridiculously high and I can't exactly keep up with him. So, instead of wasting the rest of today's time with training that'll probably be useless to him, I decided that we're done here for the day. We're going to watch an old championship match in his cabin for the rest of the training session," said Tewa.

"Do you mind if we watch the match?" asked Kabec.

"No, I don't mind. You're all welcome to watch it with us," said Tewa.

"That sounds fun, but I have to go. My little sister should be back from her trip in about twenty-five minutes," said Samara. "Let me know where you guys are after dinner."

She kissed Quincey on the cheek and left the room.

"Everyone else good to go?" asked Elias.

Everyone nodded and they all left for Elias' cabin.

"I didn't believe Quincey when he said you were an amazing fighter, but clearly he wasn't exaggerating this time," said Siara while they flew through the hallways.

"Thanks, Siara. I've been trying to get better every day. It's nice to know the practice is working," said Elias.

"Oh, I almost forgot, I think I might've found something to help you try and find out about your dad. My parents still had a few pages from their explorers' journal with them in our cabin. I can give them to you later if you want," said Siara.

"Yes, that'd be great. Thanks again. So far I've had no luck and it's getting frustrating. I just don't get how he isn't in the Cliern database," said Elias.

Up ahead, Quincey, Kabec, and Tewa were having a separate conversation.

"I'm glad you're friends with us now," said Kabec.

"Yeah, you guys are alright," said Tewa.

"You know, in a way, it was a blessing in disguise that Alera unlocked Elias," said Quincey.

Tewa looked over at Quincey.

"I mean, if you think about it, we ended up getting to meet Elias, who has his own cabin where we can all hang out together. From him learning how to fight, we became friends with you. And, as an added bonus, our sector no longer has to worry about any more yellow diamonds," said Quincey.

"And Alera having to stay at the academy for nine yeldings?" asked Tewa.

"Well, I mean other than that, of course. Obviously that's the bad part about all this," said Quincey.

Once they arrived at Elias' cabin Tewa left them to go get her copies of the old championship matches. She had purchased the hard copy version rather than one transferable via HoloTele because it was much cheaper and even though most people found them obsolete, they still worked.

"Tasich make this?" asked Kabec, taking a cup of food from the cabinet.

"The funky looking mashed clumps in the cups? Yeah, Tasich made that yesterday. He said it's called cadrawey," said Elias as he sat down in the lounge. "I'm not sure what they taught him at that cooking school he went to, but his food looks awful when he's finished making it. It tastes amazing though."

Kabec put a small chunk into his mouth and chewed.

"Mmm. You're right. This is amazing," said Kabec.

"Didn't you eat supper?" asked Siara.

"Yeah, but I only got to finish half my meal. If I had taken the time to eat it all, I wouldn't have made it to Elias' session in time," said Kabec.

"Oh, why'd you eat so late?" asked Siara.

"Someone went to Itta during my shift and they had some animals and devices that aren't native to this area. I had to go through a bunch of special procedures so it made me late to the restaurant."

"Special procedures?" asked Elias.

"Well, since they're not native to the area, there's the possibility of them disturbing the ecosystem or creating unknown diseases so we have to keep tabs on them. And if we know that there's going to be a problem, we have to give them a special designation and assign them to a specific area of the planet," said Kabec.

"What is taking Tewa so long to get those videos?" asked Quincey.

"She's been gone for less than ten minutes. Calm down, Quincey," said Elias.

"You don't understand. These are championship matches. The best of the best," said Quincey.

Tewa came into the cabin five minutes later with the videos.

"Sorry, but I ran into Beclean in the hallways,"

"Oh, really. Wasn't he on vacation in the Snowflake Galaxy in octant two?" asked Siara.

"Mmhmm. He just came back a couple hours ago. He was telling me about the liquid artists they have there," said Tewa.

"Liquid artists. Why can't we have any cool things in our sector? All we have are libraries, trivia historians, and sketch artists," complained Quincey.

"Our sector's only ten serays old, Quincey. In forty serays' time, we'll have all the cool things you could ever want," said Kabec.

"I'm going to start one of the videos now, if you all don't mind," said Tewa.

Tewa started the video and sat down on a lounge chair next to Elias. Every now and then, she would pause the video and replay something over to teach Elias the tactics they were using, but for the most part, they watched it uninterrupted for the next hour.

After watching the video, Kabec left Elias' cabin for his shift and Tewa went to go have dinner with her family.

"I'll see you tomorrow. Siara and I are having dinner with Samara and her sister so I have to go get ready," said Quincey. He waved to Siara and said, "I'll see you there."

"See you later, Quincey," said Siara. She turned to Elias just before flying off. "Remind me to bring the journal pages the next time I see you."

Elias waved goodbye and went back into his cabin. He lay down on his bed and just stared at the ceiling. Dinner time was still two hours away for him and he had nothing to do for the rest of the day. After a while, he got up and decided to go to the Explorer's Library to read more of Pulcher's writings.

When he got to the library, there was no one there as usual. Most people preferred watching videos about famous explorers on the teletrons rather than reading their journals in a library. Elias would've done so himself, but he was told that the videos were always edited and shortened so he could miss something important.

Elias got Pulcher's journal and sat down at a table. Unlike Serpico, who had written detailed and descriptive accounts of everything he had seen on his journey, Pulcher's writing was bland and lacked any imagery. Elias had been reading for twenty minutes, but it felt like an eternity.

My crew and I have finished with the search of the outskirts of what will be the Lighthouse Sector and have found nothing out of the ordinary. Two stars away on all sides of the borders and we have found no suitable planets or life forms in the area other than those found by Jeeho. We will now start to scan the area in quarters as we hope to finish our search quickly in a span of no more than sixteen more days. The first quarter will be that of the upper right left half of what will be the future Lighthouse Sector...

Elias was bored, but he continued to read. After a while, Elias came to the part where Pulcher's journey had gotten him to Mars.

We have finally neared the end of our journey near what will be the central location for the Lighthouse Sector. There are two suitable planets nearby, one of them being a red planet with a barren surface. The lack of a flourishing surface and the existence of energy deficient human life on the next planet, where part of the Ketejesuse Tamachristron famously landed, are reasons why this planet should only be lived on in the underground areas. My crew will stay underground on this red planet while I examine the planet of humans by posing as one of their own...

I have lived on this planet of humans for two days now and they are primitive in their ways. They have vehicles that they drive from place to place either on the ground or in the air at extremely slow speeds, taking them hours to get places that would take us mere seconds to reach at our slowest speeds. Their people create crimes at an alarming rate despite their punishment, which although similar to ours, seems ineffective...

Elias' eyes were tired and his head bobbed down before he woke himself up. He was sleepy, but he kept plowing through the dull descriptions written by Pulcher of his own planet. Elias dozed off five or six times while reading, but he managed to reach the last page of the journal.

This is the last day I'll be on this planet and our last day of the exploration. These people seem to know very little about anything outside this planet and will be only a small nuisance to the Lighthouse Sector because of their space probes.

There had been nothing interesting in anything Pulcher had written, let alone useful. Elias was drifting to sleep as he came upon the last paragraph.

As I leave this planet, I will also note that I have sensed an extremely small amount of energy throughout my time here, which I have determined must come from parts of the Ketejesuse Tamachristron that were not able to be recovered by the Cliern expedition crew...

Elias' eyes closed and he fell fast asleep with his head on the table.

Chapter 12: The Aurora Room

Elias' eyes opened as he woke up in his bed. He could see the light coming from the teletron, but he closed his eyes and tried to go back to sleep, pulling the covers over his head.

"What are you doing in my cabin, Quincey?" asked Elias, sensing Quincey sitting in the lounge.

"Oh, you're awake," said Quincey.

Quincey turned off the teletron and turned on the main lights in the room. Elias pulled the covers off his head and turned over. He looked at Quincey.

"I'm making sure you don't oversleep. Wouldn't want to have another mishap. Especially not today," said Quincey.

Elias rubbed his eyes as he adjusted to the light in his room.

"That was over a yelding ago," said Elias, getting up and going to the bathroom.

"Yeah, but you were an hour and half late for work that morning and it would've been more had I not found you sleeping in the library," said Quincey.

It was true. He had knocked out on the library table and when he showed up to work that day, Sredia had put him on probation for two weeks.

"By the way, how did you get in here?" asked Elias, starting to brush his teeth.

"You know, it's really not proper etiquette to have a conversation with someone while you're in the lavatory," said Quincey.

"You were in my cabin watching the teletron in the morning while I was sleeping. Are you really going to talk about proper etiquette right now?" asked Elias.

"I suppose you have a point," said Quincey. "I used the card you gave me, remember."

Elias put his toothbrush away and shook his head. He changed into a fancier spacesuit and came out of the bathroom.

"I gave that to you so you could use my cabin when I'm not in it or for emergencies. Not when I'm sleeping," said Elias.

"The risk of you oversleeping today qualifies as an emergency to me," said Quincey.

Elias sighed and sat down in the lounge.

The gateway signal rang throughout the room. Elias opened the gateway and Tewa was standing outside his cabin dressed in a colorful, elegantly lighted spacesuit.

"You look nice," said Elias.

"Thank you. So do you," said Tewa as she walked into the cabin.

"Mihalus isn't coming with us for the morning banquet or to watch Elias get seeded for the local matches," said Quincey. "He's busy directing traffic at the shipping bay."

Tewa stopped, looked up at the ceiling, and let out a long sigh. Then she plopped on Elias' bed and just lay there staring at the ceiling.

"What's wrong?" asked Elias.

Tewa continued staring at the ceiling.

"She likes Mihalus and I'm guessing she wanted to impress him today with that suit," said Quincey.

"Wait, you like Mihalus? I didn't know that. Why didn't you tell me?" asked Elias.

Tewa got up from the bed and sat in one of the lounge chairs.

"I don't know. It never came up I guess," said Tewa.

"Hmmph. My trainer and one of my best friends doesn't even tell me that she likes the guy whose family owns the restaurant that I've been getting her food from for the last yelding's worth of training sessions..." said Elias.

"You don't have to make me feel guilty about it," mumbled Tewa.

"Sorry," said Elias. He gave Tewa a hug. "It's just--you're like a little sister to me now."

"Thanks," said Tewa.

"Besides, you're only twelve and a quarter serays old. Isn't there a rule that you can't start dating until you're fourteen or something?" asked Elias.

"Wow. You sound like a dad," said Quincey.

Tewa laughed.

"He's right. You do sound like one. But no, some parent probably made that up back in the day," she said.

"Oh, okay," said Elias. "Let's get going. I don't want to be late or Quincey here will have a fit."

◆

Elias, Quincey, and Tewa got out of their transport ship and stepped onto the ship's platform. They had arrived at the Condor, the special institution of the Sunset Sector, where the local matches would be held. A handful of people were with them in their transport ship since they had come early to tour the ship before making their way to the Aurora Room for the morning banquet.

"This is where we part ways," said an older lady named Kamelah, who had been on the transport with them. "It's been nice to have you on this trip."

Her two children followed behind her and they said goodbye before going back to their mother.

"Yes, good luck to you, Elias," said her husband, Trullock.

Trullock then waved goodbye to all of them and their family went off into the ship. The only other person in their transport ship, a man named Cibee in his early twenties from the nearby Imagery Sector, came out of the transport.

"I bid you a good day, lady and gentlemen," said Cibee.

"And to you the same, my good man," said Tewa.

"Have fun with your friend," said Elias.

Cibee shook their hands and also left for the innards of the Condor. The transport ship had left the platform and moved to another area of the Condor, leaving the three of them standing alone.

"Try the fapeloure drink that Cibee talked about and then go tour the ship?" asked Tewa.

"Sounds like a plan to me," said Quincey.

"I want to sign in before we tour the ship," said Elias.

"Okay, how about after we try the drink, you go sign in, and we'll wait for you near the fapeloure booth. I heard there's a booth nearby there where you can learn to play music by smashing glass," said Tewa. "We'll watch that while you sign in."

"Okay," said Elias.

The three of them went inside the Condor, which was not all that different from the Shockwave. The Condor was larger in size and the hallways were filled with much more intriguing and interactive booths, but other than that there were minor differences between the two. Quincey pulled up a map of the ship on one of the screens and found out the fapeloure booth was located near the entrance, less than a minute away.

"This place is empty," said Elias. "Why are there no people around here?"

"It's really early in the morning. I imagine most of the people on the ship will still be sleeping or inside their cabins getting ready to host today's events," said Quincey.

"Oh, okay," said Elias.

They had flown through a few hallways and reached the fapeloure booth. A smart-looking dark-skinned man with glasses dressed in a casual spacesuit tended to it.

"Early visitors, come to try my fapeloure," said the man with a smile. "Excellent. It's the best time of day to have some in my opinion. Wakes you up just right and I've yet to hear of someone having a bad day after they've tried it. So will we be having a full glass today or just a trial cup?"

"Well, if we're guaranteed to have a good day, then full glasses all around, I say," said Quincey.

The man poured ocean blue liquid from a large jug into three regular-sized cylindrical glasses.

"My name's Theros. I imagine you three are here for the banquet and seeding," said the man.

"Yes, indeed," said Quincey.

Theros gave them each a glass of the fapeloure filled to the top.

"The best way to drink this is by taking small mouthfuls. It'll make it last longer," he said.

Elias drew some of the drink into his mouth and swirled it around before swallowing. It had a sensational blend of flavors, from sweet mango to vuriar to karamor mixed with bananas and then a kick of some strange ingredient he had never had before. His chest started to tingle and the feeling spread throughout his body. Pink wisps of energy began to emanate from his body and he felt weightless and carefree. He took a deep breath, closed his eyes, and let the pleasant sensations flow all around him.

After a few seconds, he opened his eyes again and looked over at Tewa and Quincey. The pink smoking energy made them look like they were on fire. However, they too were enjoying the drink as they floated there smiling with their eyes closed. Several more seconds passed before the sensational feeling went away and the pink smoke had stopped.

"The more you drink, the longer the feeling lasts," said Theros.

"That was amazing, but I imagine we must've looked like complete fools to you," said Tewa smiling.

Theros chuckled.

"It happens to everyone when they first try it. Once you've had about three or four glasses, your body grows accustomed to it and you'll be able to act normally. Of course the pink smoke and wonderful sensation never go away," he said.

Quincey drank some more from his glass.

"Mmm, I could--I could drink this all day," he said with his eyes closed.

"Thank you. Are you three paying separately or together?" asked Theros.

"I'm paying for all three," responded Elias.

An energy scanner came up from the booth and Elias paid with his energy signal. They thanked Theros and then left the booth to go to the glass smashing music booth.

"Why do you always pay?" asked Tewa.

"You're my trainer. It's the least I can do since you won't let me pay you like a normal trainer," said Elias.

He looked over at Quincey, who had taken a third gulp of his drink. Elias chuckled to himself. He took another swig from his glass and let the happiness flow throughout his body as he floated along with Quincey and Tewa. They were a short distance from the glass smashing booth when Tewa turned and looked at him.

"Didn't you want to go sign in?" she asked.

"Oh, right. I forgot," said Elias.

"We'll be here when you get back," said Tewa.

Elias left them and made his way back to the incoming transports bay. Once there, he went into the hallway that they had not taken of the two hallways leading into the ship from the incoming transports bay. As he moved further inside he glided slower, unsure of where the sign-in was for the banquet and seeding.

"It's definitely in this hallway, but how far along is it?" Elias mumbled out loud.

Elias stopped and pulled out his HoloTele and looked up the event information he had been given from the administrators. He found the map with the sign-in location, put his HoloTele away and continued down the hallway.

The hallway he was going down led to the visitor wing of the ship that housed hotel cabins, regional specialty cuisine, and the Aurora Room. The multiple colored lights in the hallway were set up in lines along the side walls, crisscrossing in unique patterns creating captivating artistic designs showing on the walls.

There was an intersection up ahead and Elias saw three hallways leading away from it to his right, left, and diagonally to his upper left. A large see-through gateway, which had been covered from the inside, was in the middle of the far wall at the end of the intersection and a bright sign above it read *Aurora Room*.

The instructions had said for participants to sign up outside the Aurora Room, but nobody was there. All Elias could see as he came closer to the intersection was a sculpture of a young woman in the middle of it that was giving off energy.

"What do I do now?" Elias thought to himself slowing down to a snail's pace.

He looked at the marble sculpture. The woman looked very beautiful, but Elias now noticed the sculpture was not a human. She had the body and hands of a human, but her feet were like the paws of a bear except without the nails, and her ears resembled those of a rabbit, only shorter. A leafy looking garment had been placed on the woman, who was smiling as she stood tall floating above the ground. The artist had also taken the liberty to paint her hair a golden blonde, the insides of her ears a light pink, and her eyes purple. Elias marveled at the fine details the artist had put into the sculpture making it look lifelike.

Elias reached the intersection and was floating by the sculpture. He looked around at the other hallways wondering if there was anything there. As he did so, the sculpture's right arm moved from its body and extended a hand to Elias.

"Welcome to the Condor," said the sculpture of the woman.

"Ahh," screamed Elias as he jumped back.

Elias was so surprised he flipped his glass of fapeloure out of his hands and it spilled into the air. Thinking fast, he used his energy and put the falling fapeloure back into the glass before it hit the ground. He looked back at the woman and his heart was racing. She wasn't a sculpture.

"You're an alien," said Elias out loud.

"Excuse me?" said the woman sounding offended.

"I'm sorry," said Elias. "I--you're not an alien, your just not a human. You see, I'm--I'm not from—"

The woman chuckled.

"It's alright. I know who you are. Elias Rayhan, the yellow diamond from Earth. I hope I said that right. My name is Tera Deline. I'm in charge of signing in all the fighters so I've read all about you," she said.

"Oh,uh, yeah, you said it right," responded Elias. "How did you know who I am?"

"You were holding your glass in your hands instead of having it float in front of you. I've never seen anyone do that, so naturally you must've been a yellow diamond, which I might add is quite rare," said Tera.

"And I'm the only yellow diamond that's fighting," whispered Elias to himself. "I see. Um, so how do I sign in?"

She pulled out a HoloTele that had been camouflaged in the side of her clothes and projected the screen, showing a page with Elias' name on it.

"All you have to do is confirm the information," she said. "And you can also add my contact information to your HoloTele if you need any help later on."

Elias read what was on the screen and confirmed the information. Then, he added her contact information to his HoloTele.

"Do you have any questions?" asked Tera.

Elias paused and looked at her. He smiled and looked at her face and her marble looking skin. He wanted to ask her what she was, but he wasn't sure if he'd sound rude.

"Oh, I'm sorry. I forgot. You're probably wondering about my skin," she said. "Your Earth people think I look like a statue, right? Or is it a sculpture? The books aren't very clear on that. Anyways, I'm a treeston. We're native to the Sunset Sector and our skin is made of a different material than humans. It's not like granite or marble though. You can feel it if you want," she said.

She put her hands out.

Elias took a deep breath, floated his glass of fapeloure in front of him and he touched her hands. He moved his fingers around her hands, feeling her fingers, the back of her hands, and her palms. It didn't feel anything like what it appeared. Her skin was soft and smooth, almost like he was touching a human hand.

"Wow," said Elias under his breath. He let go of her hands.

Tera smiled at him.

"I'm sorry. I interrupted you. Did you have any questions?" she asked.

"Oh, no, thank you. My friends are waiting for me at another part of the ship. I should get going," said Elias.

He said goodbye to Tera and left to go meet back up with Tewa and Quincey.

♦

"Quincey, be quiet. It's going to start," whispered Samara.

"Oh, sorry," said Quincey.

The morning breakfast had finished at the banquet and the liquid artists were set to perform before the seeding would take place. Elias had been looking forward to this since both Quincey and Kabec had talked so much about it.

"Ladies, gentlemen, and young children. I present to you the Yalcar Liquid Artists," said Captain Gyaer of the Sunset Sector.

Four people floated up above a large array of liquids in glass boxes that had been placed at the front of the room. Then, each of them gathered a set of boxes and arranged them to spell out their names floating in front of them. From left to right, they read Aurel, Phena, Naceri, and Hersch.

The lights in the room dimmed down and then in a quick flash, the four of them lighted their names in green, orange, blue, and yellow before splitting the boxes from each other and scattering them around the room.

The room was lighted once more as the four artists floated in the same spot for a few seconds doing nothing. Then they split up and moved to the middle of each of the four sides to the room, beginning their show.

Aurel floated in the front moving his hands like a composer. From the variety of colored liquids strewn about the room he created weaving, glistening ribbons that danced around the room. It reminded Elias of an aurora borealis on Earth except with more colors.

After a minute passed, the ribbons from top to bottom began to release large round balls of liquid that were dropping towards the floor. Aurel had drawn back the remaining liquids from the ribbons back into their boxes and stopped moving. Elias looked up and saw three of the large, liquid balls heading straight for their table.

He closed his eyes waiting for the impact, but from the right Naceri created a huge, clear, curved sheet made of multiple different liquids and swung it like a pendulum from one side of the room to the other just above the tables, catching all the balls of liquid on top of it. Rather than mixing with the sheet, the balls rolled along on top, colliding with another ball every now and then.

Naceri controlled the sheet's pendulum movements until all the balls were no longer colliding anymore, but weaving around each other with a hair's distance to spare. She continued swinging it less and less and the rolling of the balls slowed, forming a multicolored square of balls at the center of the sheet with one clear ball in the middle of the square. The balls were getting closer and closer until all the balls just touched and created a colorful explosion of liquids that splashed into the air. As soon as the balls exploded upwards, Naceri had let her sheet drop down and cut fast, thin lines of energy into it creating a soft mist that sprinkled the crowd.

Elias looked to the center of the room and noticed that the clear ball hadn't exploded, but was floating there shining as it reflected the lights in the room. To his left, Hersch kept the clear ball spinning in the same spot for a few seconds before letting it drop and taking control of the colorful puddle falling below it that had been created after the explosion of all the other balls. He spun the puddle into a small sphere around the clear ball, which bounced around inside, reminding Elias of when he had been unlocked by Alera.

While they all watched Hersch, from the back, Phena let out four separate energy beams at the sphere. They cut into it on four different sides at the exact same time, colliding together in the middle, hitting the clear ball, and creating another explosion. The explosion of the clear ball caused the sphere to explode outward as well, lighting up the colors, and making them glow.

The four of them then flew to the center, gathered all the boxes, and placed them just below the falling liquids in time for them to drop right back in like rain. Then they all went back to back, gathered their own sets of boxes again, and each of them floated the words *Thank You* in front of them as they spun in a circle around the center of the room.

Elias was amazed. They had performed their routine with such precision and elegance. Everyone started clapping and the four artists bowed before taking their seats. A chatter started up in the room again. The seeding would begin in ten minutes after Renalt, Gyaer, and Captain Djembe of the Imagery Sector prepared the drawing.

"Wow. Their timing was so perfect," said Siara.

"Yeah and that was only the introduction part of their normal shows. I can't imagine what a full forty-five minute show is like," said Samara.

"Yeah. It's a shame Kabec missed this," said Quincey.

They continued talking at the table, but Elias wasn't listening to what they were saying. It dawned on him that the seeding was next and he'd be placed into his first ever competitive fight. He looked around the room at all the other fighters at their tables. He swallowed down the saliva building up in his mouth. Which of them would he be going up against? It could've been any one of the eighteen other fighters in the room since he wasn't one of the four seeded entrants. What if he got paired up with Vardun or Jerematrius? They were the favorites and Elias knew they were two of the better fighters in their sectors.

"Hello? Elias? Are you there?" asked Tewa, breaking up his thoughts.

"Huh, what? Oh, yeah. Sorry. I'm just nervous," said Elias.

"You have nothing to be nervous about," she said.

"But what if I get paired up with one of the stronger fighters in my first match? I have no match experience," said Elias.

"Okay, I've already told you multiple times strength isn't the only thing that matters. Fighting requires more than just strength. You need smart tactics and quick thinking to win as well. Besides, you're ridiculously stronger than anyone here. You should be able to sense that," said Tewa.

"She's right, Elias," said Quincey.

"Would all the contestants please come up to the drawing area so that we may place you into the brackets," said Captain Gyaer over the crowd.

Elias took a deep breath and got up from the table. He went on over to the drawing area with all the other fighters. None of them seemed nervous. In fact, many of them were smiling and conversing with each other.

"We will now begin the seeding," said Captain Renalt.

The room went silent and there was a large hologram screen up front with the bracket being displayed. It was empty except for the four seeded fighters, who were guaranteed not to fight one another until the semifinals. Captain Djembe picked out the first two names from the pool of fighters and also another slip.

"The first match of this cycle will be between Raylon Neka of the Sunset Sector and Vela Fusano of the Imagery Sector," he said. "The winner will fight against the sixth seed to be determined later."

The crowd clapped as the two fighters went up to the front. Elias noticed that Raylon was a treeston, just like Tera. Despite having spent the past few hours in a room filled with treestons, Elias was still shocked at how statuesque they looked.

The captains continued picking names to be seeded into the bracket and Elias waited to hear his name called. He hoped it would be sooner rather than later. So far six people, one from the Imagery Sector, two from the Lighthouse Sector, and three from the Sunset Sector, had been seeded into fight-in matches, with the winners competing against the third, sixth, and eighth seeded fighters.

"Now we will start pairing the remaining nine fighters into the bracket," said Captain Gyaer. "Our fifth seed is Praytik Poljack of the Imagery Sector and he will face the twelfth seed, Zuiti Ahphreon, also of the Imagery Sector."

Captain Gyaer, Captain Renalt, and Captain Djembe took turns picking out the remaining seeds as they had done with the first six fighters. One by one they announced the matches that would take place and after Captain Djembe had announced his pairing, Elias had still not been seeded, meaning he would be up against Xelamas, Vardun, or Jerematrius.

His heart was racing as he awaited the next name to be chosen. He knew that what Tewa had said about his strength was true, but that still didn't make him any less nervous.

"And to face the fourth seed, Xelamas Etria of the Imagery Sector, will be the thirteenth seed, Ina Katake of the Sunset Sector," said Captain Gyaer.

Elias closed his eyes and dropped his head down as the crowd clapped. After a short time, he opened his eyes again and started fidgeting with his hands.

"Vardun Uruas, the second seed from the Lighthouse Sector, will be facing off against the fifteenth seed, Radama Arecem of the Sunset Sector," said Captain Renalt.

"This means that the first seed, Jerematrius Danesilar of the Sunset Sector, will face off against the sixteenth seed, Elias Rayhan of the Lighthouse Sector in our final and premier match in the first round. And with that, the seeding for this cycle's Aurora division tournament is complete," said Captain Djembe.

There were louder cheers than before when the final two matches had been announced. Elias went up to the front with the other three fighters and floated next to Jerematrius.

Unlike most of his fellow Sunset Sector fighters, Jerematrius was a human. He was taller than Elias with a similar build, but he looked more like a father figure than a fierce competitor. The two looked at each other and Jerematrius smiled.

"Well, this is quite the treat. I get to face off against a former yellow diamond in my last go around. Good luck to you, Elias," said Jerematrius.

He put out his hand and Elias shook it.

"Thank you. What do you mean your last go around?" asked Elias.

"After this cycle, I'm going to stop fighting and focus on my family. I have a beautiful wife, a two seray old daughter, and a four yelding old son that I would like to spend more time with," said Jerematrius.

"Oh," said Elias.

The captains had wrapped up the seeding and everyone in the room was starting to talk again. Elias and the other three fighters left the front of the room and were now heading back to their tables.

"Good luck to you too, Jerematrius," said Elias just before they parted ways.

"Thank you," he replied.

When Elias had reached his table again, he looked at everyone sitting there. Samara and Siara were talking to each other and Tewa was eating dessert that had just been served to everyone. Quincey was grinning at Elias as he sat down.

"The premier match against the number one seed. This is going to be interesting," said Quincey.

He knew Quincey was right, but Elias didn't answer and he just stared straight down at his plate of food anticipating what tomorrow's match would be like.

Chapter 13: The Grand Entrance

Maraye was sitting at a table inside his small ship, well away from the outskirts of the Orbital Sector into the unknown of space. Across from him was his mentor, Pellof, a senior member of the Nagen.

"Do you have the information, Maraye?" asked Pellof.

"Yes, Pellof," said Maraye.

He took the device he had been given many yeldings ago out of his suit and handed it over.

"You've gotten the data for every yelding, correct?" asked Pellof.

"Yes, but the guards at the portal extension have been drugged too many times. The Orbital Sector administrators are suspicious of them falling asleep so often that I think they may suspect something is wrong," replied Maraye.

"That's fine. We will no longer be using the Orbital Sector's portal extensions anymore. We have chosen a new location to obtain information from," said Pellof.

"Also, the yellow diamond in my sector was accidentally unlocked six yeldings ago by a girl on the ship named Alera Carinu. It is a boy who goes by the name, Elias Rayhan, but he is weak," said Maraye.

"Hmm, the yellow diamond in your sector. I will relay the news to the others," said Pellof. "Let's go to the Ghaila base now. I am hungry and Ghaila herself will be there to inform us of what has been going on."

Maraye went to the ships controls and soon the ship was gone, flying off into the unknown parts of space away from both the Lighthouse Sector and Orbital Sector.

♦

Elias smiled while he looked at the woman and child standing in front of him who were smiling back at him. He was trying hard not to act strange since they looked so different than what he was used to seeing.

"Hello. My name is Ruhari Bandor. This here is my son, Jaycil," said the woman, putting her arms around her son's shoulders. "Please, come in."

Elias walked into their cabin with Quincey, Tewa, Samara, and Siara.

"Thank you for choosing to stay with our family tonight. We are honored to be able to host all of you in our home. I hope that you have had a good time on the ship so far," said Ruhari.

"Um, yes we have, thank you," said Elias while looking at Ruhari.

She looked like a mix between an eagle, a human, and a tiger. She had wings made of feathers that folded behind her back and Elias would not have noticed them had she not turned to introduce her son. She did not have a tail, but her head, feet, and hands were those of a tiger while her mouth, arms, and rest of her body were human. Her skin also resembled that of a tiger with a small, smooth layer of orange and white fur with black stripes, which clashed with the navy blue suit she had on.

"Your rooms are around the corner and they are labeled with your names on the gateways. There is also a common area for the five rooms that you'll see when you go into that hallway. Feel free to help yourself to any snacks there for the time being," said Ruhari. "My husband, Kamron, whom you met earlier, should be home within the next hour and I will be serving dinner in about two hours, if that's alright?"

"Yes, that's fine," said Tewa.

"Okay. Make yourselves comfortable and please ask me if you have any questions," said Ruhari.

Elias and the other four went to their rooms around the corner while Ruhari and Jaycil stayed in the cabin's lounge area. As they ventured to their rooms, Elias realized that the cabin was a luxurious one that was at least five or six times larger than his own cabin.

"We're going to take a nap," said Siara.

"Okay," said Elias.

Siara, Samara, and Quincey went into their rooms and closed the gateways. Elias and Tewa put their things in their rooms and then sat down in the common area outside to go over a few things for his match tomorrow. Elias looked at Tewa, waiting for her to start, but she just looked at him.

"Haven't you taken the health class yet?" asked Tewa.

"No, I didn't really think I'd need to. I mean, I didn't think it'd be much different than what we learned on Earth. Why?" asked Elias.

"You look shocked every time you see someone that's not human. If you had taken the health class, you would've learned about the different species that exist and not just humans," said Tewa.

"Oh. You think she could tell that I looked like that?" asked Elias.

"Yes," said Tewa.

"I should go apologize to her," said Elias starting to get up from his chair.

"No, sit down. I want to take a quick nap also, so you can do it after our review. It shouldn't take more than twenty minutes," said Tewa.

"Alright. Just curious though. Um, her husband, Kamron, he's human, and well, Ruhari isn't," said Elias.

"Take the health class, Elias," chuckled Tewa.

Elias nodded and closed his eyes as he smiled. They started their review and finished after fifteen minutes. Once they were done, Tewa went to her room to take a nap, leaving Elias all alone in the common area.

Elias went to the lounge area to find Ruhari and Jaycil. Jaycil was lying on the ground with a book next to him while he and his mother talked to each other. As soon as Elias had walked in though, Ruhari looked up and smiled.

"Is there something I can help you with, Elias?" she asked.

"Uh, actually, I came here to apologize to you. I realize I must've been looking at you and your son quite strangely earlier and I'm sorry about that. You see, I was a yellow diamond just six yeldings ago and I never even knew all of this existed. In fact, just before today, I had only seen one other person that wasn't human so I'm really just getting used to seeing people that aren't human," said Elias.

"Oh, that's okay. I was worried that there might have been something wrong with the cabin," said Ruhari.

"Oh, no. The cabin is wonderful. Once again, thank you for letting us stay here," said Elias sitting on a lounge chair. "If you don't mind me asking, what species are you?"

"A bowstripe. My people come from around the Prism Sector in the Block Galaxy," said Ruhari.

"That's in zone four of octant seven," said Jaycil, looking up from the book he was reading.

Ruhari smiled at Jaycil. Jaycil had characteristics of both his mother and his father. From his father, he had inherited human skin, hair, and hands. His wings, face, feet, and stripes resembled those of his mother though.

"Wow, zone four of octant seven. That's really far away," said Elias.

"Yeah. When we went there a couple serays ago, it took us two whole days just to get there and that was the express trip," said Jaycil.

"It is a long way away from here, but we decided that this octant would be better to live in. The growing expansion here meant that Kamron would have more work available. He's a translator," said Ruhari.

"Translator for what?" asked Elias, confused.

"He helps translate languages for those who don't know them. He's fluent in over twenty-nine of them and has basic knowledge in eight others," said Ruhari.

"Wait, there are other languages?" asked Elias sounding shocked.

"Yes, many of them. I assume the planet you originated from had only one?" asked Ruhari.

"Um, no, but, um," sputtered Elias, "I'm sorry. I should've realized that English isn't the only language that exists. Uh, so do you speak any other languages?"

"Yes, I am fluent in my native language, *shhh-chë-káh-hoo*. In English it is called Wingbow. I can also speak the treeston language Treestonis fairly well, although I'm still learning to become fluent," said Ruhari.

"*Shhh-chë-káh-hoo*," repeated Jaycil to no one in particular.

Then, he moved his hand in the air as if drawing symbols.

"What's that?" asked Elias.

"I'm just drawing the Wingbow characters that spell out the word. I have a translation book in my room that teaches the language if you want to see it?" asked Jaycil.

"I'd love to," said Elias.

Jaycil got up and flew over to his room to get the book.

"So, how do you say bowstripe in uh, sha-check-awoo?" asked Elias. He sighed. "I said that wrong, didn't I?"

"It's alright. It takes time to learn a new language. It's pronounced, *shhh-chè-káh-hoo*. And we call ourselves *shh-mmm-ha-hoo*," said Ruhari.

Jaycil had come back with the book, which had a very artistic cover on it compared to most of the books Elias had read before. Jaycil floated the book in front of Elias, who took it from the air and opened it. Thumbing through, Elias saw all the different characters of the language, with their pronunciations in English underneath that were highlighted to indicate audio upon tapping. After all the pages with characters came a large dictionary of words that had hundreds of pages just like a typical English dictionary.

"You can keep it," said Jaycil. "I don't need it. I can already speak Wingbow fluently."

"Thanks," said Elias. "I'll have to read this another time though. I have the match tomorrow and I want to get some extra sleep tonight."

"Okay," said Jaycil lying back down on the floor and going back to reading his book.

"I'm going to go take a little nap now. Dinner will be served in about an hour, right?" asked Elias.

"Yes. I'll wake you and your friends when it's ready," said Ruhari.

"Thank you," said Elias.

Then he left the lounge area with his new book and went to his room. He put the book on a table and fell down onto his bed, closing his eyes and laying there for a while before falling asleep.

♦

"Thoros has learned some interesting moves," said Mihalus.

"I think Belanee was just not prepared for him to have improved so much," said Tasich.

"Well, she'll be working extra hard over the next week to make sure she takes care of Vela. Vela's been on quite the run being able to win her match against Raylon yesterday afternoon and then following that up to defeat Jainipear today," said Siara.

Jaycil looked up at Elias from his seat one level below in the booth. Elias smiled back. His nerves were growing bigger. Now there was only Vardun's match left before he would be going out to the arena and fighting Jerematrius.

"Stop being so nervous," said Jaycil. "You're going to win. I know it."

"Thanks, Jaycil," said Elias.

The light crowd noise started to pick up as the next match was closer to being announced. The people that had set up the event were able to allow the noise in the booths and stadium to be heard throughout, contrary to what Elias had thought after not being able to hear other noises in the training arena on the Shockwave. It was another distraction that he hadn't prepared for, but there was nothing he could do about it now.

"Um, so quickly about the betting thing. People are free to bet with each other on the league round robin matches only. Cliern law doesn't allow betting for the local matches or the championship round matches," said Kabec. "I think they do it so the matches remain as neutral as possible in terms of the crowd support, but also because there are usually very few upsets in those stages compared to the round robin stage."

"Oh, okay. Can't people just bet with each other anyways?"

"I suppose, but I'd imagine that rarely happens. Like I said, the matches usually turn out how they're supposed to most of the time. Besides, the Clierns' Data Loggers would notice any large transactions in the credit system and the fighters are never corrupted because their credits are heavily watched, especially those who are part of upsets," said Kabec.

Tewa sat down in the chair to Elias' right with a tray of food floating in front of her from the kitchen area.

"What are you guys talking about?" she asked.

"Betting," replied Kabec.

"Hmm, interesting. You don't hear much about that," said Tewa.

"Ladies and gentlemen. Boys and girls. Our next match will begin in three minutes," said the host of the stadium. "Please welcome our competitors. The fifteenth seed, Radama Arecem of the Sunset Sector."

The crowd applauded as Radama went into the arena and landed on her platform. She began her energy meditation while the host continued.

"And she will be facing, the second seed, Vardun Uruas from the Lighthouse Sector!"

The crowd cheered as Vardun made his way to his platform. The crowd continued cheering for a long time before stopping.

"Good luck to you both" said the host.

Elias watched as the two of them finished their meditations and were floating above their platforms waiting for the starting ball to come out. He hoped this match would last a long time like most of the matches they had watched yesterday and today, but he had a feeling that this was going to be a short one, like when Xelemas defeated Ina. So far, the only interesting match had been the one between Belanee and Thoros.

The starting ball had come into the arena and was moving to the center. Once it got there, everything was quiet for a few seconds until it burst into an array of colors and the match started.

Both of the competitiors let off blasts at each other, but Vardun was much stronger and his blast shattered Radama's and continued on through, weakening a small amount. She must've anticipated that would happen because she flipped back and blasted the platform below, making it turn ninety degrees, just in time to deflect Vardun's blast. Then, she blasted off the platform towards the opposite end of the arena moving to an area filled with tiles.

Vardun continued sending blasts in Radama's direction as she retreated, but she would alter her speed throwing off Vardun's attacks, which would just miss her, either zooming by in front or behind her. She knew she couldn't beat him with her pure strength and she began using the tiles to her advantage by deflecting the blasts coming at her while still using speed altering tactics. On occasion she would receive a small blow from some of the spherical blast tiles that would shatter, but for the most part Radama dodged Vardun's onslaught.

This match was unlike most of the matches Elias had watched, other than Xelamas' match. It was rather boring to Elias so far, and by the look of it, it also seemed to bore most of the other people in the booth. Most of the earlier matches had been more direct battles with a small amount of tactics included. However, given the lengthiness of those matches and the lack of creativity, they turned out to be quite boring to watch as well. Elias hoped that Radama would fight back soon and make this a match worth watching.

As if sensing what Elias was hoping for, Radama stopped retreating and did a cartwheel in the air sending a kick of energy right back at Vardun and then she took two of the tiles and hurled them to his right and left before flying at him as fast as she could.

Vardun was not thrown off by Radama's sudden attack. He blasted through her energy attack and then flipped back, averting the energy coming inward at him from both of Radama's tiles that had shattered just moments before. Radama was still coming at him at full speed though, and she sent a fast, powerful blast at him aided by her current speed that he was able to deflect with an attack of his own.

Now, the two were battling face to face. It reminded Elias of fighting videos he had seen on Earth, except fast forwarded times a thousand and they weren't touching each other, but using energy blasts as their fists and feet instead. Vardun had the upper hand as he was able to get hits on Radama every now and then when she wasn't able to deflect one of his attacks. About six minutes had passed in the match and she already seemed to be wearing down.

"Vardun's setting her up and Radama knows it too. She's looking for an opportunity to get out," said Elias out loud to no one in particular.

"Hmm, you're right," said Tasich.

Radama had just gotten a combination of hits on Vardun, albeit small ones, but after she did so, she had also taken a big hit.

"I don't think she's going to get out. She just took a big hit right there," said Kabec.

"She did that to get out. Right there," said Tewa.

Radama had indeed gotten away and was retreating again, this time in the opposite direction. Instead of using tactics to avert Vardun this time, she tried attacking him with her energy and tiles while retreating. Perhaps she was hoping he would make a misstep, Elias thought.

"She's turned blue. This match is going to be over soon," said Cufri, two levels down.

Radama's techniques were not working as she continued to get hit by a barrage of Vardun's attack. She bounced off one of the arena walls as she came upon it and started attacking Vardun again, flinging as many tiles and blasts at him as she could as they started battling directly again. The attack however, proved ineffective as Radama was now smoking purple. Sensing that she needed to get out from next to the wall, Radama did a pirouette, spinning energy around her to deflect Vardun's attacks before letting off a blast that ricocheted off the wall. Then she zoomed downwards.

Vardun wasn't prepared for the incoming blast that came off the wall. He deflected most of the blast though while taking a small hit. Despite taking a few hits from Radama so far, Vardun did not seem to be the least bit tired and maintained the same speed and strength as he had throughout the entire match as he pursued an exhausted and hurting Radama across the arena.

"See, that kind of lapse by Vardun is why he lost to Jerematrius last cycle," said Mihalus.

Radama was moving slower now and Vardun must have sensed that she was one or two big hits from turning neon green, which would give him the victory. He started sending large and powerful beams of energy in her direction, not worried about his own defense. Radama tried avoiding them, but ended up colliding with a tile that shattered and set off a blast that stopped her in her tracks, allowing one of Vardun's beams to get a direct hit on her. Radama went flying towards the wall, hitting it and falling fast to the ground before mustering enough strength to gather herself.

She was too slow, though. Vardun had sent an array of tiles at her, which unleashed a combination of energy that she didn't have the speed or strength to avoid anymore. After she had been blasted by the attacks, the energy around her body began smoking in a neon green color and the two had stopped fighting.

The crowd cheered and Vardun helped Radama get back towards the entrance platform while the host spoke.

"And our winner, Vardun Uruas of the Lighthouse Sector. A well fought battle, Radama," he said.

The crowd clapped in appreciation as she waved a hand back at the crowd as she stood on the entrance platform looking rather worn out.

Tera had come up behind Elias' seat.

"Elias, you're up next. If you'd please come with me," she said.

Elias took a deep breath and got out of his chair. Everyone in the room wished him good luck as he left the booth. Jerematrius was in the booth next to his and Tera asked Elias to wait by the gateway as she got him as well. In one of the booths nearby, Quincey came out and flew up to Elias.

"Hey, good luck, Elias. And relax," he said.

"Thanks, Quincey," said Elias.

"Alright. I gotta get back to Vardun's booth. Oh, and Samara and her family wish you good luck as well," he said as he flew back.

Tera had come back with Jerematrius and the three of them headed down towards the entrance platform to the arena. Both Elias and Jerematrius stayed silent on the journey to the platform that took about two minutes.

"Elias, you'll be going out first. Jerematrius, you'll be second. Good luck to both of you," said Tera, who then left the two of them there.

Elias looked at Jerematrius, who did not seem nervous at all.

"Um, I thought I should let you know, I'm a lot stronger than what you can sense from me. I'm not trying to intimidate you or anything, but for some reason, I've been told my strength far surpasses what can be sensed by others," said Elias.

Jerematrius smiled. "Thank you. I don't take any of my opponents for granted and though there was not much information on you, I've been told something of the sort by your sector leaders," he said.

"Oh, okay," said Elias.

He floated on the platform and waited a few minutes for the host to introduce the match.

"Ahem. And now, our premier match for the day, featuring our number one seed, Jerematrius, winner of last cycle's local matches" exclaimed the host. The crowd roared. "His opponent today, a first-time fighter, the sixteenth seed and former yellow diamond from the Lighthouse Sector, Elias Rayhan."

Elias floated out to his designated platform and heard a few cheers from the crowd. Elias knew he was the least known of all the fighters in the entire bracket.

"Ladies and gentlemen. Boys and girls. The first seed from the Sunset Sector, Jerematrius Danesilar," said the host.

The crowd cheered and then began to clap while chanting his name in unison as he went out to his platform. The noise they made was the loudest thing Elias had ever heard in the past six yeldings and it didn't stop.

Talking over the crowd, the host spoke.

"The starting ball will be out in one minute, folks. Good luck to both fighters!" he said.

Elias looked around the stadium, past the cubed, see-through arena he and Jerematrius were inside. There were booths all throughout and he tried spotting his booth, but to no avail. He looked back over at Jerematrius, who had just finished his energy meditation and was now staring at Elias, waiting for the starting ball.

He looked out towards the entrance and saw the starting ball approaching. He took a deep breath and waited as it reached the center of the arena. Several seconds passed, and then it went off, starting the match.

Jerematrius let off a large beam of energy right at Elias, who reciprocated with a stronger beam, turning his body to his left after sending the attack. Now with his hands facing down towards his own platform, Elias shot upwards, began flying upside-down, and flipped over once he had reached a star-shaped tile. He flung it at Jerematrius using his senses as he continued rocketing upwards towards the ceiling of the cubed arena.

Elias' first blast had gone through Jerematrius' blast and forced Jerematrius to flip back and then deflect the remainder of the blast before turning up to ward off the energy from the star shaped tile. After deflecting the attack, he started to come up to go after Elias, but by then, Elias had almost reached the ceiling, and had already let off a beam that bounced off the wall. Elias moved out of its way as he flipped around it and bounced off the ceiling himself, heading straight for Jerematrius along with the beam he had just deflected off the ceiling.

Jerematrius spun around just in time while using his energy and blocked the beam that had deflected off the ceiling, but after coming out of the spin, he left himself unprotected. Elias sent a huge blast right at Jerematrius that hit him square in the chest, sending him blazing to the floor. Jerematrius hit off the floor and he was smoking blue. Elias was surprised as he hadn't expected Jerematrius to turn blue so soon into the match. At the same time, Elias heard the crowd gasp and instead of the loud cheering that had been prevalent at the start of the match, there was now more of a low whisper coming from the crowd.

Elias sensed Jerematrius recover from the hit and fly off towards the other end of the arena. He was upset at himself for losing focus and paying attention to the crowd instead of the match. He chased after Jerematrius, but he didn't need to, since almost as soon as Elias had reached the center of the arena, Jerematrius had come back at him, attacking him with five different tiles. Then, Jerematrius began spinning rapidly and created a sphere of energy around him while shooting out intermittent blasts aimed at Elias.

Elias wasn't fazed by his tactic though. He shattered the three successive square blocks of energy that had come from first of the five tiles with a large beam of his own energy. Then, he released more rounds of energy while doing a set of spins and flips in succession to take care of the remaining four tiles, which were all spherical blast tiles.

It seemed that Jerematrius was able to fly around and still maintain his spherical attack aimed at Elias. The five tiles had given Jerematrius enough time that he had already sent seven bursts of intermittent energy at Elias, and continued sending more.

Elias continued spinning after destroying the tiles and let off large amounts energy to fend off the barrage of intermittent blasts coming from Jerematrius until his stronger energy beams cut through all of them and were now weakening Jerematrius' spherical shield. Elias then aimed for Jerematrius' starting platform, making sure to have his burst deflect off it so that it would attack Jerematrius from behind even though this allowed Jerematrius to build up his shield again and send two intermittent beams at a time to Elias' one.

However, with Elias' one beam being so strong, he was able to have it blast through Jerematrius' two beams and continue on to attack Jerematrius from the front. Elias shot down towards a triple, spherical blast tile and threw it at where he expected Jerematrius to have to go to avoid Elias' previous two attacks before following the tile from behind after he had let it go.

Jerematrius was smart enough to realize that the blast that Elias had sent at the platform behind him would penetrate his shield once he deflected the attack coming through from the front. He came out of his spins after deflecting the frontal attack and sped upwards to avoid the attack coming from behind, only to sense the triple, spherical blast tile's energy come right at him. Three blasts of energy rocked him further upwards and left him smoking purple.

The triple spherical blast tile was followed by a rapidly approaching Elias, who sent another huge beam of energy in Jerematrius' direction. This one hit him squarely again, just like the previous time and Jerematrius was sent crashing into the ceiling. He was smoking neon green after the hit.

Elias stopped and his heart beat was racing . He had just won. He couldn't believe it. He floated there for a few seconds, but then he saw Jerematrius struggling and went to go help him back to the entrance platform.

"Are you alright?" asked Elias.

"Yeah, I should be fine," said Jerematrius taking slow breaths. He looked up at Elias and whispered, "Wow."

At this point, Elias realized that the crowd was dead silent. He looked towards the booths and saw that almost everyone had gotten up and were just staring at them on the entrance platform with shocked looks on their faces.

"And the winner is, um, Elias Rayhan of the Lighthouse Sector," the host said.

There was a smattering of claps throughout the stadium.

"A valiant effort from Jerematrius," said the host.

Jerematrius waved his hands to the crowd before both he and Elias started to move off of the platform to head back to their booths.

As he and Jerematrius took the journey back, all the people in the other booths had opened their gateways and watched them as they went by in the stadium hallways. Some people were whispering to each other as they went by and some small children were peeking out from behind their parents trying to catch a glimpse of the two.

When they had reached their booths, they parted ways. As Elias walked into his booth, he noticed that it was much louder than all the others he had heard on his way back.

"I did it," said Elias to everyone inside.

They all looked at him. Most of them, including Kamron, Cufri, and Mihalus appeared to be in shock while Kabec and Siara smiled at him.

"Congrats. Like I said, you had nothing to worry about," said Tewa.

Elias chuckled. Tewa looked like the only one in the room who wasn't surprised in the least. Quincey came into the booth from behind and Elias turned to look at him.

Quincey didn't say anything for several seconds and just kept blinking at Elias.

"You set the record for the Aurora division tournament with the fastest time to finish a match at one minute and eighteen seconds. The record before that was four minutes and thirty six seconds," said Quincey.

"Oh wow," said Elias. "That's great."

Everyone continued to stay silent in the booth until Tewa spoke up.

"Okay, we should get going everyone. The faster we get out to one of the shuttle transports, the faster we'll get back home," she said.

Tewa and several others began filing out of their booth and Elias followed with the rest. Numerous people filled the hallways as everyone else was also making their way to the transports since the last match had ended. As they went along, they came across Jerematrius and some people from his booth. Most of the people from Jerematrius' group were leaving as well and then Jerematrius signaled to Elias.

"I'll meet up with you guys at the outgoing transport bay," said Elias to Tewa and the others.

He went over to Jerematrius, who was still glowing neon green, and they shook hands.

"Great match, Elias. I want you to meet some people. This here is my wife, Galinda, my daughter, Dasida, and my young son, Kexin."

"Hello," said Elias to Galinda.

"Hi," said Galinda, holding Kexin in her arms. "Thank you for knocking my husband out so early. This means he'll finally be able to spend more time with us."

She smiled and Elias looked at Jerematrius who was also smiling with his eyes closed while he shook his head. He opened his eyes again and sighed.

"Yes, that's the good thing about the loss I suppose," he said continuing to smile.

"Hi," said Dasida looking at Elias in awe.

"Hi," said Elias.

"You must be really, really strong to beat my daddy," said Dasida.

"Yeah, your dad's a really good fighter," replied Elias.

"Thanks," said Jerematrius. "We should let you get going now. I don't want to hold you up too long. Good luck the rest of the way, Elias. We'll be watching you."

"Thank you," said Elias.

He left Jerematrius' family and went to the outgoing transport bay. He couldn't help but feel excited as he went through the hallways. He had just won his very first match.

Chapter 14: Alera's Return

Elias arrived at the manufacturing floor and reported to Sredia. She had been mentoring him for the past three and a half yeldings and he would become one of her assistants after completing his training. It wasn't a hard job since he worked three hours a day and his tasks weren't difficult, but it was enough to earn him a below average salary of nine thousand credits per yelding while he was still in school.

"Why are you still coming back to work?" asked Sredia after Elias had put on his headset.

"What do you mean?" asked Elias.

"You beat Xelamas handily yesterday and you're going to the league qualifiers. You'll have made more than five-hundred thousand credits from the local matches alone to support you," said Sredia. "I told you a week ago that I don't mind if you stopped working here now."

"I've already been training for three and a half yeldings. I'm not going to quit now just because I have a lot of credits," said Elias. "And also, I'm not taking Vardun lightly. There's no guarantee that I'll go on to league qualifiers."

"Alright then. Let's get started," she said.

Sredia and Elias flew up over the tile makers and made their way towards the map making section of the room.

"I'm going to have you look over the specialized maps this week," said Sredia. "So as you learned from last week, we receive information all the time from the Clierns and other sectors on what we include in our maps to keep them updated, to add new features, and to add new places. However, a part of the information we receive we put away into a specialized file. That file contains information from explorers and spaceway transport system analysts. We use that data to create specific maps that are built just for explorers, the Cliern counsel, and Standards."

They had arrived near the end of the long workstation for the map makers and Elias noticed that the last line containing two hundred workers were working with maps that looked different from the rest.

"We'll have you set up at the end of the line here today," said Sredia.

She took out a HoloTele and map projecting device from her pocket and placed it on the workstation, ten feet away from a young woman, who was the last person in the line.

"Hello, Meredith," said Sredia to the young woman. "Did you enjoy your vacation last week?"

"Huh," Meredith responded still looking at her HoloTele and map before looking at Sredia and Elias. "Oh, yes. Yes, I did. Got to spend time with my entire family." She paused for a second. "I'm sorry. I don't mean to be rude, Sredia, but I really need to work on this. I received news that the Clierns have completed reclaiming and securing all the sectors that Jaru had a hold of and they'd like for this map to be as updated as soon possible."

"Finally. That's great news," said Sredia. "We'll move down some more then. Carry on."

Sredia moved the HoloTele and map projecting device down to the very end of the workstation so that Elias was sitting on a hover chair looking down the last line of workers. Then, she pulled up a specialized map and spent about fifteen minutes explaining a few of the general aspects of it.

"I'll let you look around at all the features of these maps and I'll come back in an hour to see how well you're doing. Send me a message if you have any issues and I'll help you as soon as I can," said Sredia.

"Okay," said Elias.

Sredia left and Elias started going through the specialized map. While he was going through different parts of the map, he looked at the HoloTele that Sredia left on the workstation, which contained the specialized file. At the top, was the story that Meredith had talked about, *Jaru's forces removed from galaxy group, Milky Way - Clierns*. Below that story were three other lines, *Explorer Reports*, *Spaceway Systems Analyst Reports*, and *Miscellaneous Reports*.

Elias looked through each of the three sections included in the file and realized that all they contained were journals, news articles, or formal reports, which the workers could use to update the information on the maps. He went back to the map and started using his hands to manipulate the projection, which was showing a sector and its traffic density. He tried turning the projection, but for some reason it wouldn't budge. He was going to try harder, but a voice rang out.

"Don't do that. You'll probably mess up the device," said Meredith coming over to his area. "You locked the projection in place by keeping the added features options still selected. If you read the help directions, it tells you that the map won't move while you're still adding features. So to get the map to move again, you just have to lower the options down, and, there you go. You can move the map easily."

"Oh, thanks," said Elias.

"No problem. By the way, that was a great match yesterday," said Meredith.

"Thank you," said Elias. Just as she was about to go back to her area Elias asked, "If you don't mind me asking, how did you get the name Meredith? It's just…you're the first person I've met since I've been here with a normal Earth name."

Meredith smiled.

"My parents decided that rather than giving me a unique English name like most people do nowadays, that they'd rather give me one of the older ones used in England, where I'm from. It's actually more common to do so around there," she said.

"England? Wait, you lived on Earth too?" asked Elias.

"No. I lived in the England Sector, where the English language and humans originated. It's usually just called England though. It's in zone one of this octant, close to Sanize," Meredith said.

"Oh, okay" said Elias feeling deflated. "There's a place called England on my home planet too, so yeah, that's why I got confused."

"Interesting," said Meredith. "Anyways, I need to get back to my station. Remember, if you have any more trouble with the map, look at the help directions first."

She went back to her station and Elias continued looking at the map in front of him for a long time, exploring all the features that were included in it.

◆

The starting ball went off and Elias was now fighting in the finals match against Vardun for the right to move on to the league qualifiers, where the contestants for the Orace Petrans championship rounds would be determined.

Vardun came at Elias with a flurry of attacks aimed in all directions. Vardun was trying an aggressive approach to the match, which was the opposite of what the other fighters who had faced Elias tried to do. It was effective at keeping Elias busy, but he was still able to evade every attack, either by avoiding them, deflecting them with his own energy, or deflecting them with a tile.

Elias gained the upper hand and was on the offensive after carving through Vardun's initial onslaught. However, Vardun did not back down or try to fly away. He continued trying to attack, every now and then taking the blunt of one of Elias' energy beams. Despite Vardun's valiant efforts, he had already started smoking blue within seventeen seconds. After another four seconds, in which he had taken two beams square on, he was smoking purple.

Realizing his tactics weren't working, Vardun tried moving around the arena while attacking Elias, but this made things worse for him as Elias was much more skilled and powerful. Thirty-three seconds into the match, Elias had smashed him into the arena wall on the opposite end and Vardun had lost, smoking the ever famous neon green.

The crowd cheered. Now, after a yelding of matches, they knew who Elias was and everyone seemed to be rooting for him. He had heard people buzzing throughout the Shockwave about him. Many people seemed to think that he could be the first person in over eight cycles from the Aurora division to have a decent showing in the league qualifiers, although most people still didn't think he'd have a good chance to win or finish in the top three of the league he'd be put into.

As Elias found out from Tewa and others, dominance of this nature wasn't all too unfamiliar in some sectors in the Universe. However Tewa and Quincey seemed to show the utmost confidence in Elias' ability, having been the ones that had seen him train most often. They believed after a few matches that Elias would be recognized as the favorite in league qualifying with a chance for a decent showing in the Orace Petrans championship rounds.

With each passing day, Elias felt as though his energy was growing stronger and stronger and his senses were so good that when he concentrated, he could sense individual people moving in and out of the ship with ease. However, the more Tewa realized how strong and perceptive Elias was, the less she seemed to train with him so he didn't tell her about his increased abilities. Instead, he made it seem like he was gradually progressing from their usual routines.

Elias had made his way back to his booth and sat down in one of the chairs.

"You're going to the league qualifiers. This is awesome," said Quincey.

"Yeah, it's exciting. Surprisingly, I'm not all that nervous anymore either. After that first match with Jerematrius, it's just been all fun," said Elias.

"You did a great job, Elias. We'll take this next week off from training as a congratulations," said Tewa.

"Thanks, but I really don't need any time off," said Elias.

"Come on, we can hang out. We don't get to do that as much when you're training," said Quincey.

"That's true. We don't," said Siara.

"You make a good point," said Elias. "Alright, I guess I'm not training this week."

"Want to hang out on Oorag? Or is Biwu a better day for everyone?" asked Kabec.

"I have a test on Biwu that I want to study for on Oorag, so let's say we all meet up at my place for supper on Biwu," said Elias.

Everyone nodded in agreement. As they all left the arena to go back to the Shockwave, Tasich floated next to Elias.

"If you want, I can come over a little earlier and help you cook that day. I learned a new recipe from the restaurant recently," he said.

"Yeah sure, that'd be great," replied Elias.

They all boarded the shuttle transport back to the Shockwave and Elias looked back at the Condor. The Aurora division tournament was over and league qualifying lay ahead.

♦

Elias glided through the hallways making his way back to his cabin from Emium's grocery store. After stopping to talk with a few people along the way, Elias had reached his cabin and went inside, where Quincey and Kabec were waiting for him while watching the teletron in the lounge.

"Captain Renalt came by earlier. He says to go see him when you're free," said Quincey.

"Oh, really. What about?" asked Elias.

"Well, it's been, what, about nine yeldings since you were unlocked and your family still lives on Earth so he wanted to talk to you about visiting them," said Kabec.

Elias put his box of groceries on the counter.

"Oh, I'll go see him now then. Just send me a message telling me where you guys go for dinner and I'll meet up with you," said Elias.

"Alright," said Quincey.

All three of them left the cabin and went out into the hallway. After a short while, Elias parted ways with the other two and made his way to the captain's ship deck. The last time he had been there was when Raina had scanned his energy levels.

Elias acknowledged some of the people he passed with quick gestures. He was a few hallways away from the captain's ship deck and he wasn't focused on his surroundings as he began thinking about seeing his family again. He missed them while he had been on the ship and he wondered what they had been up to since he had left.

All of a sudden, Elias was hit on his side with a strong beam of energy that sent him flying to the ground. As he regained his balance, he looked up and saw Alera floating there, glaring at him.

There was another woman in the hallway that had seen the attack unfold and she spoke up, sounding quite startled.

"Alera. What was that? Did you not learn anything being in the academy? Perhaps you need to spend more time there," said the woman.

Elias hadn't met this woman before, but he wanted to calm her down. Tewa had already made Elias feel bad enough about getting Alera in trouble before and he didn't want her to get into any more trouble because of him.

"It's fine, ma'am. Really it is. Please, just let me talk to her alone," said Elias.

"Are you sure?" asked the woman.

"Yes, thank you," replied Elias.

The woman left the hallway, leaving Elias and Alera there. Alera continued to glare at him. Elias hadn't recognized her energy signal from before. Her energy level was much higher now than when Elias had followed her from Earth to the ship.

"Okay, what was that for?" asked Elias.

"For getting me into the academy," said Alera.

"You were the one that unlocked me. I didn't do anything," said Elias.

"You didn't slip on a rock and almost faceplant on the ground?" asked Alera.

"Okay, yes I did, but there was no reason for you to be there. You weren't even allowed on Earth anyways," said Elias.

"Well I was, so consider that hit what you would've felt had I not been there to save you," said Alera.

"I would've barely felt anything if you had let me fall," said Elias.

"I added some interest to it for making you wait so long," said Alera.

"Look, there's no reason to argue about this. It's already happened and it's over. I'm sorry about you going to the academy and all. Can we just move on from it? I have to go meet with Captain Renalt right now," said Elias.

Alera took a deep breath and exhaled.

"Fine. Just leave me alone," she said before leaving the hallway.

Elias watched her leave and shook his head. He didn't understand her.

He continued making his way to the captain's ship deck and the hallways were empty as he approached closer to it. Reaching the gateway, Elias rang the bells to announce that he was there. The gateway opened and Elias saw Captain Renalt sitting by the hologram projector table.

"Come in, Elias," said Captain Renalt.

Elias went over to the table and sat down across from Captain Renalt.

"I wanted to talk to you about visiting your family. It's been more than one of your Earth years now and you haven't seen them since you came aboard the ship. I assume you'd like to see them?"

"Yes, I would, Captain Renalt, but it's too early for me to visit them. You see, to explain my leaving, I told everyone I'd be gone for almost two years," said Elias.

"Well, your league matches start in about one yelding and there's only one break during the league qualifiers when you'd be able to visit them. Otherwise, you'd have to see them after the league qualifiers are over," Captain Renalt told him.

"Yeah. I guess I'll go see them during the league break then. I should be able to make something up about being back a few months earlier than expected."

"Okay. I'll have someone contact you to help you plan the trip since Earth is a restricted area," said Captain Renalt.

Just as he was about to leave, Elias remembered something. "Is it possible for me to invite people to come with me? They want to see what it's like on Earth."

"Hmm," said Captain Renalt. "Wouldn't it draw attention to your people if your friends came with you?"

"No, the people on my planet wouldn't be able to tell unless someone used energy, but I can make sure that they don't unless they're inside my house," said Elias.

"I suppose it's fine then. Remember though, your people are not to find out about us. Make sure the person that I have contact you knows about everyone that will be going. I do not want any mishaps," said Captain Renalt.

"Thank you," said Elias.

Elias left the room and closed the gateway behind him, flying in helixes around the hallways. Then he remembered he was supposed to meet Quincey and Kabec for dinner. He checked his HoloTele for his messages and saw that they had gone to Lefold's restaurant. He changed his course and headed there, waiting to tell them the good news.

Chapter 15: League Qualifiers

Elias and Quincey were in Elias' cabin while he packed for his trip to the Wave Galaxy, where his league matches would start in three days.

"You buying any new suits for your league matches?" said Quincey.

"Yeah, I was going to buy two or three of them," responded Elias.

"Hmm, okay. Did that lead on your dad get you anywhere?" asked Quincey.

"I'm not sure. I feel like I'm just finding a bunch of things that lead to something only to turn out to really be nothing. Maybe it's all related. I don't know. It's frustrating," said Elias. "How can there not be any trace of him anywhere?"

There was a long pause as Elias continued to pack.

"I know you might now like to hear this, but I just thought of something. Maybe he used a different name when he was living on Earth. That might explain why you can't find any mention of him," said Quincey.

"I just—I just don't believe that he would do that. What would that do for him? What did he have to hide from us?" asked Elias.

"I don't know, but it just seems unlikely that the Clierns didn't know about him especially given that he lived on Earth. We're nearer the outskirts here, but still it'd still be strange for someone from outside our Universe to venture to our area without seeking us out or us finding out about them," said Quincey.

A notification sound came from Quincey's Holotele.

"I should get going," he said as he looked at his Holotele. "I have to write up some information about the fighters in your league for the news."

"Alright, I'll see you tomorrow for breakfast then. I've got a full schedule today," said Elias.

"Okay. By the way, you should go buy those new suits you wanted today so that you can practice in them at least once before your first match," said Quincey.

"Right. Thanks," said Elias.

Quincey left the cabin and Elias continued packing for his trip.

◆

Elias read the screen in front him that was showing the daily news among other things. He was aboard a shuttle transport on his way to the Wave Galaxy. The transport looked like a cross between a train and an airplane, except much larger and much more luxurious. The seats were paired in twos, one across from the other with plenty of room in between and they were first-come first-served. Each seat had its own mounted HoloTele and a tray next to the aisle for any food a passenger ordered. The seats also transformed into a bed at the push of a button so a person would be able to sleep.

Elias was sitting near the back of the shuttle transport and hadn't met anyone else. This was his first time riding a shuttle transport alone and he had decided to arrive earlier than usual to make sure he wouldn't miss it, so the vehicle was empty when he had gotten on.

"Hi there. My name's Marcos Anand. Do you mind if I sit here? The rest of the shuttle is rather full," said a man who looked to be in his forties.

"No, I don't mind," said Elias. "My name's Elias Rayhan."

"Well thank you, Elias," said Marcos sitting down in the seat across from Elias. "Usually this transport isn't that full even with the league matches starting up. Most people don't usually take their vacation to go watch the matches because the fighters around here don't stand much of a chance against the other fighters in the league." He paused. "I'm sorry, I must be boring you with stuff you already know. I'll keep quiet now."

"No, it's fine. I actually didn't know that. I was a yellow diamond just over a seray ago so I really don't know much about anything outside the Lighthouse Sector," said Elias.

"A yellow diamond you say," said Marcos. He began mumbling to himself before looking excited. "Now I know where I've heard your name before. You're the fighter from the Aurora tournament that qualified for the league."

"Um, yeah, that's me," said Elias.

"Well now, it really is quite the pleasure to meet you. Although I must say, you don't seem like a fighter. Your energy level is quite low. May

I ask, how you managed to win all those matches with such a low energy level?" asked Marcos.

"Oh, right, I forgot about that," said Elias to no one in particular. He looked at Marcos. "My energy level is actually much higher than people can sense. I'm not sure why, but I've been told that it might be a special property of a yellow diamond, although they haven't been able to really confirm anything."

"Hmm, I'll have to see that for myself then. I'll watch one of your matches later," said Marcos.

"So why are you going to the Wave Galaxy?" asked Elias.

"I go to the league matches every cycle. I'm the event organizer for everything that's not related to the actual fighting," said Marcos. "The Aurora division is always my last stop so I'm always on this shuttle back home."

"Oh, okay."

The two of them sat there in silence for a while attending to their own things. Elias continued reading the screen in front of him and Marcos unpacked his belongings for the long journey to the Wave Galaxy.

"I'm sure you get asked this question a lot so if you don't feel like answering it, that's fine, but may I ask, what's it like living on a planet where nobody has energy?" asked Marcos.

Elias looked up from the screen and smiled. Marcos was right. He had been asked that same question numerous times.

"It's fine. Feel free to ask me anything," said Elias. "From my experience, living on a planet without energy is like living here except you don't have the benefits of energy to do a lot of things. But if you don't know about it, it doesn't feel like you're missing anything."

"Hmm, interesting. So how do you move around for long distances or move heavy objects?" asked Marcos.

"We've created technology that helps us do those things. We have things like, um, hmm...wheeled vehicles and bird-like vehicles that help us move around. And for heavy objects, we built special machines to move them. They aren't nearly as fast or efficient as using energy obviously, but they still work fairly well," said Elias.

"Well, at least with your planet, I'm sure your government doesn't have to regulate your speeds since you don't have to keep yourselves a secret," said Marcos who then chuckled.

"Actually, they do, but only for safety reasons. And there's more than one government on my planet. There are hundreds of governments," said Elias.

"Hmm, what you're describing doesn't sound anything like what we have here. I thought you said they were similar?" asked Marcos.

"I meant in general," replied Elias. "A lot of things are different, but the way people live is similar."

"Okay," said Marcos. "Have you ever heard of the Moral Dilemma argument?"

"I can't say that I have. What is it?" asked Elias.

"It's an argument that has been going on for thousands of years among the people in our Universe about the planets that contain Untouched Ones. I'd like to hear your take on it since you've been a part of both sides," said Marcos.

"You see, as a species with energy we realize that we have powers that are superior to what Untouched Ones are capable of and therefore, we can most certainly be of assistance to them in many aspects of their lives. However, there is a moral dilemma about revealing ourselves and helping them."

Marcos paused. "It stands to reason that one of us could stop the crimes that Untouched Ones commit on their planets. However, the question is then, what is considered a crime and to who is it considered a crime? Who should we help first, and why should we help them first? Is one person really more important than another? Some laws on planets are outdated, some are peculiar, and some are forward thinking, but should all of them be enforced the same?

"There are more questions like these that are part of the large Moral Dilemma argument, but I think you understand what I'm trying to get at, so I ask you, what are your thoughts on this?"

"I've wondered for a while now why we didn't help my planet," said Elias, after taking a few moments to get his thoughts together. "I didn't understand why not, but I never bothered asking my friends about it. I haven't thought about those perspectives you mentioned though. I'd say it'd be better to help because there are already some terrible things going on right now and I'm not sure it can get much worse if we were to help them."

"Okay, so what would you do first on your planet?" asked Marcos.

"Um, I guess I would stop the genocides and dictators that are on the planet first," said Elias.

A female voice came over the onboard speakers, interrupting their conversation. "Ladies and gentlemen, boys and girls, thank you for being aboard our shuttle to the Wave Galaxy today. We appreciate your business and would like to make your trip as enjoyable as possible. I am your pilot, Merrimer Itho. We will be leaving now and our journey should take us around fourteen hours and three minutes to complete. If you need anything at all, please simply use the signals on your seat and one of our attendants will be with you shortly. Thank you."

The shuttle began to move and as Elias looked out the window he could see the spacescape changing.

"If you stop the genocides and dictators first," Marcos said, "then some of the people with diseases might die. Why not help them first? And what about the people that are victims of crimes that only hurt individuals such as assault or murder?"

"Right, um, then have multiple people working to tackle multiple problems at the same time," said Elias.

"Is there a point where we would be invading people's privacy by constantly watching over them with many people? Would we seem like dictators that support one cause, but not another? Are people entitled to their privacy and to what extent? People have brought about the possibility that we only help them when they need it, but then the question becomes, how would they let us know they need help in a way that we could detect from far away when they themselves possess no energy to sense? Would there be people that may abuse the system with things that are unnecessary? How long would someone help Untouched Ones? Surely those with energy would need to live their own lives as well. And what happens if Untouched Ones become dependent on us to live their lives?" asked Marcos.

Elias just looked at Marcos for a while and said nothing while he thought about everything that he had just heard.

"Hmm, it's a much bigger topic than I thought and there's definitely a lot to think about," said Elias. "I would need more time to come up with an answer for you that I feel confident in."

Marcos smiled. "It's quite alright. People have spent many years on this and there are still questions to be asked. I was just wondering what your initial perspective might be," he said. "If you don't mind, I am going to take a nap now. If I don't wake up in two hours, would you be so kind as to wake me up?"

"Oh. Yeah, sure. No problem," said Elias.

Marcos converted his seat into a bed and a sound blocking curtain came up in a semicircle to cover up half of his bed. Elias sat in his seat and looked out the window. After a few minutes, he remembered he hadn't studied Tewa's notes. He took out his HoloTele and began to read while the shuttle continued its journey to the Wave Galaxy.

♦

Elias looked around the room reading the signs above all the booths as people kept flying by him. A loud chatter sounded throughout and Elias could sense the energy of the thousands of people inside. Even some of the machines and random objects that Elias passed by earlier seemed to being giving off small amounts of energy and the crowds of people marveled at the displays of great skill they were watching.

Elias' eyes stopped upon a woman at a booth creating glasses for people to drink from. He recognized her species as one of they ones they had gone over in his health class so far.

"Fly on over, folks. Get a one-of-a-kind glass here from the Wave League commons. Only seventy credits a piece," said the woman.

She banged her fists down on the table creating a jarring noise. Then she brought them back up as blue, yellow, and green pieces of material popped up from in front of her, which she molded into the shape of a round glass. She rolled the glass around on a tray of paints creating an artistic design around the outside and inside of the glass. Elias noticed that the shape of the glass also continued to change as the woman worked with it more and more. After several more seconds, the woman had finished and brought the glass upright, spinning it to dry the paint before floating it up in the air in front of a boy watching her.

"There you go," she said floating the glass over to the boy.

Elias was impressed at the woman's mastery of art as he looked at the glass. It showed the Wave League's special institution faded in the background with several of the fighters flying about amid a rainbow of colors swirling on the outside of the glass and the words "Wave League" was strewn about on a ribbon she had painted just above the bottom of the glass.

Elias continued watching her make a few more glasses, noticing that each one looked nothing alike. After a while, Elias floated up a little higher, looking for a place to sit and watch more of the booths around him as he waited for Marcos to meet back up with him. He saw two short, wide, stone tree logs floating nearby and sat down on top of one of them.

As soon as Elias sat down on it, the top turned and then leaned back making Elias float up off of it.

"Well, that's just rude. You don't sit on a person's head," said a male voice coming from the stone log.

"Oh, wow. I'm sorry," said Elias as he realized what he had done.

"Just trying to listen to the music at the booth next to us and people start sitting on me," said the stone log as some of the stone on his body shifted revealing his eyes.

The man started to change form. The stone shifted around so that it protected parts of the skin around the man's body although the top of his head remained the same and his two feet formed the opposite halves of a yin and yang circle.

"I'm really sorry about that," said Elias. "I haven't learned about your species so I didn't know you were a person."

The other stone log transformed too.

"Well haven't you taken a health class yet?" asked the man, who no longer seemed grumpy anymore.

"People keep asking me that," said Elias blushing. "I just started taking one last yelding."

"Hmm, you look quite old to me lad. Why are you taking a health class so late?" asked the man.

"Um, well I was a yellow diamond so I just started my second set of classes," said Elias.

"A yellow diamond," repeated the man. He looked over to the stone log person next to him. "You hear that, Usa. A yellow diamond."

"Melvin, I'm floating right next to you. Of course I heard it," said Usa.

"Oh, right. Sorry," said Melvin a bit flustered. He turned to Elias. "Wow, a yellow diamond. Where are you from?"

"The Lighthouse Sector," said Elias. "But I was born on a planet called Earth."

"Well, I'm sure glad you sat on my head then. Who knows if I would've ever met a yellow diamond in my lifetime if I hadn't met you," said Melvin. "This is my wife Usa. We're from England by the way. Old souls if you will."

"Oh, okay," said Elias remembering that England was actually short for the England Sector. "You wouldn't happen to know a place I could sit down that isn't on top of a person would you?"

Melvin chuckled.

"Yeah, right on over there," he said pointing to an area of the commons about a half mile away.

"Thanks," said Elias.

Then he flew off to where Melvin had directed him. Just as he was about to reach the seating area, he saw someone he recognized from the Shockwave. Cozart was floating by himself and watching some of the booths nearby. Elias went up to him.

"Hey, Cozart," said Elias. "What are you doing here?"

"Oh, hey, Elias. I came by to watch a few of the league matches," Cozart said. "I'm guessing that's why you're here too, right?"

"Um, no. I'm actually fighting in the league matches. Didn't you know that?" asked Elias.

"Oh, really. I've been travelling for the last four yeldings so I haven't been able to catch up on any news back on the ship," said Cozart. "Congrats on making it to the league qualifiers though. How'd you get past the likes of Vardun and Jerematrius?"

"I'm actually a lot stronger that it looks. I don't know why, but I think it might be a yellow diamond thing," said Elias.

"Oh, okay. So when's your match?" asked Cozart.

"The very first one," said Elias. "I'm kind of nervous about going first now after seeing all this here. It's a whole different atmosphere than the Shockwave."

"Yeah, I know what you mean," said Cozart. "Unfortunately I won't be able to watch you fight. I'm only seeing the last three matches of the first round."

"Oh, okay," said Elias.

"I'm gonna get going. Good luck on your fight," said Cozart.

"Thanks," said Elias.

Cozart left and Elias continued to make his way to the seating area. This consisted of thousands of tables with hover chairs around them. There were plenty of people there talking to one another, playing games, and eating at the tables. He didn't see an empty table anywhere nearby.

"May if I sit here?" Elias asked a man wearing a hooded suit sitting at two person table alone.

Elias could not see his face at all as the hood of the man's suit made it too dark to see the parts that were not covered.

"Yes, go ahead," said the man without moving to even look up at Elias.

Elias sat on the empty chair opposite of the man. Elias found the man to be strange. His energy signal was very low although it seemed to radiate all around him.

"Thanks," said Elias. "My name's Elias Rayhan."

"Rayhan," said the man in a low voice taking a long pause. "Hmm, so you're the yellow diamond from the Aurora division. Your parents must be proud of you."

"Uh," said Elias, "um, parent actually." He paused for a brief second. "My dad passed away shortly after I was born."

"Oh. I'm sorry to hear that," said the man. Then he paused for a split second. "How did he come to pass?"

"I, uh, I...I don't know," said Elias a little shaken. "Um, I'm sorry, I didn't catch your name."

Something about the man seemed familiar to Elias, but he couldn't figure out why.

"Hmm, I must be going now. Take care, Elias," said the man, who got up and flew away.

Elias watched him as he flew away. Elias was confused and thought about following the man, but just at that moment Marcos came up to the table and sat down where the man had been sitting.

"Hey, I found you, finally. I've finished my business for today. I'm ready to show you around now," said Marcos.

Elias looked past Marcos and watched the man who had just left the table move out of view. Then he turned back to Marcos.

"Huh?" Elias said a bit dazed. "Oh, yeah. Right. I'm, uh, I'm ready."

Elias and Marcos got up and went towards the food tasting booths in a section of the Wave League commons.

"Alright, so at the big events, we make sure that everyone uses the five major languages for their signs and menus," said Marcos. "This way no one gets confused."

"What if you don't know one of the languages?" asked Elias glancing at a menu on one of the booths.

"Hmm, well that's what the translator code is for. All businesses buy them. Even so, I'd say about ninety-five percent of people know the basics of at least one the five major languages so it's really not too much of an issue," said Marcos.

"Oh, okay," said Elias.

Marcos continued to teach Elias different things about the Wave League commons, but Elias had a hard time focusing on what Marcos was saying all the time. Elias kept thinking about the strange man he had sat next to, wondering who the man was and why he seemed so familiar.

♦

Alera was sitting at a table eating breakfast with Tewa, Quincey, Samara, Siara, and Kabec while they watched the match on the large teletrons at the Nitorhe Restaurant.

"Who's Elias up against?" asked Siara.

"Justin Arba. He's from the Clover Sector in the Crescent Galaxy," said Tewa.

"That's in zone one, isn't it?" asked Quincey.

"Yeah, that is weird," said Kabec.

"They instated a new allocation system this cycle because of the expansions that have been going on in zone two. They had to have some of the zone one competitors join our league to balance out the competition," said Tewa.

"Here you guys go," said Tasich.

He placed their plates of food onto the table saying what each one was as he placed them down.

"And lastly, for Alera, the chef's special. You're the only one to order that today so hopefully it tastes good," said Tasich.

"Hopefully?" asked Alera looking a little worried.

"Well, we followed the recipes, but pancakes and sausage links are an Earth food. We don't normally make them," said Tasich.

"You didn't try one yourself before putting it on the menu?" asked Samara.

"Um, no, I didn't think about that," said Tasich slowly looking slightly embarrassed. "Sorry, I've just been really stressed out lately. I only put it on the menu yesterday." He paused briefly. "Tell you what. If it's bad, just let one of us know and I'll get you something else."

"Okay, thanks," said Alera.

"It's starting. It's starting," said Quincey.

From the teletron, an announcer could be heard speaking.

"Hello everybody out there. My name is Baysayly Erizo and I'm glad to be announcing this round's first day of matches," he said. "We have a total of thirty five contestants in our league for this cycle at the Wave Galaxy's OP Stadium."

Alera sliced a piece of a pancake on her plate, dunked it into syrup and ate it. To her surprise, it wasn't that bad. She looked around the restaurant as she ate the pancake. It was much busier than usual with so many people excited about Elias' prospects in the Wave Galaxy league.

Then she looked back at her plate and cut a slice of the sausage. As she chewed, she noted that the sausage had much more flavor than the pancake and was more salty than sweet, which made it blend well with the pancake.

"How is it?" Kabec asked Alera.

She slowly chewed her food on purpose and looked over to her left, giving Kabec an emotionless look.

"I said I was sorry," said Kabec.

Alera finished chewing.

"You want to try some?" she said, offering the food to Kabec.

"Thanks," said Kabec.

"All these people here to watch him and it's all thanks to me. But what do I get for it?" asked Alera. "Nine yeldings at the academy."

"Well, we appreciate you for what you did," said Kabec. "And I know he does too."

"And here we go," said Baysayly. "The first match for this cycle between Elias Rayhan and Justin Arba is about to begin."

Alera watched the teletron in front of them as she ate her food. Both Elias and Justin were standing on their platforms watching the starting ball come out in the center.

"Wow. He forgot again. I tell him everytime and he always forgets," said Tewa sounding unhappy.

"What'd he forget?" asked Kabec.

"His energy meditation right before the match starts," said Tewa.

"Ah, he's just nervous. Besides, he's been doing fine without it," said Quincey.

"They're off," exclaimed Baysayly.

Elias and Justin showered each other with powerful bursts of energy trying to gain the advantage in the match. After a few seconds, Elias managed to land a soft hit on Justin, but neither one had been able to gain a significant advantage.

"See, this is what I mean. He's not focused. He should be dominating this fight already," said Tewa.

"It is a league fight. The fighters are much stronger than the ones we have here," said Siara.

"I'm sure Elias has some sort of trick up his sleeve," said Quincey. "He's probably just setting him up."

Elias flew around the arena with great agility landing three of his many blasts on Justin. Soon Elias started flipping forward while spinning his body in the process, aiming large, powerful, diagonal swaths of energy at Justin before sprinting off to attack him from another angle.

"Elias seems to have gotten the upper hand so far," said Baysayly.

The crowd in the restaurant got louder as Elias landed several more hits on Justin. As Alera watched the match she couldn't help, but feel jealous of Elias' inherent skills. She had been training everyday for over the last seray and was strong enough to hold her own with some of the fighters that took part in the local matches, but Elias had already made it to the Orace Petrans league in that same amount of time.

"He's keeping Justin on edge by moving around so much," said Samara.

"Yeah. This is so exciting," said Siara.

Elias stopped moving around after every flip now, aiming two or three bursts every so often before moving to another spot. At this point, it was clear that Justin was outmatched. Elias and Justin were flying near a corner of the arena now and Elias aimed two spherical blast tiles below Justin before moving a separator tile at him. Then he shot himself towards the corner just above Justin.

"What? Why'd he go into the corner? He had Justin trapped in there," said Kabec.

Justin reacted by heading towards Elias and both of them aimed equal bursts at their opponents as they passed by, but now Justin was facing the separator tile which had split into four separate rectangular walls of energy. He avoided them by making a ninety-degree turn and shooting up above them. Then Alera saw what Elias was doing. He had bounced a beam off the wall and flipped around it, letting it zoom straight at where Justin had just moved to before aiming a powerful burst right behind it also at Justin.

Justin deflected the first blast from off the wall, but got hit by Elias' second blast. It was so powerful that Justin was now smoking purple, and Elias started to go after him.

There was a loud cheering in the restaurant, which changed to confusion. Elias had stopped moving and was looking out of the arena towards the booths around in the stadium. It didn't make any sense. Justin recovered from the hit that Elias laid on him and started aiming blasts and tiles at Elias, taking advantage of Elias' position in the corner.

"What's he doing?" asked Tewa confounded.

The restaurant went quiet.

"Not sure what's happening here folks. Elias cleverly managed to put Justin in some serious trouble, but now Elias looks out of it. He appears to be staring at one of the booths," said Baysayly.

Justin's first beam hit Elias rocking him into the corner, but he stopped himself from hitting the wall as he looked back at Justin, now focused on the match again. Elias aimed a flurry of beams to deflect the salvos coming from Justin and soon he had evened out the battle, although he was still in the corner. He spun around and deflected a blast off the wall towards Justin before bouncing himself off another wall in the corner and blazing down away from Justin.

"Elias managed to get out of that jam folks, but it looks like the tides of this match have suddenly turned," said Baysayly.

Justin chased Elias to the other corner of the arena and fired off shots at him. Elias somersaulted forward, repeating the move over and over again, shooting of bursts of energy from both his feet and legs, one moving towards the walls in the corner and the other deflecting Justin's attacks.

"Interesting move," said Samara.

"Why's Elias flying away from him? He's stronger. He should just go after him," said Quincey.

"He's being flashy," said Tewa.

Elias neared the corner and changed course by jettisoning himself off the wall. The bursts he had sent at the walls before had all deflected at angles and were aimed at and around Justin, who had noticed what Elias had done. Justin was retreating from the beams that hadn't smashed into tiles and Elias was close on his tail sending powerful bursts in his direction, but they hit tiles around the arena as Justin weaved around them.

"He's struggling now, but he's not tired at all," said Alera confused.

Tewa shook her head.

"He's holding back. He's fighting just above Justin's level on purpose," she said.

"Why would he do that?" asked Siara.

"He thinks that if he becomes too strong that I'll stop training him. He's been showing himself getting incrementally better all the time for the last three yeldings thinking I wouldn't notice it," said Tewa.

"How do you know he has more than what you've seen though? The energy level we sense from him is the same as always," said Kabec.

"I've put him to the test before in one of our training sessions. He should've gotten tired at the very least, but he didn't even glow gray. He's hiding his true powers from us," said Tewa.

The people in the restaurant roared. Alera looked at the teletron and saw that Elias had connected with one of his attacks.

"There it is folks. Elias Rayhan has defeated Justin Arba in our very first match," said Baysayly.

"Well, he did it. One match down, only thirty-three more to go," said Kabec.

Alera smiled as she watched Elias wave to the crowd. After a few seconds she looked to her left and Kabec was smiling at her.

"What?" she asked.

"You like him, don't you?" asked Kabec, still smiling.

"What do you mean?" asked Alera sounding confused.

"Maybe I'm wrong then. Nevermind," said Kabec turning back to watch the teletron.

"Does he like me?" asked Alera.

"What difference does it make?" asked Kabec.

"She likes him. That's why she wants to know," said Tewa who had been listening in on the conversation. "I'm going to the traning arena if anyone wants to join me."

Then Tewa got up and left the restaurant.

"So you do like him then," said Kabec.

"I--please don't tell him," said Alera.

"I won't," said Kabec. "I take it you've forgiven him for getting you into the academy then?"

"No. I mean, sort of. I know it wasn't his fault or anything, but I'm still not happy about it. I'll get over it though. Since Tewa's his trainer and she's my best friend, the three of us hang out together fairly often now. He's just, I don't know," said Alera pausing. There's just something about him."

Chapter 16: A Family Affair

"Are you serious? We take all sorts of precautions so that we don't get seen and yet all eight of us can just fly down here in the middle of the night and not have to do anything," said Quincey in disbelief.

It was early Wednesday morning, the day before Thanksgiving and Elias was visiting his family during the break in the league matches. Quincey, Kabec, Tewa, Samara, Siara, Alera, and Tasich had come with him for the next Earth week as part of their vacations. They were walking through Elias' backyard towards his house, which was dark. He had talked to his mother a few hours ago via a HoloTele that had been delivered to her a week back. She told him that she didn't want to arouse any suspicions by having the lights on in the house so late at night, but she said she'd be awake when they arrived.

"Yep," said Elias.

"Wow. Did we even need the transport or was that just a waste too?" asked Quincey.

"No, we kind of needed that. There's an extremely small chance they would've seen us if we didn't have one, but there's still a chance," said Elias.

Quincey shook his head.

"Yeah, I didn't realize you were supposed to fly the transports by the planets. I always flew mine into the ocean, but they didn't notice anything" said Alera.

Elias chuckled.

"That's a little surprising. People here are always looking out for killer asteroids or UFOs," he said.

"What are UFOs?" asked Alera.

"Unidentified Flying Objects," said Elias. "Basically alien spaceships."

"Oh," said Alera.

They reached the back door and Elias opened it, knowing that his mother had left it unlocked. He walked inside the house and the rest followed as he turned on the lights in the kitchen. They all put their bags on the floor around the kitchen table and stood there while Elias started making his way out of the kitchen to find his mom. Before he made it out of the kitchen though, his mom had appeared from the office room.

"Hello everyone," she said.

They all said hello back to her and Elias began to speak.

"Hi mom," he said while hugging her. Then he turned to the others. "Guys, this is my mom. Mom, these are my friends. Samara, Tewa, and you remember Kabec. Then there's Tasich, Siara, Quincey and Alera. She's—"

"The girl that unlocked you," finished his mother as she smiled.

"Yeah," said Elias.

"It's nice to meet all of you," said his mother.

"So mom. How exactly are we going to have room for all of them?" asked Elias.

"Oh right. You all must be tired. Come with me and bring your things with you," she said.

She led them down the hall on the first floor past the office and laundry room stopping in front of the garage door. Like all the other doors in the house, this one was a mahogany-colored one with markings etched onto it.

"Hmm," she said while looking at the door. "I really wish your father had made this a little easier."

She was running her fingers over the markings and mumbling to herself as Elias looked at her.

"Okay, I'll need the tools then," she said out loud, turning around and going back towards the laundry room.

Then she stopped and looked at Elias.

"Silly me. I forgot you have energy," she said shaking her head. "Okay, listen to my directions Elias. Put your hand here just between these two markings."

Elias put his right hand on the door between the two markings.

"No, no. To the left of the door. Not on the door itself," said his mother.

Elias moved his hands over to the wall just to the left of the door.

"Okay now hammer that spot lightly once," she said.

Elias did so and a small, inch-long, vertical crack appeared about a foot to the left of where Elias had his hand.

"Now use your energy to go from bottom to top through the crack," his mother said.

Elias did just that and as he did so, he felt a slight bit of resistance from something he seemed to be moving upwards. As he reached the top of the inch-long crack, another crack appeared about a foot higher and six inches to the right. He looked at his mom waiting for further instructions. What had his father done with the house? He couldn't sense any energy coming from the house, but this was strange.

"Keep doing the same thing. Right to left for the horizontal ones and bottom to top for the vertical ones. There should be six more of them," his mom said.

Elias continued using his energy inside the small cracks and after finishing with the seventh and final crack, he looked back at his mom.

"Okay, what now?" he asked.

"Be patient. It's happening. It'll just take a minute or two," she said.

He looked at the others standing by him and they all seemed intrigued by what was going on as they looked at the wall with him, waiting for what his mother said would happen. A minute passed by and still nothing happened. Elias looked at his mom, who was still watching the wall.

Suddenly there was a loud creaking noise and a section of the wall in front of them began to move inward. The section fell down and there before them were stairs leading down under the ground and a light switch at the entrance.

"I told you your dad wanted to impress me with this house," his mom said while turning on the light switch.

The stairs lit up with bright lights making it look welcoming and at the bottom of the stairs was a white, carpeted floor, but Elias couldn't see the rest since it was blocked by the walls to the sides and top of the stairs.

"Everyone please follow me," said Elias' mom as she went down the stairs.

"You didn't know about this?" asked Quincey.

"No. No idea," said Elias behind everyone else as they followed his mom into this new area of the house.

When they reached the bottom of the stairs, they all stood at the entrance to a huge room that reminded Elias of a fancy hotel lobby. He looked around and saw seven small hallways spread about in the shape of a Christmas tree, three on the left, three on the right, and one up ahead. The hallways that Elias could see each had five doors, two on the right, two on the left, and one at the end.

"So you all can choose whichever rooms you'd like to stay in," said Elias' mother. "The middle two rooms in each hallway are the bathrooms. Everything you need should be in the rooms, but if it's not just let me know."

They all said thank you and went to separate rooms while Elias stood near the bottom of the stairs with his mom. He looked at her in shock.

"Why didn't you tell me about this last time?" he asked.

"I wanted it to be a surprise," his mom said.

"I'm pretty sure it would've been a surprise if I had seen it last time too," said Elias.

"I know, but--I mean last time you learned about all this stuff and sure it would've been surprising, but it would've been just part of everything else I told you about him. I wanted to make sure you knew how amazing your dad was--you know, in case you didn't believe me that he didn't leave us," said his mother.

Elias took a deep breath, looked down at the floor and exhaled, taking in what his mom had just said.

"Did you have any luck finding anything about him?" asked his mom.

Elias looked back up at her and then shook his head.

"No. He's not in their database and I haven't been able to find anything about him," said Elias. He paused for several seconds looking around the room. "You're not keeping anything else from me are you?"

His mother looked at him for another short period of time before answering.

"The doors in the house. They all have markings on them. The markings are all in the secret language your father taught me. I was reading the garage door for the instructions that your father left on how to unlock this area," she said.

"So all the doors have something he wrote on them?" asked Elias.

"Yes," said his mom. "I can tell you what they say tomorrow if you want."

"Yeah, I'd like that. Anything else?" Elias asked.

"Hmm, there is one more thing, but I'll let you find out tomorrow night when the rest of the family arrives," said his mother.

"Wait, what? The whole family's coming here for Thanksgiving?" asked Elias.

"Yes, I invited them this year. I didn't know you'd be coming down too, but I'm glad it worked out that way," she answered.

"But what about them?" asked Elias, pointing to the rooms that the others had gone into.

"Don't worry about that. I have that all taken care of," she said. "Come on. Let's go upstairs and get some sleep. It's late."

"Okay," said Elias.

They both went upstairs to their rooms after turning off the lights and locking up the house. Everyone in the house was soon fast asleep as the sun started to rise on the day before Thanksgiving.

◆

Elias was getting the food his mother had askd for at the grocery store. Because they lived in a rather isolated area, the store wasn't too crowded. Pumpkin filling was the last thing left to get from the list his mom had given him. Elias moved his cart through the aisle until he had reached the canned pumpkins. He put four of them in his cart and headed to the registers. The self-checkout was open, but Elias had too many items so he went to the open register. He pushed his cart behind a woman, who was paying for her groceries and looked at the cashier.

It was Isaiah. He hadn't noticed Elias yet since he was still helping the woman paying. Elias smiled and loaded his groceries onto the conveyor belt.

"Thank you for shopping with us," said Isaiah to the woman before turning to the next customer, who was Elias. "Hi, wel—"

Isaiah's mouth was open and he just stared at Elias for a few seconds. Elias laughed.

"Hey, Isaiah," he said.

"It's really you?" asked Isaiah in disbelief.

"Yeah, it's really me," Elias chuckled.

"But you're not suppose to be back from 'The Amazon' until the summer," said Isaiah, making clear he didn't believe for one second that that's where his friend had been.

"Uh, oh yeah, well I got out early," said Elias.

"Oh nice. So you're going to be coming back to school then?" asked Isaiah.

"Um," said Elias.

"Oh, I get it. You're going to have to leave soon again aren't you?" asked Isaiah.

Elias looked behind him and another person had gotten in line behind him.

"Look, come by my house tonight and I'll tell you about it," said Elias.

"Okay," said Isaiah, who began checking out Elias' groceries.

"So, when'd you start working here?" asked Elias.

"Um, about four months ago. I got a car over the summer so I wanted to earn some cash for gas and stuff," said Isaiah.

He finished bagging all of Elias' groceries and Elias paid.

"What kind of car?" asked Elias.

"I'll show you when I come by tonight," said Isaiah smiling.

"Okay, see ya Isaiah," said Elias as he rolled his grocery cart away and out of the store.

Elias drove home in a good mood and went into the garage. As Elias got out of the car, his Uncle Chris' car pulled up behind him in the driveway and his uncle got out of the car. Aunt Sarah, his cousin Remy, and his cousin Marissa unpacked the trunk.

"Elias," said Uncle Chris. Uncle Chris went up to him and hugged him. "It's been a long time since we've seen you."

Elias smiled. Uncle Chris was as happy as always. He was a tall man with messed up poofy hair wearing his old college sweatshirt and blue jeans.

"It's nice to see you guys," said Elias. Aunt Sarah came up to him. "Hi Aunt Sarah." She gave him a hug and a kiss on the cheek.

"You're all grown up now," she said while looking at him.

Aunt Sarah was as tall as Elias and she acted like a mother to all her nephews and nieces as if they were her own children.

"Do we really have to carry all these inside?" asked Remy taking two of the suitcases out of the trunk and putting them onto the driveway. Remy looked at Elias. "Can't you just take them all inside?"

"Uh," said Elias looking at Remy.

Remy was a year younger than Elias and from the looks of it had gotten a lot stronger since the last time Elias saw him. Elias and Remy always competed against each other in everything when they met for family occasions, but it was always in good fun.

"No, Remy. We're not going to have Elias use his energy out here," said Aunt Sarah. "It's not that hard to bring the luggage in. It's on wheels. Chris, go help your son."

"Wait, you know?" said Elias sounding shocked.

"Of course we know," said Marissa, who came up and gave him a hug. "We're family."

Marissa was several years older than Elias and she attended college in Pennsylvania majoring in animal sciences. She was a popular girl and according to Elias' mom, she had a boyfriend and they had been together for four months.

Elias followed them in without getting the groceries.

"But how?" asked Elias.

"Your mother told us," said Aunt Sarah

"Where's Fuzzy?" asked Marissa.

"He's, uh, he's inside with—" Elias said pausing.

"Your friends from the ship I assume," said Aunt Sarah.

Elias' mom had come to the garage door to greet everyone.

"You told them?" Elias asked his mother.

"Yes, a long time ago. That's the last secret I've been keeping from you. All your family members know," said his mother.

"Since when?" asked Elias.

"Well, your aunts and uncles knew when your father and I got together. We told them then. And they told all your cousins whenever they asked about what happened to your dad. But don't worry, nobody in the family's ever told anyone outside of ourselves," said his mother.

"So everyone knew, but me and nobody told me?" asked Elias.

"Well, we did it for your own good, dear," said Aunt Sarah. "We didn't want you to become arrogant growing up thinking you had all these special powers. And it worked. You're a fine young boy."

"I don't know about that. He seems pretty arrogant to me. Too high and mighty to take our luggage inside for us," said Remy.

Elias looked over at Remy, who was smiling at him. Elias would've come up with a clever retort, but he was still in shock about his entire family knowing all about him all along.

"Where are the groceries, Elias?" asked his mother.

"Uh, they're in the car. I'll go get them," he said.

Elias walked back into the garage and saw that Uncle Richard, Aunt Jennifer, and Kayla had pulled up in the driveway next to Uncle Chris' car. Kayla got out of the car holding a teddy bear in her hands and ran up to Elias. He picked her up and gave her a hug.

"Hi, Elias," said Kayla. She was the sweetest and nicest little girl Elias had ever met.

"Hey, Kayla. Who's this?" asked Elias about her teddy bear.

"He's my new teddy, Snuffy," said Kayla. "What's new with you?"

Elias looked at her and smiled. After seeing Kayla, Elias couldn't help but feel happy that his family was here even if they had all known about him and not told him.

"A lot," he said laughing.

He put Kayla down and she went inside the house while Elias got the groceries. He said hello to Uncle Richard and Aunt Jennifer and then he caught up with everyone inside for a few hours.

Sometime around 6:30 that night, his Uncle Caleb, Aunt Alice, and younger cousin Henry arrived at their house. Elias was helping them take their luggage inside and was surprised when Aunt Alice took out a stroller from the car.

"What's with the stroller, Aunt Alice?" asked Elias.

Aunt Alice smiled at him and went into the back seat. She came out and was holding a beautiful baby girl.

"Meet your new cousin, Abigail," said Aunt Alice, putting Abigail inside the stroller. "She's sleeping though, so please be quiet."

"Wow, cool," whispered Elias as he looked at his newest little cousin.

"She's eight months old," whispered Aunt Alice.

An old, unfamiliar car parked on the side of the street next to Elias' house and he looked towards it.

"I'm going to go inside. Can you handle all the luggage or should I ask Henry to come help you?" asked Aunt Alice.

"No, I've got it," said Elias.

Aunt Alice took Abigail inside with the stroller and Elias went to go see who was in the car that had just parked by the house. As he walked towards it, the passenger side window opened and Elias saw Isaiah smiling in the driver's seat.

Elias nodded while closing his eyes. He opened them back up and smirked at Isaiah.

"Of course you'd have some beat up old car. I should've known," said Elias.

"It's great. Hop in. We'll take a ride around for a few minutes so you can see what it's like," said Isaiah.

"No way. I don't want to get in that thing anymore than I want to watch all my shows with those VHS tapes," said Elias.

Isaiah turned off the car and got out.

"Ah well. I tried," he said.

He and Elias hugged each other.

"Looks like your whole family's here," said Isaiah.

"Yeah, they all came for Thanksgiving. I can't remember this ever happening before," said Elias. "Anyways, I was gonna tell you what I've been doing since I left."

"You mind if we go inside first? It's kinda cold out here," said Isaiah.

"Right," said Elias as he headed towards the front door.

"What about your aunt's luggage?" asked Isaiah.

"Ah right. Thanks," said Elias going to the three suitcases on the driveway next to Aunt Alice's car. "Wanna help me with this?"

"Yeah, I got this one," said Isaiah grabbing one of the suitcases.

They went inside the house using the front door instead of the garage and put the suitcases down in the foyer. It was quiet inside and there was nobody around because everyone was in the basement.

"Where is everyone?" asked Isaiah.

"They're in the house," said Elias. "So anyways, as for what I've been doing for the past year and a half. You can't tell anyone about this." He paused as Isaiah nodded. "Hmm, okay. Watch this."

Using his energy, Elias picked up one of the suitcases and floated it in the air to their right. He saw Isaiah's eyes open wide as he watched the suitcase floating there.

"Oh my god," said Isaiah. He looked at Elias. "What in the world?"

Elias put the suitcase back down.

"It's called energy," said Elias.

"How?" asked Isaiah.

"Turns out my dad wasn't from Earth," said Elias. "I don't know where he's from, but I think I inherited this from him. I only found out a little while before I left."

"That's crazy. It's like you're Thor," whispered Isaiah. He paused trying to take it all in. "An alien. I don't believe it. But, why'd you only find out about it a year and a half ago? I mean, if you've had it all along, that doesn't make sense."

"Yeah. The night I got this energy it was because a girl from another civilization in the Universe unlocked it by using her energy. That's the only way I could've gotten them apparently so I owe her a lot. Just don't tell her that," said Elias.

"So, when you said you went to the Amazon jungle, you were really going to like, the sombrero galaxy," said Isaiah.

"Um, no. Actually they have a huge ship. It's right next to the asteroid belt. Right behind Mars," said Elias.

"How's that possible? We have telescopes that could see that," said Isaiah.

"Yeah, but it's literally behind Earth's view of Mars all the time so you guys would never see it unless you send a probe nearby there," said Elias.

"You know this sounds impossible to believe, right?" asked Isaiah.

"Okay, well what would prove it to you then?" asked Elias.

"Lift something heavier and then move it around," said Isaiah.

"Like what?" asked Elias.

"I don't know. Pick something," said Isaiah.

"Okay," said Elias.

Using his energy he picked up Isaiah and lifted him a good two feet off the floor and tilted him at a forty-five degree angle.

"Woah, woah, woah. Not me. What's wrong with you? Put me down man," Isaiah said.

Elias chuckled and put Isaiah down.

"Jeez man. That's not cool. I could've been seriously hurt," said Isaiah taking a few steps back from Elias.

"You believe me now?" asked Elias.

"Yeah, I believe you alright. Just don't lift me up again. Jeez. Didn't even warn me," said Isaiah. He calmed down. "So, these aliens you live with now. What do they look like?"

"They're human," said Elias.

"What?" asked Isaiah. "Your telling me all these aliens are human?"

"Well, no, there's a bunch of other alien species, but the ones I live with are mostly human," said Elias.

"Oh, I get it now. These 'humans' you live with only got like funky ears or weird feet or something so compared to all these other aliens, they're normal," said Isaiah.

"No, I'm serious," said Elias. "They're normal humans. You can see for yourself. A bunch of my friends are down in the basement."

"Basement?" asked Isaiah. "What basement? You don't have a basement."

"Funny thing. Turns out we actually do have one. Not only was my dad an alien, but he built a secret basement inside our house," said Elias. Isaiah looked at him like he didn't believe him. "You can check it out yourself. Just go over by the door to the garage. You'll see."

Isaiah started heading towards the garage.

"You coming with me?" he asked.

"I'll be with you in a second. I gotta take these bags upstairs first," said Elias, taking the all three suitcases with him as he went upstairs.

"Alright," said Isaiah. Elias was now out of sight as Isaiah continued towards the garage.

Isaiah reached the corner and turned into the hallway leading to the garage only to bump into Siara right as he did so, knocking him back.

Siara was startled.

"Oh, I'm," she said, slowing down as she looked at Isaiah, "sorry."

Siara smiled. She couldn't stop looking at him. Isaiah regained his balance.

"It's alright. It was my fault. I should've been more careful," said Isaiah. "My name's Isaiah. You must be a friend of Elias'."

"Huh? Oh, yeah. I'm a friend of his. My name's Siara. I'm from the state of Nashville," she said without hesitating.

Isaiah looked at her and smiled.

"The state of Nashville," he repeated.

"Yep. Right next to Hawaii," said Siara looking back at him and smiling.

"You sure about that?" asked Isaiah, who was holding back from bursting out loud with laughter.

"Um," said Siara.

Isaiah chuckled.

"It's alright. Elias told me about you guys. I know you're from outer space," he said. "And for future reference, Nashville is a city, not a state. And Hawaii is nowhere near it."

"Oh, thanks. Yeah, I just heard his family talking about those places downstairs so I made something up. He didn't mention anyone else was coming over," said Siara.

They stood there for a few seconds in awkward silence.

"Uh, so I'm gonna go down there and say hi to the rest of them," said Isaiah.

"Oh, right. I'll see you down there in a bit," said Siara.

They went past each other and Isaiah went down to the basement while Siara went into the kitchen to get a drink. She looked back down the hall to make sure Isaiah was gone and then she took a deep breath.

♦

It was late in the afternoon on Thanksgiving Day. The house was bustling with people moving all over preparing the dinner, playing games, and telling stories. Elias had just taken a shower and came down the stairs into the living room. Fuzzy and Kayla were playing behind the couch and Elias went up to them.

"How's it going, Fuzzy?" he asked while petting the top of Fuzzy's head.

"We're busy preparing for the circus," said Kayla while holding a red rubber ball in her hands.

"Sorry," said Elias smiling.

He went into the kitchen, which was busier than Elias could ever remember. His mom and Aunt Jennifer were by the oven with the turkey and Aunt Sarah was cutting vegetables on the island. Aunt Alice was feeding Abigail in her stroller and Uncle Richard had an apron on, stirring something in a big pot. Remy was sitting on the opposite side of the island from Aunt Sarah and he looked at Elias as he walked in.

"One of your friends is out there in the cold sitting on a tree," said Remy.

"Who?" asked Elias as he started sensing in that direction.

"Alera, dear," said his mother. "Would you please go tell her to come inside? Everyone's inside having fun. She should be a part of that."

"Okay," said Elias, making his way out to the backyard.

He sensed her sitting near the top of the tree she had sat on the night he had been unlocked. He reached the tree and flew up, sitting on a branch next to her. She was still looking out in front of her.

"What're you doing out here?" asked Elias looking at her.

She continued looking out for a few seconds before turning to look at him.

"I like it out here," Alera said. She paused for a second and looked back out at the town. "It's so beautiful."

Elias looked out over the town. The sun's rays were shining through a few clouds, reflecting off the water on the lake and the hillsides were lush with plants and trees. He saw a few families playing football outside in their backyards and even saw one smoke trail from someone that was barbecuing outside.

"You're right. It is beautiful. I've never seen it from up here before," said Elias.

They both sat there for several minutes just watching the landscape.

"So why'd you come to see me?" asked Alera.

"My mom wanted me to tell you to come inside," said Elias.

"Oh," said Alera as if she had been expecting a different answer. "Right. I'm gonna go then."

She got off the branch and flew back down before walking towards the house. She seemed upset to Elias, but he didn't understand what he did. Everything seemed fine for the past few minutes. He flew down from the tree himself and went back to the house.

When he stepped inside, he saw Isaiah sitting at the table in a dress shirt, tie, and khakis, but his pant and the bottom of his shirt were covered in cranberry sauce. Fuzzy was licking the floor by him, which had small bits of the sauce in a line.

"Go away, Fuzzy," said Isaiah.

Fuzzy left the kitchen and Isaiah looked up and saw Elias enter the kitchen.

"What happened to you?" asked Elias.

Siara flew into the kitchen with a towel in her hands.

"Here you go. I'm so sorry about this," she said handing Isaiah the towel.

"Thanks," said Isaiah as he wiped the cranberry sauce off as best as he could.

Siara looked at Elias.

"Oh, hey, Elias," she said. "I, uh, I accidentally spilled the bowl of cranberry sauce on him."

"How?" asked Elias, who was very confused.

"Well, I was going out the kitchen over there and I was taking it to the dining room. I turned the corner and he was right there. I got startled. I dropped the bowl, the sauce landed on him, and the bowl broke on the floor," said Siara.

"Why didn't you just catch it with your energy?" asked Elias.

"Look, it all happened very fast alright. He was like, less than a foot away and I didn't have time to react. You know, you should just stop asking questions about it," said Siara.

"Okay, jeez, I'm sorry," said Elias.

Siara left the room and headed down the hallway towards the basement.

"That's weird," said Elias.

"Today does not seem to be your day. Alera went by here earlier and she seemed pretty unhappy as well," said Isaiah.

"I don't get it. I have no idea what I did to either one of them," said Elias.

"Well, I'm gonna get some new clothes from my house. You wanna come with?" asked Isaiah.

"Yeah sure," said Elias. "Where is everyone?"

"They're all downstairs waiting for Kayla to perform in the circus with Fuzzy," said Isaiah.

"Oh, okay," said Elias.

They were just about to go out the front door when Kayla came down the stairs.

"Where are you guys going?" she asked. "Aren't you guys gonna watch me and Fuzzy in the circus?"

"Huh, oh, well we have to go to Isaiah's house and get some new clothes for him," said Elias. "Tell you what though. If you have someone tape it, we'll watch it later."

"Okay," said Kayla.

She made her way to the basement. Elias and Isaiah went out the door and Elias got into Isaiah's car as the two of them went to Isaiah's house.

Chapter 17: The Nagen's Discovery

Maraye took a seat next to Pellof, who was conversing with Derela.

"He is indeed a special one," said Pellof. "But he is strange. He comes from a place we do not know."

Maraye knew Pellof was speaking of Elias as they prepared to watch his final match in the league qualifiers.

"He has gotten much stronger recently," said Derela.

"His mother is an Untouched One. His father must have been a great one to pass such powers to him," said Maraye.

"He is a yellow diamond and we are unaware of how they come to be, but it would seem so," said Pellof.

"It's a shame his father passed away," said Maraye.

"Yes, and he doesn't know how it happened," said Derela. "It's hard to believe such a thing could happen to a person."

The three of them stopped talking and waited for the match to begin. Their booth was empty, but others they did not know would be arriving in several minutes. Maraye went up to the food station and ordered his food via a panel. As he retrieved his tray and sat down, several others entered the booth including Ramses and Subedai.

"Ah, hello Cozart," said Subedai sounding surprised. "I didn't know you'd be here."

"Oh, yes," replied Maraye. "I came to watch Elias' match. He is the first one from our sector to ever make it this far."

Maraye smiled and shook both Subedai and Ramses' hands.

"Hello," said Ramses to Pellof and Derela.

"Oh, right. This is Ballon and Luel," said Maraye pointing to Pellof and Derela, respectively. Then he looked to Pellof and Derela and introduced them to Subedai and Ramses.

"Nice to meet you," nodded Pellof.

"Yes, Cozart tells us that you have a spectacular ship," said Derela.

"Thank you," said Ramses. "Although it seems like Cozart is hardly ever on board. He's always busy traveling for work."

"Ladies and gentlemen. Children of all ages. Please take your seats. The final match will begin in four minutes," said the announcer, her voice resonating throughout the arena.

"It was nice to meet you two," said Subedai. "I wish we could talk more, but we should get our food and have a seat though. Don't want to miss the start of the match."

Subedai and Ramses went over to the food station and Maraye took a deep breath. He always worried that the Shockwave's hierarchy might find out the truth about him. Maraye looked over at Pellof and Derela, but both of them were staring straight ahead into the arena. Maraye took a bite of his addon loaf and chewed, glancing at Subedai and Ramses as they went to their seats with their food trays. Maraye listened in on their conversation.

"You know, I heard one of the finalists from the second octant say that the Wave League was weak this year because Elias has been able to go undefeated so far," Subedai said.

"Maso Fazaile was his name. I have been lucky enough to watch a few of his matches though. He lost to Ashar Dene two cycles ago. Remember Ashar? He was the runner-up," said Ramses.

"Yes, but still, Maso says he can easily beat any of these contestants with just one blast. Sounds like he's a little too cocky to me," said Subedai.

"Please welcome our competitors for the final match. From the Lighthouse Sector in the fourth zone, Elias Rayhan with an undefeated record," the announcer said as Maraye watched Elias move out to his platform.

Maraye and the others in the booth clapped and throughout the stadium loud cheers could be heard, musicians began to drum, and a set of five light ribbons were shot into the stadium outside of the arena. The lights circled around before hitting the walls of the cubed arena, causing it to glow. Elias waved his hands to the crowd and then began his energy meditation. The cheering died down to a lower level as the announcer introduced his opponent.

"From the Innovation Sector in the third zone, Aercia Lald with a record of thirty-two battles won and one lost!" said the announcer.

Maraye watched as Aercia flew out to her platform, her blonde hair flowing through the air. She was a beautiful woman and the cheers throughout the stadium for Aercia were louder than the ones for Elias. A minute passed as the crowd continued cheering anticipating the start of the match.

"There it is folks. The starting ball is out," said the announcer. She paused until the ball burst. "And let the match begin!"

Both Elias and Aercia let off blasts, but Elias' blast was enormous, more powerful than Maraye had seen him ever use before.

"What in the world?" said Subedai in disbelief as he stood up from his seat.

The crowd became dead silent. Elias' blast was so strong that Aercia's blast had blown clean by it and she got hit so hard she was smoking neon green. Maraye was about to clap, but Pellof grabbed his right hand and stopped it from moving. Maraye looked over and saw Pellof shake his head before letting go of his hand.

"Uh, wow," said the announcer also in disbelief. "Elias defeats Aercia to win a spot in the Orace Petrans Championship."

The crowd stayed silent.

"That wasn't exactly a shabby blast from Aercia," said another person in the booth.

"That concludes all the matches we have for this cycle's Wave League," said the announcer. "Thank you to everyone who made this possible and we wish Elias the best of luck in the championships."

There was soft applause throughout the crowd and in the booth. Maraye saw that Pellof and Derela were clapping and Pellof looked at him as if telling him to do the same. Maraye obliged and clapped for a few seconds. Then, the people in the booth began to file out. Subedai and Ramses passed by them again.

"Quite some match wasn't it, Cozart," said Subedai.

"I'll say," responded Maraye trying to sound surprised.

Subedai and Ramses left the booth while Maraye, Pellof and Derela stayed in their seats staring straight ahead into the arena. After a short while, they were the only ones left in the booth.

"It's him," said Pellof.

"And it's a darn shame his father isn't around to see it," said Maraye.

"Were you able to find out what bothered him in his first match?" asked Derela.

"He said it was nothing to worry about. Just a lack of concentration," said Maraye.

"We should go now. We have much to do," said Pellof.

The three of them left the booth, led by Derela with Pellof and Maraye close behind.

◆

"I've told Jaru your information," said Ghaila.

"And?" asked Derela.

"His orders are coming in as we speak. Laris should arrive soon," said Ghaila.

They all sat silently for several minutes. Then, Laris entered the room and looked around.

"Ghaila, the orders from Jaru," said Laris handing over a device similar to the one Maraye used to hack into the Cliern database.

Ghaila put the device into another machine and went about unlocking the information. After a bit of reading, Ghaila looked up at the group in the room.

"How well is your relationship with him?" she asked.

"Well enough that he knows who I am and trusts me," said Maraye.

"You'll need to extract him from the Lighthouse Sector to a place where we can avoid the Cliern troops quickly intervening," said Ghaila.

"That'll be difficult given the boy's status now that he's a finalist," said Pellof.

"Yes, I agree," said Laris. "Even the people in my sector have grown to like him. Intrigue of a yellow diamond and all."

"Actually, if I'm able to borrow a Cliern ship, it should be easy to get him outside of the range of the Cliern's known Universe," said Maraye.

"You have a ship," said Ghaila.

"I'd need one large enough to fit him and his friends for at least two weeks. He's been looking for any signs of his father as you all know by now. One of the old explorers has an adventure for him that interests him. If I could get a ship, I could easily get him and his friends to join me," said Maraye.

The room went silent for a minute.

"Well?" asked Ghaila.

"It can't be done anytime too soon," said Derela.

"Jaru prefers it be done before the championships begin," said Ghaila.

"It would raise suspicion doing something of the sort so quickly with no reason especially in an area that is already under heavy watch because of the Orbital Sector incident," said Derela.

"How long then?" asked Pellof.

"At the least a little over four yeldings. To be safe, five yeldings and a week," said Derela.

"Fine. Put it in motion as soon as you can," said Ghaila turning around and adjusting a screen connected to the device.

Then she took the device out of the machine and handed it back to Laris.

"Back to Jaru. Tell him of the plan. We'll need most of the force then," said Ghaila.

"Yes, Ghaila," said Laris, who then left the room.

"Back to the normal schedule," said Ghaila. Everyone got up and left the room, but Ghaila. "And make sure your end is complete, Maraye."

"Yes, Ghaila," responded Maraye.

♦

It was three days after Elias had won his match. Elias and Tewa were flying through the halls of the ship when Maraye saw them and started a conversation with them.

"Yeah, I was at the stadium for your last match. You did amazing. Only needed one hit," said Maraye.

"Thanks, Cozart," said Elias.

"He should've been doing that all along, but he's been holding back this whole time," said Tewa. "It would've shut up that guy Maso Fazaile for sure."

"Oh, don't worry about that," said Maraye. "He's probably just unhappy that he had to face tougher competition in his league. He's still got a top eight seed so I don't know what's bothering him anyways."

"Yeah. Anyways, I need to get to class," said Tewa.

"Bye," said Elias.

Tewa left down the hallway leaving Elias and Maraye alone.

"I have to go too," said Maraye. "In case I don't see you, good luck in the championships."

"Thanks," said Elias. "Hopefully I'll see you around though."

◆

Eleven weeks had passed since Elias had won a spot and in the Orace Petrans Championship. Now back on the Shockwave and back to his normal schedule, Elias was sitting at a table in the far end of the Explorer's Library alone as he studied for his classes. He had several books open on the table and a historical timeline was projected above the table.

"This doesn't make any sense," he whispered in frustration as he poured over the books.

He continued looking at a map on octant expansion for explorers. There seemed no feasible reason why octants one and eight continued to be unexplored. The books he read hadn't mentioned anything about it either.

Elias sensed Alera approaching the room. Over the last four weeks, they had been studying together quite often and Elias grew to like her, but he couldn't bring himself to tell her.

"Hey," said Alera as she entered the empty room and sat down across from Elias.

"Hi," said Elias looking up from one of the books.

"What's with all the books?" she asked.

"Huh, oh well I'm working on my class project plan for exploring and octant expansion and I can't figure out why there's essentially no expansion in octants one and eight. It seems like there's something there stopping it because octant four has the fourth least expansion after our octant," he replied.

"Hmm, let me see," said Alera as she came over to his side of the table and sat down next to him.

Alera had told him and Tewa two weeks ago that she would become an explorer upon leaving school since she had increased her energy level enough to qualify for the position. Elias waited as she read different sections of the books feeling nervous as he watched her.

"Well, you're right. It doesn't say much about it," said Alera. "I've been to octant eight for vacation once and it's not that crowded there as it is in our octant and octants two and three. I think they just don't need to expand."

"Oh, okay," said Elias looking at the timeline above the table. After a few seconds he continued. "Why doesn't our octant have more expansion then? I mean, we're one of the most populated octants of the eight."

"The destruction of the Ketejesuse Tamachristron. It really messed up things in our octant until recently. Even the other zones weren't as safe as moving to other octants," she said. "Shouldn't you have learned about that by now?"

"Oh right. That seems to be kind of a big deal around here," said Elias.

"Not really. It's just common knowledge. The biggest thing that's happened to us around here is probably you actually," Alera said as she looked at one of the books.

"Me?" asked Elias sounding surprised.

"Yes, you," Alera said looking at him now. "You're by far the strongest person to come out of this galaxy since who knows when and you're a former yellow diamond. It also helps that you look halfway decent."

"Only halfway decent, huh?" asked Elias.

"Yeah," said Alera smiling at him. Then she started to laugh at him.

"Thanks," said Elias sarcastically.

"I'm sorry," said Alera who was still laughing. Elias looked at her and shook his head before going back to one of the books. Alera put her right hand on his left shoulder. "I'm just kidding. Really." Her laughing had died down and she smiled at him. "You look great."

They both stared into each other's eyes. Elias' heart was racing and he was filled with nerves. He didn't know what to do. Alera began moving closer to him. They were about to kiss when Alera pulled back and started looking at one of the books in front of her. Elias turned around and saw Quincey fly into the room and take a seat opposite of him. Elias wanted to yell at Quincey for interrupting, but he acted as if nothing had happened.

"What's up?" said Quincey as he sat down.

"Nothing much. Just studying," said Elias hoping that Quincey would go away.

"Oh cool. What class?" asked Quincey.

"Modern Civilization," said Elias.

"I'm gonna go," said Alera getting up from her seat.

"You just got here," said Elias.

"I forgot I had to do something for my parents," she said. "See you guys later."

She took her things and left the Explorer's Library. Elias looked back at Quincey.

"Why'd you have to come in here?" he asked.

"Something wrong?" asked Quincey sounding confused.

"She was going to kiss me, but then you came by," said Elias sighing.

"Oh, sorry man. I didn't know," said Quincey.

"You and Kabec are my best friends. You two are the only ones I've told that I like her and yet you two manage to stop in every time," said Elias.

"I said I was sorry," said Quincey. "Why don't you just ask her out?"

"I would, but I'm so busy that I don't have time for it. I have to make up for all the time I missed with my classes and Tewa's making me watch every single video on the other finalists in the champsionships. And on top of all that, Sredia's given me more hours at work since I've been there long enough now," said Elias.

"Why don't you just quit? You definitely don't need the money anymore. You're set for the next ten serays at least," said Quincey.

"I don't want to quit. I actually like work. And besides, that's only three hours of my day," said Elias.

"Suit yourself," said Quincey who then sat there looking at the timeline while Elias went back to studying.

Chapter 18: Sanize

Quincey, Samara, Siara, Tasich, and Mihalus were sitting down in the Nitorhe Restaurant eating their supper.

"So are any of you going to go to Sanize to watch Elias' match?" asked Tasich.

"He'd have to pay for me to go. The tickets are fairly expensive and I'd rather not spend my next two serays of vacation savings on it," said Siara.

"I'm sure he will. He just donated ten million credits to the ship's general funds for activities and commerce last week," said Quincey.

"He donated credits?" said Samara sounding shocked.

"Yeah, ten million of them. You think you're shocked. You should've seen the look on Subedai's face when Elias told him," said Quincey.

"Speaking of which," said Mihalus looking over to the entrance of the restaurant.

Elias glided to their table and he looked to be in a good mood. Quincey had seen Elias happy before, but for some reason he seemed more jubilant today.

"I'm surprised you have time for us," said Quincey as Elias sat down at their table.

"Ha ha," said Elias. "You'll be happy to know that Sredia and I both agreed that I'll stop working in the manufacturing room after tomorrow. She'll be able to give my position to someone else and I can come in anytime if I really want to."

"That'll only mean that Tewa can train you longer," said Samara.

"Yeah, I don't understand. She's training me more the further into the Orace Petrans I've gotten. You'd think she'd have confidence in me being able to hold my own after everything I've done," said Elias.

"She does. That's why she trains you so hard now. She believes you're going to be the next Elite Ilay," said Mihalus. Everyone was silent for a few seconds. "Just because we stopped dating doesn't mean we're not still friends."

Everyone had finished with their suppers and Linur their waitress came by the table.

"Would anyone like anything else?" she asked.

There was a consensus no among everyone.

"You're not going to eat?" Quincey asked Elias.

"No, it's alright. I don't want to keep you guys here just so I can eat. I'll just get something from a vendor," said Elias.

"Okay then," said Linur as she gathered their dishes and left.

"You need to come with me afterwards," Elias told Quincey.

"What for?" asked Quincey.

"Well, Subedai wanted someone to oversee spending for the donation I gave and he asked me, but I told him that I'd rather have you do it. You know since you're always complaining how boring this ship is and all," said Elias.

"Oh, please don't enable his crazy ideas," said Samara. "I have enough trouble as it is keeping him in line."

Quincey smiled at Samara.

"Crazy ideas?" asked Quincey. "I don't know what you're talking about."

"Anyways, he wants to see both of us as soon as possible," said Elias.

"Alright," said Quincey getting up from his chair. He kissed Samara on the cheek before he and Elias left.

He and Elias flew through the hallways to Subedai's Administration Deck and Quincey had to know what it was that made Elias so happy.

"What's with you?" he asked. "You seem happier than normal."

"Huh," said Elias. "Oh, well—"

"You and Alera 'studied together' again, didn't you?" asked Quincey.

A notification sound came from Elias' HoloTele and he looked at it. Quincey watched him as he read the message.

"Hmm, interesting. Cozart just sent me a message saying that he's getting a ship commissioned for a journey on Jeeho's old explorer's path through this area to find the planets that Jeeho says are still out there and he says that he can take me with him if I wanted to since he has room for seven more people," said Elias.

"That's awesome," said Quincey. "When is it though?"

"A few weeks after the first round of the Championships," said Elias.

"That works out nicely," said Quincey.

Quincey slowed down as they had arrived outside Subedai's Administration Deck. Elias put his HoloTele away and they both went inside. Subedai was busy at one of the machines, but he turned around as they entered the room.

"Hello, you two," said Subedai.

Quincey had seen the ship's hierarchy far more often during the past two serays that Elias had been on the ship. He was no longer nervous around them now that he knew they were just like everyone else.

"Hello," said Elias and Quincey almost in unison.

"Elias told you about why you're here, correct?" Subedai asked Quincey.

"Yeah," replied Quincey.

"Good, so I along with several other members usually decide how to spend the funds we have for activities and commerce based upon weekly meetings with numerous adults on board the ship. We meet once every Thayke and hold votes on specific suggestions brought about during the meetings and it usually takes about two hours," said Subedai.

"Right, I got a message to attend my first one in several weeks," said Quincey.

"Yes, had you not been chosen by Elias to be included in the decision making, you'd have gotten those messages every few weeks or so," said Subedai. "Nevertheless, you are now expected to come to every meeting if you are up to the task."

"I most certainly will," said Quincey.

"Excellent, then I shall send you the information you'll need via HoloTele and you may read it at your convenience," said Subedai.

"Okay, thanks," said Quincey.

"As for you, Elias, Captain Renalt wanted me to give you this," said Subedai handing over a map.

"Oh, thanks," said Elias, "but I really don't need anything in return."

"Nonsense. We all agreed that you should have it," said Subedai. "It's not a regular map by the way. This particular map has every option available. It's a deluxe master map. Only the Clierns order these."

"Wow, thanks," said Elias. "But for the future, please don't feel the need to give me something in return. I just want to help everyone out since you guys have helped me out so much."

"In the future?" Quincey asked a little shocked.

"Well, I mean, I really don't need as many credits as I'm getting so I'll likely donate more later on," said Elias.

There was a long, awkward silence as Quincey and Subedai both stared at Elias.

"Well, once again, thank you, Elias. I wish I could talk longer, but I have to get back to work," said Subedai. He and Elias shook hands. "And I'll see you next Thayke, Quincey."

Quincey also shook Subedai's hand and then he and Elias left Subedai's Administration Deck. Quincey looked over to Elias.

"I'm going to go back to Samara," he said.

"Okay. I'll see you tomorrow then," said Elias.

They parted ways and Quincey went on his way to Samara's cabin.

◆

Elias and Kamron had arrived in Sanize after a two and a half day journey. They were in the center of one of the nine special institutions that comprised the capital city and upon arriving in Sanize Elias noticed that everything was well organized.

"Good morning to you, Elias and Kamron," said a welcoming human woman. "My name is Soihel Maan."

"Good morning," responded Elias.

He let Kamron handle their accomodations while he took in the spectacles of the Cliern capital. Elias was glad he had completed his health class because there were so many different species of people flying around that he would have been gawking at a few of them otherwise. There were vendors everywhere in the spherical enclosure of the special institution they had entered after deboarding their transport ship. After reading the signs on the vendor booths, Elias realized they were organized into several categories: food, travel, entertainment, lodging, and miscellaneous.

Kamron tapped Elias' shoulder.

"We're going to follow Soihel now," he said.

"Okay," said Elias.

He and Kamron followed Soihel as she weaved through the traffic and into a hallway that was labeled for lodging in the five major languages. They made their way outside a gateway that was even larger than the one to Captain Renalt's ship deck.

"Here we are. Your cabin for your duration at the Orace Petrans Championship. You should find the essentials inside," said Soihel.

"Thank you," said both Elias and Kamron.

"Should you need anything more, please do not hesitate to contact me via HoloTele," said Soihel before leaving back from where they came from.

Once Elias and Kamron entered the cabin, Elias' raised his eyebrows surprised at the size of the cabin. To call the place a cabin was a gross understatement. The entrance alone was as large as Elias' cabin aboard the Shockwave and the floor was lighted with three shimmering pathways that led to the different areas of the cabin.

The pathway on the right led to the kitchen and inside was an array of shelves full of hundreds of different foods in boxes. Elias could see everything from milks to meats to spices. The kitchen lay to the left of the shelves and along with numerous tables for eating, it contained two of every item Elias had in his kitchen on the Shockwave and some devices he had never seen before.

The pathway on the left led to a lounge area that could seat at least twenty five with three teletrons the sizes of which made it feel more like a restaurant and not a cabin. Past the lounge, there was a library similar to the Explorer's Library Elias except there were several hundred more videos and books available.

Straight ahead, the pathway led to a T-intersection, at the end of which Elias could see a small training arena was inside their cabin. He guessed it to be about one hundred miles long on each side. The two hallways that led out of the intersection weren't visible, but Elias assumed that's where the bedrooms were and based on the size of the cabin, he guessed there had to be at least thirty bedrooms inside.

"So what would you like to do first," asked Kamron.

"Uh, I don't know," said Elias as he thought about it. "I guess we could eat breakfast if you're hungry?"

"Oh please don't worry about me. I'm here to help you out," said Kamron.

"Well, I'm not terribly hungry, but why not eat breakfast now so that's one less thing to worry about," said Elias.

"So is there a specific type of breakfast you'd like? We can order it, cook it ourselves, or go out to one of the restaurants to eat," said Kamron.

"I'd rather go out to one of the restaurants. My friend Mihalus told me about this place--I don't know the actual name, but it translates to *Clouds on Water*," said Elias.

"Ah yes. I know the place," said Kamron. "Shall we go then?"

They left their belongings in the cabin and Elias followed Kamron as they flew through the hallways of the ship making their way to the restaurant.

"This ship is built to represent a map of the eight octants with the spherical room we first came from representing Sanize. The restaurant we're going to is in the 'fourth octant' of the ship. It's a rather unique place," said Kamron.

"How so?" asked Elias.

"You'll find out when we get there. Anyways, the food there is native to the Delicants," said Kamron.

They continued flying until they reached the restaurant and Elias noticed that the name of the restaurant was shown in Tranquilon, the Delicant's language and one of the five major languages. It read

ᘒᕽ ᐊ Ꭵ .

"How come it's not labeled in the other four languages?" asked Elias.

"All the restaurants are only labeled in their native language. Same with the entertainment," said Kamron. "It lets people feel the culture of each octant."

They were greated by a Delicant as they entered the restaurant. Most adult Delicants were around eight feet tall, but this one was at least nine feet tall with three legs in the shape of a tripod and rough, orange skin. The Delicant's fingers, toes, and ears were long and wide, but proportionate to his body due to his large size and other than his wider eyes, the rest of his face was similar to a human.

"*Huru ahh doh-doh-dok nay dak-dak shoopsh,*" said the male Delicant. "*Nay-um nay suu paap ju-ju. Um-dak* Matai Joahn."

Elias recognized a few words here and there from what he had studied on the other four languages the week before coming to Sanize.

"He says an early good morning, gentlemen. Welcome to Clouds on Water," Kamron translated for Elias.

"*Ahh doh-doh-dok,*" said Elias saying good morning back. He had studied some basic phrases in all the five major languages on their way to Sanize.

"*Tup, ahh doh-doh-dok nay dak-dak. Weesh haa eh-nay huh-huh, hay-uh,*" said Kamron.

They followed the Delicant into the restaurant and Elias was surprised as they flew in to find that the restaurant was all just one giant lake with high ceilings. All the walls consisted of a continuous projection making it seem like they were outdoors on a very scenic planet with three suns.

"*Nay-woosh dak-dak,*" said Matai his hands pointing at a cloud on top of the water.

Elias wondered how the cloud was able to stay on top of the water.

"Here you are," translated Kamron.

Kamron flew onto the cloud and sat down on a seat. Immersed within the cloud, were a table and eight seats, all of which were made of the cloud as well. Elias looked at Matai, who was smiling. Elias then flew onto the cloud taking a seat opposite of Kamron. He hesitated as he sat down. He was sitting on a cloud.

"*Hia dak paap tu-tup-paap nay no-no-nay tu-tupsh. Shah dak-dak ehh aww oh shah dak-dak oom-ha nay uh-oom, pa-poom wah dak-dak oh-hmm shoo bop,*" said Matai.

"He says to see a menu just wave your hand over the table. If you need any help or if we're ready to order, just send a small burst above us and someone will be with us shortly," Kamron translated once again.

Then he let go of his grasp on the cloud and it began moving with the currents of the lake. Despite seeing their cloud moving, Elias didn't feel the cloud's movement.

"I told you this place is unique," said Kamron smiling.

"I'll say. They actually mean clouds on water," said Elias looking around the lake at others on different clouds. "How is this possible? Why aren't the clouds dissolving into the water?"

"The water in the lake is denser than the clouds. A slightly different chemical composition. But they are both water and both drinkable, although it's not polite to eat the clouds," said Kamron before waving his hands over the table.

A colorful menu lighted up on top of the cloud table surface in front of Kamron. Elias followed suit, waving his hands, and the same menu came up in front of him. He looked around wondering where the light came from to create the menu, but he couldn't see anything that would explain it. Looking back at his menu he saw that all the menu items were written in Tranquilon, but there were pictures for each item that helped him get some idea of what each dish contained.

"See anything interesting?" asked Kamron.

"This one here looks good," said Elias pointing to a menu item labeled 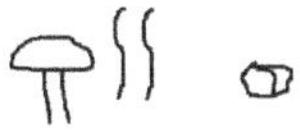 .

"That translates to 'Waterfall Loaf'. It's a type of bread that can be dipped into numerous sauces. If I didn't know better, I'd say they have a different kind for every single person's palate out there," said Kamron.

"I think I'll get that then," said Elias. "Oh and Rainbow Uthenve Milk if they have that.

"Yes they do," said Kamron. "Looks like we should order then." He shot a small burst into the air above them which soon dissipated.

"What are you going to get?" asked Elias.

"The Pink Petal Fruit Soup," said Kamron showing Elias the item on the menu.

They waited for another Delicant to come over and they ordered their food, which came a few minutes later. While the two of them ate they chatted about different topics including Sanize, Jaycil's new classes, the donation Elias made and what it was being used for on the ship. A half hour had passed before their cloud had floated on by a different entrance to the restaurant and four other people they did not know joined them on their cloud. Elias recognized them to be Sonars, their distinct features being slender bodies, flat feet, and long thick ears.

"*Boom-ba,*" said the one that sat next to Elias. "*Boo-thump boom ba-doom-ba-doom bum-bum dhe-un.*"

"He says, 'Hello, you are one of the finalists fighting, right?'" Kamron translated.

"Yes, I am. My name's Elias Rayhan," said Elias.

Kamron translated Elias' sentence. Then everyone else became acquainted with one another and they had a pleasant conversation before the other four ordered their food. Elias and Kamron decided to leave for their cabin to get a quick nap before Elias had to go out to the Sanize Champions Stadium for the championships ceremony.

Elias went to his room and without changing, lay down on his bed staring at the walls of his room as he thought about everything that was going on in his life. He was here in Sanize. He would be taking part in the Orace Petrans Championships. It was all just amazing. Then there was the last time he and Alera had been studying. His mind continued to wander as he thought about the trip that he'd be going on with Cozart and the others, the clouds floating on the water in the restaurant, and then back to the possibility that he could be an Elite Ilay. Soon, he fell asleep in his bed for the quick nap before the ceremony would start.

♦

Elias was floating in a room with all the other finalists that would be competing in the championships. The five rounds would each take place over two days except the Finals and the rounds would each have a two yelding break in between. Consisting of the sixteen lowest seeded fighters fighting single elimination, the first round would begin tomorrow. However, Elias was one of the top eight seeded contestants having been able to get through his league undefeated so he would be watching the matches to study his potential opponents.

"You seem nervous," said Werevol, a finalist from the league in zone one of Elias' octant.

"A little," said Elias. "Not about the ceremony though. Just about the matches."

"It's normal for your first time," said Werevol. "What was Maso talking to you about earlier?"

"He was just apologizing for what he said before. He got to see my last match and realized I'd been holding back the whole time," said Elias.

"Why'd you hold back?" asked Werevol.

"I was trying to trick my trainer. It's kind of a strange story," said Elias.

"Oh, okay," said Werevol.

They floated next to each other in the room as they waited for the ceremony to begin. After another ten minutes, the finalists were being called out to enter the stadium's arena to be introduced to the crowd inside and the rest of the Universe that would be watching. Elias could see parts of the arena from the room they were in and the hosts were pulling out all the stops when introducing each contestant, from ribbons of light, glowing tiles in the background, thundering music playing, and each persons name being flashed in different forms and languages using a larger than normal stadium screen.

Elias' name got called as the fifth seed in the Championships and he went out into the arena where the other nineteen contestants that had already been called were floating around.

"The fifth seed from zone four of octant six, Elias Rayhan," screamed the announcer. "Elias finished the Wave League with an undefeated record and defeated his last opponent with just one blast. He's only fifteen serays old, one of the youngest contestants we've ever had and an interesting fact, he used to be a yellow diamond less than three serays ago."

Elias waved to the crowd and clapped his hands in acknowledgement of their loud cheering. He moved to a random spot in the arena and waited while the remaining four finalists were called out. The number one seed, Ashar Dene was called out last and she went out into the stadium to loud cheers. Ashar and Suu Zahn, a female Shiftane who was the number two seed who had lost in the semifinals two cycles ago, were both considered heavy favorites to face each other in the Finals of the Orace Petrans Championships.

"Ladies and gentlemen. Boys and girls. There are your twenty four finalists for this cycle!" said the announcer. The crowd clapped for them again before the announcer continued. "Our first round starts tomorrow with four matches throughout the day. Thank you for tuning in to watch this ceremony and I wish you all a great day."

The finalists waved to the crowd again as they left the arena and the crowd in the stadium started to disperse. Elias said goodbye to the other finalists and then found Kamron before going back to his cabin to have his daily training session via HoloTele with Tewa. Knowing that he had a bye in the first round made it difficult for Elias to concentrate on the training session. Tewa realized this so she cancelled the training session for the day and decided talk to him after the next day's matches.

Chapter 19: The Battles Begin

Elias watched the starting ball as Makenu and Ibere stood on their platforms. Then, they were off in a flash as the starting ball went off. Each unleashed the common opening blast at each other, but Elias sensed the power from them was at least twice as powerful as the one he had leveled at Aercia in his last match. Neither of them was holding any energy back. Their two beginning blasts collided and cancelled each other out, but that did not stop both Makenu and Ibere from sending more blasts at each other as they moved around the arena.

Makenu moved closer to a series of tiles floating in the arena and grabbed them. He deflected one of Ibere's attacks with three spherical blast tiles and sent the fourth tile he had at her. She kicked her speed up a notch and headed towards the ceiling of the arena. The tile Makenu had sent at her exploded into a hurricane of energy spewing out random bursts of energy particles in different directions. At this point, Makenu had sent another blast upwards at Ibere, but she balled herself up and spun around, now facing the direction of the hurricane. Then she sped down towards it.

"Makenu shouldn't have thrown that tile," said Ashar from her seat in the booth Elias sat in with several of the other finalists.

Ibere continued moving downwards as Makenu continued to aim blasts that zoomed right where she had just been the instant before. Makenu must've assumed Ibere would try to head towards the other wall at some point because he did not send any blasts to stop her from heading into the hurricane. The moment before she did, Elias sensed her spinning with the vortex of energy until she was riding on top of the hurricane of energy. It began to move in the direction of Makenu, who retreated towards the opposite end of the arena. He threw several tiles at Ibere as he did so, but the energy from them seemed to fuel the hurricane even more.

"Stop chasing him Ibere and just release it," said Ashar.

Makenu retreated all the way to the wall of the arena and looked to be trapped as Ibere's vortex of energy was set to engulf him inside, but he bounced off the wall and moved like a speeding bullet cutting through the hurricane. Ibere recognized this and sent a blast below at him as they crossed paths. With the hurricane of energy gone, Makenu deflected the blast and balled up into a spinning sphere as he and Ibere were within ten feet of each other. Despite Ibere's attacks in an attempt to stop Makenu, Makenu managed to spin faster with each revolution. Ibere was outmatched and within seconds, Makenu's spinning deflection turned into a barrage of attacks, one of which leveled Ibere sending her flying across the arena.

"Rookies. They never anticipate their opponent's actions," said Ashar followed by a sigh.

Elias expected Ibere to be disheveled, but he was surprised when he saw her already in a defensive position and glowing gray.

"There's the first big hit," said the stadium announcer.

Makenu went after Ibere after leveling her and was putting on quite a display by forcing Ibere closer to a corner of the stadium. Ibere had a set of tiles nearby and she took full advantage of this by hiding behind them as she jettisoned them towards Makenu. This made their battle even again as they once again started sending barrages of energy bursts at each other.

Ashar got up from her seat and went to the food station. Elias was confused why she did so in the middle of the match. Was the match so uninteresting to her that she did not feel like watching it. Why was she here then?

Ibere and Makenu were near a cluster of tiles now as their battle raged on. Makenu launched five different ones in Ibere's direction, an exploding fan tile, a horizontal striped tile, a tri-separator tile, a blaze tile, and a triple spherical blast tile. Elias realized that the combination of those tiles in that order would leave Ibere in a precarious situation. She had one out and she didn't realize it. She had a set of three tiles and while they were powerful ones, they would not save her from the upcoming onslaught. Could that have been why Ashar had gotten up from her seat? She had been anticipating every move throughout the entire match, albeit a rather short one.

"This match is going to be a rather disgraceful one. Disappointing to say the least," said Maso from his seat.

Ibere's three powerful tiles were released at the same time as Makenu's tiles. Makenu's blaze tile created a large burst of energy which deployed at twice the speed it was launched at, fueling the three tiles in front of it to overpower the three tiles from Ibere. Makenu's triple spherical blast tile was left in its wake to attack Ibere. She saw it coming too late and could not avoid it, getting hit by two of the three spherical blasts of energy followed by an onslaught of blasts from Makenu. Ibere was smashed further into the corner with no escape as she changed from her glowing gray state to light blue to purple and then neon green.

The crowd inside the stadium cheered, although it seemed like a good number of them knew the performance by Ibere wasn't a very good one in terms of quality as the cheers were tempered.

"Well, looks like I'm next," said Cecenta. "I'll be sure to give a much better show than that."

"I would certainly expect no less, Cecenta," said Ashar.

"Thanks, Ashar," said Cecenta smiling before she left the booth.

Ashar went back to her seat with her food. Elias was surprised by Ashar. She seemed arrogant and yet was well respected by all the other finalists. Fifteen minutes passed in silence in their booth before the next match was ready to start. Cecenta sat on her platform opposite of Ruyali performing her energy meditation. The winner of this match would face off against Ashar two yeldings from now in the second round.

"And there they go!" said the announcer as the starting ball exploded.

The beginning of the match started with the usual fighting only this match felt more intense than the previous one. Elias knew from his training sessions that both Cecenta and Ruyali had fought in several Orace Petrans Championships before, but never against each other. Their tactics were flawless as one's attack was blocked by another's moves. They had gone several minutes into the match without either one giving up any air space.

"Looks like they both might wear each other out before they get a chance to challenge you, Ashar," said Maso.

Ashar stayed silent and Elias went back to watching the match. Ruyali sent a blast in the direction of Cecenta before taking a spinning hemispheres tile and launching it as well. The tile exploded and the released energy formed two hollowed hemispheres of energy one above the other separated by about six feet. Ruyali followed behind it and deflected the blast coming at her that Cecenta had sent flying through the two hemispheres. Cecenta didn't seem worried in the least about the impending attack from Ruyali's tile. She continued to send more blasts through the two concentrations of energy directly at Ruyali who continued blocking them with attacks of her own. As the two hemispheres reached Cecenta she quickly spread her arms and legs as far as she could sending out a surge of energy from her body completely destroying the two hemispheres of energy.

At the same time, Ruyali sent an attack her way from close range, spotting that Cecenta was vulnerable. Immediately after destroying Ruyali's tile attack, Cecenta started to turn her body counterclockwise rapidly while dispersing energy from her spread out arms and legs making her appear to be an energy disk. Cecenta quickly turned this disk of energy she had created using her own body at Ruyali's close range attacks, but Ruyali had been able to get much closer as a result and was piercing through Cecenta's defense. Ruyali would break through and Cecenta could easily see this along with the rest of the crowd. Cecenta began to back up while still in disk form and this kept Ruyali at the same distance, but Cecenta was backing her way into a corner.

"That's it," said Ashar.

Elias saw what Cecenta was doing as well and so did Ruyali as she backed off of Cecenta. Had Ruyali kept her attack up, Cecenta's attacks would have been coming at Ruyali and been bouncing off the corner walls at her creating a multiple blast attack that would have put her at a great disadvantage.

Several more minutes passed as the intensity of the match stayed the same throughout while the two battled. Cecenta sent a burst to Ruyali's right side, which Ruyali deflected while spinning to her left. Cecenta moved around to a set of three tiles floating in the arena and Ruyali had come out of her spin firing two bursts on either side of Cecenta that would clip her arms, giving Ruyali enough of an advantage to get in a direct hit. Ruyali knew this wouldn't work though as she flipped and rocketed away in a diagonal, and she was right. Cecenta deflected the two bursts coming at her with two simple, small disk tiles and sent the third tile, an expanding star tile, in Ruyali's direction.

The expanding star tile released its energy, forming a star of energy flying in its intended direction. The star then split into five different stars and continued to multiply, becoming a net of stars chasing after Ruyali. However, the downside to the tile's attack was that the energy of it remained the same so the longer the attack travelled and expanded, the weaker each star became. After a few seconds Ruyali stopped and wiped out the stars' energy with little effort and continued her fight with Cecenta who floated near the bottom of Ruyali's starting platform. Elias had not seen such smart movements and tactics last so long at this high intensity in any match he had watched live before. It was a pleasant surprise as it kept his senses sharp.

Makenu came into their booth and sat to Elias' right.

"That was a terrible display," said Ashar from her seat ahead in the booth. She had not even turned around to look at Makenu as she spoke.

"I defeated her rather quickly. What was I supposed to do?" asked Makenu.

"You got lucky. That tile you threw was ill-advised to say the least. She just happened to be as unwise as you with her moves," said Ashar.

"Why are you giving him crap?" Elias blurted out at Ashar. She was so arrogant and Elias did not like it.

There was an awkward silence in the room for a while.

"She is my mentor," said Makenu. "She is simply teaching me to be better."

"I may seem arrogant to you, Elias," said Ashar pausing, "but those who know me know that I am far from it. I criticize to help them become better. And yes, sometimes it isn't pleasant criticism."

"This is Ashar's last cycle fighting," said Makenu to Elias. "She is the only one among us who has made it to the Orace Petrans and we all wish to take the knowledge she can give us and use it to help ourselves."

"What do you mean? We're all in the Orace Petrans," said Elias a little frustrated and confused.

"To the fans and novice fighters, yes, we are all in the Orace Petrans. But to those of us who are finalists, who are strong enough, the Orace Petrans means only the final battle. That is what the competition was named after and that is always what it shall be," said Maso.

Ashar got up from her seat and came over to Elias, sitting in the seat to his left. She continued watching the match rather than looking at Elias. They all sat in silence again for a short time.

Ashar then turned to Elias and smiled. "I know that Makenu and the others are good fighters or they would not be here. I think the same of you too," she said. "This match is over. Ruyali will win, but I'd like to know your thoughts."

"Well, with all due respect," said Elias, "Cecenta will win."

"How so?" said Ashar not seeming the least surprised.

"I've watched Cecenta's matches. She'll allow herself to be hit to gain an advantage. You see they're currently battling evenly one blast for one blast, but soon Ruyali will gain the advantage via the set of tiles she's moving towards. Cecenta knows this, but continues to fight without adjusting. Why? Because she wants to get hit. She's throwing Ruyali off her guard. When Ruyali reaches the tiles she will use them in the most strategic way and Cecenta will only be able to partially block the attack. But, Cecenta knows her momentum will carry her to another set of tiles, a more useful set of tiles," said Elias.

"Go on," said Ashar.

"Cecenta will use the exploding ball tile to deflect all of Ruyali's subsequent attacks and then fire the spring helix tile at Ruyali to keep her occupied. And instead of using the remaining ribbons tile, Cecenta will move above Ruyali and have her retreating to the floor where she will slowly, but surely be outmatched and eventually defeated," said Elias sounding satisfied.

"Hmm," said Ashar. "I'll admit, I did not see Cecenta not using the ribbon tile. As I said, I am not so arrogant. However, Ruyali will still win."

"What?" asked Elias sounding shocked.

"It's true. Ruyali will not retreat. She'll realize her only chance, albeit a painful one will be to blaze right through Cecenta's attack," said Maso.

"Right, she's just slightly stronger than Cecenta and that's what'll be the difference," said Makenu.

Elias realized what they were saying. He had not thought of such a drastic move, but given the circumstances, that would be the only option left to even achieve victory. They continued watching the battle and it unfolded exactly as they had seen it. Ruyali was now at a disadvantage. She retreated for a split second as Elias had expected her to do, but then as Ashar had seen, Ruyali rocketed in the direction of Cecenta taking a bombardment of attacks before blazing upward and above Cecenta now. Ruyali was glowing purple and looked tired as everyone in the stadium gasped and the noise level increased as the chatter picked up from the strange maneuver. However, as Elias and the rest of the fighters could see, Ruyali was in position to win as long as she executed her moves without any hiccups.

Ruyali deflected Cecenta's next blast and then sent a growing spear tile in Cecenta's direction. Cecenta started flying after Riyali, realizing her precarious position now. The growing spear tile release its energy in the form of a spear and grew larger in size as it travelled making it easier to get a hit on Cecenta, but Cecenta completed a large flip forward around it and continued on her way to Ruyali. Cecenta then began to spin her body while sending out bursts as she moved around looking like a knuckle ball in baseball. Ruyali anticipated the move and sent an expanding star tile in the direction of Cecenta.

"She's done it," said Ashar.

Ruyali's star tile had been placed with enough precision that as it expanded it just clipped Cecenta before she could get out of its way and to the center of the arena. Cecenta was knocked off balance and it was enough for Ruyali to finish her off with a triple spherical blast tile followed up with several powerful blasts that landed direct hits on Cecenta, who began smoking neon green. The crowd went wild as the match, which had lasted for just over half an hour, ended.

"I apologize for what I said earlier," Elias said to Ashar.

"No need to apologize. I'd expect nothing less from a rookie," said Ashar as she smiled.

"I look forward to fighting you in the semifinals, should we both get there," said Elias.

"The same to you," said Ashar.

Chapter 20: An Explorer's Adventure

"I don't know how you guys finagled me into letting you come on this trip. There's no reason for you to go. It'll be really boring and we're just going to be looking for clues to find my dad," said Elias.

"You've been looking for clues about him for over two serays. The more eyes looking the better," said Quincey.

"I didn't finagle you into anything. I'm going to be an explorer. This trip is a rehearsal for me," said Alera.

They were loading their things into Cozart's ship for a two week exploration along Jeeho's old route. Quincey, Samara, Alera, Siara, Kabec, and Tasich would be going with Cozart and Elias.

"Have you seen Kabec? He hasn't loaded anything on board and we have to leave in twenty minutes," said Elias.

"No, I don't know where he could be," said Quincey.

Samara and Siara were sitting inside the lounge in the ship and Cozart was at the controls ready to depart. He had been getting restless since his clearance to leave would be ending soon and then they would have to wait another hour otherwise. Tasich arrived with a box of food and went into the ship.

"We ready to go? I got our supper and dinner here," he said putting the box on a table inside the ship.

"We're waiting on Kabec, but if he doesn't get here soon, we might leave without him," said Elias.

"Couldn't you just sense him on the ship and go to him?" asked Quincey.

"I'm not that good. I can single people out when they're close by or isolated, but not inside this entire ship," said Elias.

"How close is close by?" asked Quincey.

"Fine, hold on. I'll try it," said Elias.

He didn't need to though. As he said that, they saw Kabec flying towards them with his belongings.

"Sorry I'm late," said Kabec as he came to a halt in front of the ship's entrance.

"It's alright. We're still in the clear, but we should move quickly," said Cozart from inside the ship.

"Right," said Kabec. He loaded his belongings into the ship. "Which one's my cabin?"

"The second one on the left," said Elias.

"Everyone's ready?" asked Cozart.

A consensus yes was heard throughout the ship. Cozart closed the ship entrance and then began to move the ship into position to leave the outgoing transport bay. Kabec went into his cabin and put his luggage inside before coming back out to the lounge where everyone else sat as they awaited their departure.

"We'll be stopping by Itta for the first day before we start exploring the unmapped areas of Jeeho's old route," said Cozart.

They sat there for a few minutes until they left the Shockwave and were flying out of the solar system heading to Zelnar station 649-21.

"What took you so long?" Quincey asked Kabec.

"Oh, right. I'm officially no longer a training guardsman anymore. I passed my sensing tests for the last seray and I am an official guardsman now," said Kabec.

"What does that mean?" asked Elias.

"It means I can be a guardsman anywhere, not just for the Shockwave," said Kabec.

"You're going to move?" asked Elias a little surprised.

"No, no. Not now at least. I just have the option to do so if I want," said Kabec.

Elias watched the spacescape go by outside the windows of the ship. He had never seen this portion of the solar system before. The brown zone, the area outside of Jupiter's orbit, was past them and they were going by Neptune's orbit as shown by the technology installed in the window, though it was currently on the other side of the sun. His eyes began to droop as the rest of the group continued conversing. Before he knew it, Elias fell fast asleep on the chair he was sitting on in the lounge.

♦

Elias woke up and looked around him. He was in his cabin, but he didn't remember how he got there. Alera was floating by the gateway to his cabin.

"Elias," she said. "We're on Itta. You want to come and see it or do you want to sleep some more?"

Elias got up from the bed and rubbed his eyes. He was still a bit tired, but he wanted to see what Itta was like.

"I'm coming with you guys," he said. "How long was I asleep?"

"Three hours," blurted Quincey as he passed by the cabin in the hallway.

"Yeah," said Alera.

Elias left his cabin with Alera and they moved out into the lounge. Everyone was waiting there except Cozart, whom Elias had assumed was making preparations for the ship to stay overnight on the planet. Elias looked out the window and realized they were not on the ground, but rather high up in the air with the white and green ground of the planet several miles down below.

"Why aren't we on the ground?" asked Elias.

"We're on Itta's air colony. Most of the people live up here rather than on the ground," said Alera.

"Is something wrong with the ground?" asked Elias.

"Nope," said Alera.

Elias waited expecting her to explain more, but she didn't.

"Um, would you care to expand on that?" he asked.

She smiled at him.

"Nope," she said.

Elias didn't understand what was going on, but then Tasich spoke up.

"They need to preserve the planet as best as possible to keep the resources they excavate from diminishing. The ecology on the ground is important for that so there's only a small portion of the population that actually lives down there," he said.

"Thanks," said Elias. He looked to Alera. "Why couldn't you just say that?"

She just continued smiling at him and shrugged. Elias moved from a state of confusion to complete befuddlement. Was she mad at him? What did he do?

Cozart came by the entrance.

"Alright, we're good to go," he said.

Everyone filed out of the ship and onto a large platform that stretched for several miles and in the distance a few clouds could be seen above the floating city they were on.

"What'd you do?" whispered Quincey as he and Elias were flying in the back of the group.

"I didn't do anything," whispered Elias. "It's so weird. She doesn't even look mad. I don't get it."

"Nevertheless, your girlfriend's not happy with you. That's not a good thing," said Quincey.

"Technically, she's not my girlfriend. I mean, we've never really talked about that or anything," said Elias. "To be honest, we've never even been on an actual date."

"Ohh," said Quincey as he raised his eyebrows. "A little awkward."

They all went inside a semi-transparent, lobalce hexahedron building. Lobalce was a building material common to the planet Toreal that was super strong and yet breathable, allowing air to pass through while also repelling most liquids upon contact including water. The city consisted of numerous buildings connected via lobalce tubes three times the size of train tunnels.

"I'll be getting supplies and making preparations for my part of the exploration. I'll meet you all back on the ship," said Cozart.

Everyone said goodbye to him as he left into the depths of the city. Then they all looked at each other wondering what they should do.

"So, does anyone have any suggestions?" asked Tasich.

"I've always wanted to see the white anga that are on the ground," said Siara.

"Yeah, that sounds fun," said Elias. He noticed Alera glaring at him as he said so.

"Anyone know how we can see it?" asked Quincey.

Nobody responded.

"Guess we're going to have to find out," said Samara leading the group into the city towards an oversized teletron.

She waved her hand in front of the screen and the words *"Welcome to Itta. You are in the city Davance."* showed up. Then, an interactive map of Davance appeared in on the left side of the screen while the right side contained a search logo. Samara searched the words *white anga* and upon the screen was a smiling woman.

"Hello," she said. "I presume that you wish to see the white anga on the ground, correct?"

"Yes please," said Samara.

"I can arrange a journey. The cost will come to fifteen credits per person. Do you wish to continue?" the woman asked.

"Yes," said Samara.

"Very well," said the woman. "Please enter the pertinent information on the screen and have all participants input their energy signals."

They followed the instructions on screen and waited there as they were told an Orbital Series 9 would arrive to escort them to their required destination.

"That was easier than I thought it'd be," said Samara.

"Yeah, I was surprised by the woman on the screen setting everything up," said Quincey.

"They make half their credits off tourism on Itta. You'd be amazed how many people pass by the Shockwave just to visit here," said Kabec.

"I don't know if I'd come all the way out here just to see the white anga," said Siara.

"Oh it's not just the white anga. They have several delicious foods here that they can't take anywhere else because it spoils within only eight hours after cooking it," said Kabec.

"Doesn't hurt that it's cheap as well," said an older man that came up to them. "My name is Denesd. Your Orbital Series 9 is here."

A vehicle larger than, but similar to the Orbital Series 6 was hovering nearby. As they took their seats, Elias realized that the number signified the number of seats inside the vehicle. With everyone seated,

Denesd took command of the controls on the side compartment and they were off.

"We will arrive at our destination in three minutes folks," said Denesd.

"Now that Kabec's told me about the food on Itta would you guys mind if we saved the supper I brought for another time? I'd much rather try the local cuisine," said Tasich.

Everyone agreed.

"There are a couple restaurants here in Davance where you can find said foods," said Denesd. "I'd suggest Unity."

"Thanks," said Tasich.

They arrived outside a set of tubes and Denesd slowed the vehicle down to a stop.

"Here you go," he said. "Egami over there will take you all down to the surface."

The young woman whom they had seen on the teletron screen before was smiling and waving at them. They all thanked Denesd while getting out of the Orbital Series 9 and went over to Egami.

"Hello everyone. As I'm sure Denesd has told you, my name is Egami. I'll be showing you the white anga today," she said. "If you all could please follow me, we'll be going down this channel."

Egami turned around and went down into the tube behind her at a moderate pace. They followed her down the tube which turned left and right every now and then. After about two minutes, they had reached the floor. Elias saw the openings to numerous other tubes leading to the same floor he stood on. There were hundreds if not thousands of people around them floating beneath the openings of the different tubes and they all appeared to be waiting there.

"We'll have to wait a few minutes here before we're given the go ahead," said Egami.

Every few seconds Elias would see a circle light up underneath one of the tubes and the people on it would then fly up and out to one of the openings around them leading to the outside.

"This place is so different than the Shockwave," said Quincey. "I like it."

After ten minutes a light circle flashed underneath them.

"Follow me," said Egami.

She led them to one of the openings and they flew out into the open air of the planet.

"Please try to fly as much as you can for now. We like to preserve the ground as much as possible and there will be a designated zone along the ground which will let you know that it's alright to walk along the forest floor," said Egami as they flew towards the forest of white anga.

The ground was covered with green grass several inches long and a few animals were roaming about nearby. As they flew closer to the forest, more animals could be seen on the ground below.

"I'll give you all a brief history of the white anga forests if you would like?" asked Egami.

"Sure," said Samara.

"Okay. The white anga is native to our planet Itta and our planet alone as far as anyone knows. It has been here since the discovery of the planet about twenty serays ago and we have continued to preserve the plants as they are the main catalysts that allow this planet to thrive. White anga is a unique plant if one can even call it that," said Egami. "As you may notice during our journey, they can in fact move on their own despite having a base similar to that of a tree. They will do so, not because they dislike being next to you as some may have you believe, but because they wish to find a more ideal spot in which to grow."

They reached the forest of white anga. They were pure white and as far as Elias could tell, they resembled trees. The branches coming from the trunk were much thicker than typical trees though and rather than extending outward, they weaved around one another making each one look unique. There were no leaves on the branches of the the tree either, but numerous animals could be seen climbing along them.

"The white anga lives in symbiosis with the grass on this planet, however, it is possible for the white anga to survive without it," said Egami as they started flying below the white anga branches and into the depths of the forest. "The plant itself has several unique characteristics." She landed on the grass nearby one of the white anga. "Those of us who live down here have learned to live with the life among us as best as we can though we are learning new things every day."

One of the white anga branches with no animals on it began to untangle itself from the other branches and hung above where Egami stood on the ground. Then the branch unfurled itself and spread out into a shade over Egami as it rested on several other branches for added support. Everyone gasped in surprise.

"Wow," said Siara looking awestruck.

"That's amazing," said Samara.

"How?" asked Quincey as he stared up at the branch.

"We're not really too sure how the white anga know what's going on around them, but we are certain that somehow they do," said Egami. "You all can come underneath here if you wish."

They all joined Egami and as they did, the air felt colder. Elias looked at the others and noticed that they all appeared to be rubbing their shoulders as if they were freezing.

"What's wrong with you guys?" asked Elias.

"It's really cold under here," said Kabec.

"You serious? It's just a few degrees cooler under here," said Elias.

"I'm so sorry. I forgot. Most people aren't used to temperature changes so this must be quite cold for you all. We can move out of here," said Egami as she flew outside the shade of the branch. She waited for them to fly over with her. "What makes the air several degrees cooler underneath the branches is that the white anga are actually quite cold themselves so when one of them unfurls it makes the air around it cooler."

"But we don't feel much of a temperature change due to our energy. This doesn't make sense," said Tasich.

"I agree," said Egami. "We have been unable to figure out why, but it would appear as though the cold temperatures from the white anga are able to penetrate through energy and upset our temperature balance."

"Can I touch one?" asked Elias.

"Go ahead," said Egami.

Elias went over to a different white anga that was closer to them and placed his palms on the trunk. He felt an even greater temperature change than before as the white anga cooled his hands like an air conditioner. A branch above Elias shook and water began falling down, drizzling like rain onto Elias' clothes. Elias lifted his hands off the white anga and covered his head with his arms as he retreated from it. He heard everyone else laughing.

"Guess it doesn't like you," said Alera laughing.

"I take it you're rather hungry," said Egami.

"Um, yeah. A little hungry, but how did you know that?" asked Elias. He looked back at the white anga that had rained on him. "Wait, they know when you're hungry?" asked Elias.

"Only if you're in contact with them. That's why it started raining water," said Egami.

They heard a loud thundering noise in the distance and looked further into the forest. One of the white anga was moving several feet to the right before stopping.

"Like I said, sometimes they'll move around," said Egami.

She took them further into the forest as they asked more questions. The white anga were numerous and of different sizes throughout. Animals were roaming about all over the forest as well. Some of the animals stopped to observe their group while others ignored them as though they weren't even there.

"This place is amazing," said Alera. "I could stay here forever."

"We can stay as long as you all would like. Just let me know when you would like me to lead you back and I will do so," said Egami.

"I'm fairly hungry," said Tasich.

"Me too," said Samara.

"Does everyone want to go back and eat then?" asked Kabec.

Although Alera seemed reluctant, they all agreed to go back to Davance. Egami led them out of the white anga forest and they thanked her for guiding them before going back up to the city.

◆

Elias lay down in his bed. They had all just come back from Davance after eating their supper at Unity. He looked to the ceiling and closed his eyes. He was at ease for now having enjoyed a delicious meal and resting, but he knew once the search for his dad started he would be anxious and uneasy most of the time. He had spent over two serays reading books, watching videos, asking people for explorer's journals or stories in the hopes he would find something, but despite all his efforts he was nowhere closer to knowing any more about his father than the day he had come on board the Shockwave.

He took a deep breath and exhaled. Then there was the strange man that he had sat next to on his first day at the Wave League. Who was he? Why had he left after Elias started asking him questions? And the man's energy signal. It wasn't normal either. Elias hadn't stopped thinking about him since that day.

Elias sensed Cozart coming back to the ship. After a few minutes Kabec came by Elias' open gateway.

"Cozart's back. He says we're going to leave at 3:00 tomorrow so we can make it to the first unmapped planet by 11:00," he said.

"Okay, thanks," said Elias.

Kabec left to tell the others. Elias got up from his bed and sat the foot of it. He looked back out into the hallway and noticed Alera's gateway was also open and he walked over to it. As he looked inside her cabin he saw her reading a book, which he assumed was another explorer's book for her training.

"Are you mad at me?" asked Elias.

Alera sighed, marked a page in her book, closed it and then looked at him. She signaled to him to close the gateway so they could talk in private. He did so and then looked back at her waiting for her to say something.

"Do you like me?" she asked.

Elias gulped and opened his mouth to try and something but nothing came out.

"Wow," said Alera looking shocked. "You're joking, right. I don't get you. One second you really like me and the next you act like I'm just someone that's there."

Elias exhaled. "Sorry. I do. I do like you, it's just…" he said stopping before finishing the sentence.

She shook her head.

"Forget it, Elias. Just go," she said.

"You want to go with me for dinner to Aximu's Restaurant when we get back to the Shockwave?" Elias asked.

Alera stared at him.

"Finally asking me out after what, seven yeldings?" she said. She paused for a few seconds looking down at the bed as she thought about it.

"Please say yes," said Elias.

"I'm still mad at you," she said.

"I'm sorry, but I don't know why," said Elias.

"You act like you've never heard a thing about this planet before," said Alera.

"I haven't really. We never studied it in classes," said Elias. "Besides, what does that have to do with anything?"

"I'm not talking about classes, Elias. I told you about this place a few yeldings ago and you don't even remember a thing I said," said Alera.

Elias closed his eyes feeling stupid. He remembered their conversation now. She was right. She had told him everything about Itta and Toreal because it's where she wanted to go on her next vacation.

"Sorry," said Elias. He opened his eyes after a few more seconds, looked at Alera and then turned to leave her cabin.

"You didn't give me a day and time you know," she said from behind him.

Elias turned back.

"Aria at 24:00," he said.

"Don't be late," said Alera.

Elias turned back around and left her cabin. He wasn't too sure what just happened, but he made sure he wouldn't forget. *Aria at 24:00* he kept repeating over and over to himself in his head. *Aria at 24:00...Aria at 24:00...*

Chapter 21: Nayreen

"You should be able to see it now," said Cozart.

Everyone looked out the windows. The first unmapped planet on Jeeho's route was becoming visible. It looked larger than Earth although more barren like Mars. There were a few patches of blue on the planet, but otherwise it seemed unattractive.

"Jeeho said there are people on the planet. Should we really be flying so close without anything to disguise ourselves?" asked Kabec.

"It's fine, Kabec. Jeeho said they didn't have any technology to see out into space when he was there. There's no way they could develop it between now and then," said Elias.

"So they're even more primitive there than you guys on Earth," said Quincey.

Cozart stopped the ship outside the of the planet's orbit just above its atmosphere.

"I'm going to let the ship's devices do its analysis on the planet first," he said. They waited about four minutes for the ship's devices to work their magic. "Looks like it's just like Jeeho recorded it. The planet seems in good shape and there's a decent population living down there. The city he went to is even in the same place as it was when he recorded his descent positions."

"Can we go down there then?" asked Elias. He wanted to find the rock formations that Jeeho had seen with the ancient language on them.

"Hmm, it's still risky, especially with all of us," said Cozart.

"Elias knows how they operate though," said Samara.

"Yeah, I'd be able to tell if we need to leave or not. It won't be a problem," said Elias.

"Fine," said Cozart. "I'll stay here by the ship though. If you guys need me to come down there let me know."

"Okay," said Elias. He knew this planet was useless to Cozart's search since he would not be able to use it to garner any resources for his business.

"Try and make it back by 14:00 at the latest. I want to get to the next planet by 19:00," said Cozart.

Cozart opened the ship's gateway and everyone except him went out.

"Coordinates are this way," said Kabec.

They followed Kabec as he led them down Jeeho's descent path. They entered into the atmosphere which was several miles longer than either Itta's atmosphere or Earth's atmosphere. After a few more seconds, Elias could make out the individual cities on the planet. They were spread apart and they did indeed look primitive, reminding Elias of videos he had seen of the Wild West.

"Looks like they may have expanded their city some. Perhaps we should veer off course slightly to the left just to be safe?" Kabec asked Elias.

"Yeah, sure. I'd say two miles should be fine," responded Elias.

They continued their descent until they had reached a flat land with a sparse forest and small creeks running through it. It seemed that the people in the city had left this place to itself rather than cross the canyon that separated them from it.

"There's no coordinates for the rock markings," said Kabec.

"Jeeho said it was by the canyon. We should fly over there," said Elias.

"This place feels sad," said Siara as they flew over to the canyon.

"Yeah, there's nothing here," said Tasich.

They all floated at the edge of the canyon looking around now. Elias was looking for the rocks that Jeeho had spoken of. They had to be here somewhere.

"I don't see anything," said Samara.

"Yeah, me neither," said Quincey.

"It's here somewhere. I'm not giving up this easily," said Elias.

He started flying around through the canyon and the others followed behind him.

"What are you hoping to find from the rocks anyways?" asked Kabec.

"I don't know, but finding something is better than finding nothing," said Elias.

He was on edge. He wanted to find something. Anything. Any clue about his dad would be helpful.

"There!" said Elias pointing to a series of rocks that had been jumbled together along the middle of a cliff.

As Jeeho had said, there were markings on the rocks and they seemed familiar to the few scriblings of the ancient language from their textbook.

"I'll get my recorder out, said Samara. "I can't imagine any of us knows what it says."

"Not a clue," said Tasich.

"Looks like doodles to me," said Quincey.

Elias looked at Alera who seem intrigued by the markings. If he didn't know better, he'd think that Alera was reading them. Elias moved around the rock formation and looked inside a hole lighted by the Sun outside.

"It's a cave I think," said Elias who noticed a larger hole big enough to allow a person to go through. Suddenly there was a noise from further inside the jumble of rock. They heard the sound of a rock falling and a light scream followed by running footsteps.

"What was that?" asked Kabec a little worried.

Elias went inside the sun-lit cave and saw a little girl running to the opposite end of the large cave. There was an opening at the other end that was lighted. She stopped and looked at him. She seemed frightened.

"Elias, get out. It's probably one of the people from the city. We should go," said Kabec.

Elias didn't listen however as he walked along the cave floor.

"Hello," said Elias.

The girl turned and ran again before stopping and climbing down into a hole that Elias hadn't seen due to the darkness. Elias followed her and came to a stop as he stood over the hole in the ground. He went down the hole for a few feet before he reached the dark floor. The area became illuminated by Elias' energy. The place was small, about eight by five feet if Elias had to guess and the ceiling wasn't tall enough for a normal person to stand unless they stood under the hole. Elias saw the girl sitting in a corner with her hands around her knees and breathing fast. She tried backing up further into the place, but there was no more room.

"Hi," Elias said once again, this time smiling.

The girl still didn't say anything. Elias looked behind him and sat down on the opposite side of the place from the girl. Then he looked back at her.

"It's okay," said Elias. "I come in peace. My name is Elias."

The girl appeared to calm down as her breathing slowed.

"Elias," Elias heard Kabec yell from inside the cave.

The girl's breathing picked up again.

"I'm down here," said Elias in a normal voice. "Everything's fine. Just stay there alright. He turned his attention to the girl who was stared at him. "It's okay. They're just my friends. It's okay. So who are you?"

The girl calmed down again and stared at Elias. Then she gulped.

"My...my name is Nayreen," she said.

"Hi, Nayreen. Is this your cave?" asked Elias.

She nodded.

"So did you make the markings outside on the rock then?" asked Elias.

"No," she said.

"Do you know who did?" asked Elias.

Nayreen stayed silent and looked down at the ground.

"Okay, that's fine. You don't have to tell me," said Elias.

They sat there for several seconds.

"Why are you here?" Nayreen asked as she looked up at Elias.

"I'm looking for my dad," said Elias. "His name is Brooks Rayhan."

Nayreen gulped again.

"Rayhan?" she asked.

"Yeah, Rayhan. That's my last name too," said Elias. He looked at Nayreen intrigued by her asking about his last name. "Why? Have you heard of it before?"

"You're in danger. You should go. You should leave now," said Nayreen urgently.

"What? Why?" asked Elias. Did she know about his dad?

"You need to go. The Nagen are looking for you. They will attack you soon. Please, go back home. Please," plead Nayreen.

"How do you know about the Nagen?" asked Elias. Elias sensed around him for another signal couldn't sense anyone else other than their exploration party anywhere near the planet.

"The faster you go home the better for you. Please go, Elias," she said as she got up. Then she walked over to him being short enough to stand in the place and started pulling his right arm to get him to go towards the hole.

"Okay, okay," said Elias as he went over to the hole and stood up.

He held on to Nayreen and then flew up to the cave area. The others were all inside the cave nearby the entrance and Samara had her recorder out. Elias put Nayreen down in front of him.

"You guys hear any of that?" Elias asked.

"Any of what?" asked Kabec who had been closest to them.

"Guess not," said Elias.

"Who's she?" asked Kabec.

"This is Nayreen," said Elias.

"You need to go back home, Elias. You need to go now. Please. Otherwise they'll attack you," said Nayreen.

"What's she talking about?" asked Kabec. "Who's going to attack?"

"She says the Nagen are going to attack me. She says that I should go back," said Elias.

"She doesn't have energy. How does she know who the Nagen are?" asked Quincey.

"Don't know," said Elias. "But she's insistent on me leaving. She won't say anything else."

"Yes, you need to go. For your own safety. Please," said Nayreen.

"We shouldn't have come in here," said Kabec. "She doesn't have energy. This is a breach of common Cliern code."

"I agree," said Samara. "Let's go, Elias."

Elias looked at Nayreen since he wanted to know more about what she was talking about, but he knew he wouldn't be able to convince them to stay. How did she know about all this though?

"Fine," said Elias. He walked towards the entrance of the cave.

"Wait!" said Nayreen just as Elias was about to exit the cave with the others. She ran up to him holding a piece of black clothing. "Take this with you."

Elias looked at it. It was a cloak.

"Thank you," said Elias as he took the cloak from her.

"Now please go back home. Be safe," said Nayreen.

"Let's go," said Kabec.

They left the cave and began their ascent back up the the ship outside the planet. Elias looked back at the cave and waved goodbye knowing that Nayreen could see him through one of the holes in between the rocks.

"What'd she say to you?" asked Quincey.

"Not much. She repeated my last name before telling me to go. She seemed worried that I'd be attacked by the Nagen if I stayed," said Elias. "I get the feeling, however crazy it sounds, that she knew my dad. She said my last name like she'd heard it before."

"Nobody tell Cozart that one of the people down here saw us. Just tell him we saw the markings, but they didn't lead to anything and we came back up," said Kabec. "We don't need to get in trouble for a minor breach in Cliern code."

Everyone agreed as they continued on their way out of the planet's atmosphere. Elias continued to sense as far around him as he could, but he didn't feel anyone else's presence other than theirs and Cozart on the ship. Why did Nayreen think the Nagen would attack him? And how did she know who the Nagen were?

◆

Alera looked over at the rocks Elias had pointed out on the side of one of the canyon cliffs. She followed him and the others as they got closer to them.

"I'll get my recorder out, said Samara. "I can't imagine any of us knows what it says."

"Not a clue," said Tasich.

"Looks like doodles to me," said Quincey.

Alera recognized the markings. They were the same ones Elias' mom had taught her during their trip to Earth. She started reading them. *Welcome my old friend. You have come upon a safe and simple dwelling. Take refuge here if needed.* Alera stopped reading as Elias spoke out.

"It's a cave I think," he said from another side of the rocks.

Suddenly there was a noise from further inside the jumble of rocks. They heard the sound of a rock falling and a light scream followed by running footsteps.

"What was that?" asked Kabec a little worried.

Elias went inside the rocks and disappeared. They all went over to where he had been and saw a hole there allowing people to enter.

"Elias, get out. It's probably one of the people from the city. We should go," said Kabec.

They didn't hear any response from Elias.

"Ahh, why doesn't he listen," said Kabec heading into the entrance. "Let's go find him."

They all went inside and realized they were in a cave of sorts, but Elias was nowhere to be found.

"Elias," Kabec yelled trying to find out where he went.

They heard Elias' voice coming from somewhere in the darkened part of the far end of the cave. There was another entrance at the very end of the cave that gave off some light and let them see a small hole in the ground.

"I'm down here. Everything's fine. Just stay there alright," he said.

Alera looked around the cave and realized that the markings were all over. She looked at several lines and was able to read them all in the secret language Elias' mom had taught her.

"We shouldn't be here," said Kabec.

"Yeah, I don't like it. All this writing looks like it's in ancient language. It gives me the creeps," said Samara.

"Hey, Samara," said Alera. "Can you make sure you get pictures of all this stuff? You know for my explorer's stuff."

"Oh. Yeah, sure," said Samara as she made sure her recorder collected all the wall images.

Alera shook her head as she was processing her thoughts. Elias' mom knew the ancient language that nobody else seemed to know and she had learned it from Elias' dad. Elias' dad knew the ancient language, but there was no record of him anywhere. Who was he? Then it clicked in her head. Elias' dad was one of the ancients. No, that can't have been possible. The ancients lived millions of years ago. It didn't make any sense.

"Something wrong Alera?" asked Siara.

Alera realized she looked shocked to the rest of the others.

"Huh, no, I'm just, uh, just amazed at all this," she said.

Elias popped up from the hole at the far end of the cave holding a little girl in his hands. He set her down in front of him.

"You guys hear any of that?" Elias asked.

"Any of what?" asked Kabec.

"Guess not," said Elias.

Alera wondered if what she thought could be true. Could he be the son of an ancient? How is that even possible if they existed so long ago? Maybe they lived forever.

"Who's she?" asked Kabec of the girl standing in front of Elias.

"This is Nayreen," said Elias.

"You need to go back home, Elias. You need to go now. Please. Otherwise they'll attack you," said Nayreen.

"What's she talking about?" asked Kabec. "Who's going to attack?"

"She says the Nagen are going to attack me. She says that I should go back," said Elias.

The Nagen? This was all the more confusing for Alera. Why was this little girl with no energy mentioning anything about the Nagen?

"She doesn't have energy. How does she know who the Nagen are?" asked Quincey.

"Don't know," said Elias. "But she's insistent on me leaving. She won't say anything else."

"Yes, you need to go. For your own safety. Please," said Nayreen.

"We shouldn't have come in here," said Kabec. "She doesn't have energy. This is a breach of common Cliern code."

"I agree," said Samara. "Let's go, Elias.

"Fine," said Elias. He walked towards them at the entrance to the cave.

"Wait!" said Nayreen just as they were all about to leave. She ran up to Elias holding a piece of black clothing. "Take this with you."

It was a cloak.

"Thank you," said Elias as he took the cloak from her.

"Now please go back home. Be safe," said Nayreen.

"Let's go," said Kabec.

They left the cave and began their ascent back up the the ship outside the planet. Alera flew at the head of the pack with Kabec.

"Nobody tell Cozart that one of the people down here saw us. Just tell him we saw the markings, but they didn't lead to anything and we came back up," said Kabec. "We don't need to get in trouble for a minor breach in Cliern code."

Everyone agreed as they continued on their way out of the planet's atmosphere. Alera looked back at Elias a few times while they made their way to the ship and wondered, who was he?

Chapter 22: Maraye's Attack

Elias was sitting in his cabin watching a video of his next opponent in the Orace Petrans. He wanted to keep his mind off their encounter with Nayreen, which he thought about often. It was 16:30 and they were on schedule to reach the next planet by 19:00 as Cozart had wanted.

"Hey, you alright?" asked Tasich as he looked into Elias' room from the hallway.

"Yeah," said Elias. "I'm fine."

"Okay. Well, supper's ready if you want it," said Tasich.

"Thanks," said Elias. "I'll be there in a second."

Tasich went back to the lounge area where everyone was waiting to eat. Elias paused the video he was watching and put his HoloTele away. Then he went out to the lounge and sat down at the table where everyone else was having a conversation. Well, almost everyone else.

"Where's Alera?" Elias asked.

"She said she didn't feel like eating," said Tasich.

"Oh, okay," said Elias wondering why.

"We ready to eat?" asked Quincey.

"Shouldn't we wait for Cozart?" asked Siara.

"No, he's taking a nap before we get to the next planet," said Tasich.

"Let's eat then," said Quincey.

On each person's plate lay a spread of two small retze sandwiches, three pieces of laksor bread, a bowl of worlay soup, and a glass of Rainbow Uthenve milk.

"Food looks great, Tasich," said Kabec.

"Thanks," Tasich said.

They all began to eat their food starting with the worlay soup before it changed taste by turning cold.

"You excited for your next match?" Siara asked Elias. They had all been trying to keep his mind off of the events earlier in the day.

"Yeah. Excited. Nervous. Anxious," said Elias.

"You haven't lost yet," said Quincey. "And I don't see that changing any time soon."

"Quincey, you don't have to suck up to me. I already told you I'll pay for you to watch it live," said Elias.

"I'm not sucking up to you this time. I'm serious. Me and Tewa are the only ones that have believed in you from the beginning, remember?" said Quincey.

"We supported him too, Quincey," said Samara. "But it's hard to believe that someone who'd never fought before and didn't seem that strong would be able to get this far."

"It's fine. I don't blame you. I would've thought the same thing," said Elias.

They all continued to finish their soup. Elias took a bite of one of his retze sandwiches after he finished his soup.

"Oh, Siara. I've been meaning to ask you, what were you busy with last week on Catair?" asked Samara.

"Huh, oh, um I ran into a bunch of people earlier in the day so I was running late on all the other stuff I had to do. That's all," said Siara.

"Like what?" asked Quincey.

"You know, stuff. Well, I guess you wouldn't know since you do nothing all day," said Siara.

"Wow okay. Guess I hit a nerve with you," said Quincey. "And it just so happens that I'm a lot busier with my new role making decisions on the funds Elias donated."

"You're right. I'm sorry. I don't know why I snapped at you," said Siara.

"Oh it's alright, Siara. It'll make up for all the times he really was lazy a few serays ago," said Samara.

"Can we talk about something other than me?" asked Quincey.

"I'm thinking of opening up my own restaurant, but I don't know where it should be," said Tasich.

"Wow, really?" asked Kabec. "How have you been able to get the credits for that so fast? I mean you haven't been working at the Nitorhe Restaurant that long."

"Elias' matches have been amazing for the restaurant's revenues. We've made five times what we normally would in the last two serays because of his run in the Orace Petrans," said Tasich.

"Why not have it on the Shockwave?" asked Siara.

"I could, but I don't want to compete with the Nitorhe Restaurant. Mihalus' parents gave me the opportunity to work there so it'd be rude of me to do so," said Tasich.

"Why not have it on Itta. You said it yourself that they have some amazing food to work with there," said Quincey.

"Yeah, or Toreal. You could have the food from Itta shipped there," said Kabec.

Everyone continued to give Tasich ideas on his restaurant as they ate their supper. After an hour they had all finished their supper and left for their separate cabins. Elias went to go check on Alera, but saw that she was sleeping inside her cabin. He closed her cabin gateway and then went back to his cabin to go back to watching the video of his next opponent.

♦

Elias sat in the lounge with Tasich and Siara. They could see their next destination as they looked out the windows. This planet was more colorful than the last one and the ship was slowing down as Cozart used the ship's devices to do an analysis on it. This is what Cozart had come for, a planet that could be used to harvest resources without any people on it.

"What's the analysis say?" Elias asked Cozart.

"So far everything is looking good. If this planet has any resources at all, this trip will have been worth it," he replied.

"Are we going to go down there and check it out?" asked Siara.

"Yeah, soon. Could one of you go tell the others? I plan on leaving the ship here like last time except I'll be going out to see the planet," said Cozart.

"I'll do it," said Siara.

Siara left the lounge and went down the hallway to the cabins.

"So are you looking for anything specific when you go down there?" Tasich asked.

"No. Any abundant resource will work. The business I work for deals with almost everything you can think of," said Cozart.

They sat there for a few more minutes as they waited for the ship to complete its final analysis of the planet.

"No people on the planet. Perfect," said Cozart.

Siara had come back to the lounge and was followed by the remaining members aboard the ship.

"So are we going down there now?" asked Samara.

"Yes, is everyone ready?" asked Cozart.

They all nodded. Then Cozart led them out of the ship, opening the entrance and starting the descent down to the planet's atmosphere. About four minutes had passed as they neared the top of the planet's atmosphere. Elias suddenly sensed something coming closer to them, albeit from quite a distance away from them.

"I'm sensing people coming closer to us," said Elias.

"What do you mean?" asked Cozart. "There's nobody here. The ship's devices said so themselves."

"It's not close by here, but it's getting closer," said Elias as concentrated his senses on the energy he felt moving ever faster towards them. "There's got to be at least forty of them, no wait fifty, no…this is weird. Something's wrong." He could sense each one of them now. "There's close to a hundred different people and they're closing in on us fast."

"Nayreen's warning," said Kabec.

"What?" asked Cozart. "Who's Nayreen?"

As he said it, the people whom Elias had been sensing had already arrived. They had been travelling at speeds too fast to be associated with the Clierns. They must be the Nagen.

"Stay close. Nobody separate from the group," said Elias to the others.

"Ah, Elias. So we finally have the pleasure to meet," said a female floating in front of the rest of the group. "Let me introduce myself. My name is Derela of the Nagen."

Elias was taking slow deep breaths. He did not like the situation they were in. Each of the Nagen was at least as strong as the weakest contestants in the Wave League and a few were at the same level as Aercia. While he knew he could handle them, even in their large numbers, he knew the others would be in a lot more danger.

"What do you want?" asked Elias.

"How kind of you to ask," said Derela with a wicked smile. "It's really quite simple actually. And nobody will have to get hurt if you just do what we want."

"Spit it out already," said Elias growing impatient with her.

"Alright then. We want you to come with us, Elias. And to make sure there are no difficulties, we'll take one of your friends too. In case you decide you no longer wish to be cooperative," said Derela looking smug.

"Don't do it, Elias. Don't listen to them," said Cozart.

"Yeah, we just need to find a way to get back to the ship. It'll be strong enough to hold while we escape. We need to get back inside the Lighthouse Sector and send for Cliern troops," said Kabec.

"Well, that's nice. But if we don't get what we want, we'll just have to make sure it happens," said Derela. "And believe me, we won't show any mercy to any of them, the Cliern underlings."

Elias looked down the line to his right and saw Kabec, Alera, Siara, Samara, Cozart, Tasich, and Quincey. Cozart and Alera were the only ones strong enough to stand a chance fighting for more than five minutes. He couldn't put any of them in harm's way though.

"What if I agree to come with you? You leave my friends to get back to the ship and I come with you," said Elias.

"No. We wouldn't let you do that," said Quincey.

"Neither would we. One of your friends will have to come with us. But you don't seem to want that, do you? I think I know where this is going so I'll just save myself some time," said Derela sighing. "It's a shame, really." She turned to the people surrounding her. "You seven, deal with them individually. They are weak, but do not kill them all. We need one of them. The rest of you, well, there's only one magical warrior left, isn't there."

"We have to get back to the ship," said Kabec.

"There's not enough time now. We have to just keep backing up while we fight until we get there," said Elias.

In a flash, the Nagen came after the eight of them.

"Stay in a line!" screamed Cozart. "If they single us out, we won't stand a chance."

The onslaught of people came at Elias. It was unlike any league match he had ever been in. There were no tiles, no boundaries, and no rules. He couldn't let any of them get behind him. He didn't know what they might do to the others who would not see it coming.

Blast after blast came at him and he deflected each one with no time to spare and unable to move around as the next blast was just an instant away each time. They must not have been attacking him all at once for fear of killing him. Why did they want him so bad?

Elias sent a burst powerful enough to obliterate at least thirty people with energy levels similar to Makenu. It worked somewhat, blasting through over thirty different attacks, but it was still no match for the close to one hundred people bombarding him with energy attacks.

He tried to check on the others as he continued deflecting attacks. They had been able to move back closer to the ship since they only had one person after them, but it was clear that they were struggling. The only one doing well was Cozart, but even so he looked like he was dead even with his opponent.

"He's stronger that we thought," yelled Derela. "Four at a time now."

As Derela had directed, the blasts were coming four at a time to Elias now. He was staying even with the Nagen that were attacking him and not allowing them to advance whatsoever. Perhaps they would let up soon or send some to attack the others. Then he could gain an advantage and move closer to the middle to help everyone else.

Another minute passed, but the battle still raged on. Derela was smart. She would not let anyone leave off attacking Elias, knowing that he would gain the advantage. It was as if she had known how many people she would need to fight him beforehand. Elias didn't understand how. He hadn't even shown close to ten percent of his true powers during any of the matches.

They were still far from the ship and would need at least seven minutes to back up to it. Elias looked over at the others. Quincey and Kabec were both already smoking blue and Tasich glowed gray. Elias needed to find a way to help them or they wouldn't last long enough to get to the ship.

He started to spin sending wave after wave of energy at the attacks coming from the Nagen. Soon he was a whirlwind moving through the air, but Derela would have none of it as she ordered them to send a twenty blast attack stopping him in his tracks and forcing him to deflect the attacks without being able to move.

The stronger Nagen fighters were now sending special attacks at him as they had more than enough time to prepare them. Several spherical blasts came his way as did a few expanding spear attacks. Elias was getting frustrated. If he didn't have to worry about the others, he would have gained an advantage by letting some of the Nagen to get behind him.

"We're almost there," said Samara two minutes later.

They had been retreating faster and were about a minute from reaching the ship now, but the faster retreat caused the others to be put in dire positions. As Elias looked over, he saw Kabec and Quincey were smoking purple. Everyone else other than Cozart was smoking blue, but suddenly the one battling with Quincey hit him with an enormous blast square on. Elias was worried. Quincey went from smoking purple to a yellow-orange color. Then Tasich got hit and he was smoking neon green.

"Cozart, switch with me. You might be able to help Quincey out," yelled Tasich seeing the poor shape that Quincey was in.

Tasich and Cozart switched positions as they battled their opponents.

"We need to do something. There's no way he's going to make it," said Kabec as he struggled and got hit, turning neon green.

Elias had been looking over at Quincey as he tried to think of some way to get over there and help him.

"Now Maraye," yelled Derela.

The person attacking Cozart stopped, as did Cozart. They both turned towards Quincey and sent two enormous blasts at him.

"No," screamed Elias, who stopped paying attention to the attacks coming at him.

He sent a powerful burst in Quincey's direction to try to help him. Quincey just managed to deflect his opponent's attack, but he did not see the blasts from the other two coming.

"Quincey," yelled Samara realizing what was going on.

Elias watched as his attempt to deflect the attacks on Quincey was just an instant too late. Then Elias got hit with the attacks coming at him, but he just took it as he floated frozen in the air staring at where Quincey had been. He was gone. They'd killed him. They'd killed Quincey.

Elias looked at Cozart. Cozart. The traitor. He was with the Nagen. He did this.

Samara had jumped in front of Tasich as the two of them started battling four people now. Another attack hit Elias and this time he looked back at his attackers. Shock turned to rage as Elias sent powerful blast after powerful blast in their direction. He no longer worried about them getting behind him and he advanced forward obliterating every attack coming his way.

Derela ordered everyone to attack Elias letting the others get back to the ship. Elias was still advancing some, but not as much as before with eight added people attacking him.

"Elias. Get back to the ship," yelled Kabec from just outside the ship realizing that Elias had been moving forward to attack instead of retreating back to the ship.

Elias didn't listen as he continued plowing forward, sending blast after blast in the direction of any he saw attacking him.

"Elias," screamed Kabec again moving closer to Elias.

Elias looked over and noticed that none of them had gone back inside the ship yet as they all stopped just outside it realizing Elias was still fighting. If Elias didn't go to the ship, he was sure the others would come and try to help him, putting them in danger again.

He began spinning again sending out powerful swaths of energy as he made his way to the ship. The Nagen were able to deflect Elias' attack however, staying even with him. Derela didn't seem upset that Elias was going to make it to the ship though, as she did not ramp up their attacks. Elias entered the ship through the gateway and stood there continued to send blasts at the Nagen.

Kabec was at the controls as he tried to get the ship on course for the Lighthouse Sector. In seconds, he closed the gateway just after Elias sent one last blast and then they were off. They were jolted a bit as the Nagen managed to get a hit on the ship, but it kept moving on through space as fast as possible on route towards the Shockwave. Elias looked out the window and saw the Nagen were flying after them, but not chasing them as he would have expected.

"What are they doing?" Elias asked.

"They know they won't be able to destroy it before we get to the Shockwave," said Kabec, turning on the ship's messaging feature.

"Emergency alert. Emergency alert. We need help immediately. This is Kabec. We were attacked by the Nagen. There are over one hundred of them. I repeat, emergency alert. We need help immediately. We—we..." Kabec had trouble breathing and paused for several seconds. "We have already suffered one--one casualty. We are in need of assistance."

Kabec turned off the messaging feature and then dropped down into his chair. He started crying. Elias looked around the ship at everyone else. Tasich had head was down. Samara just stared at a wall looking frozen as Siara held her in her arms.

Then Elias sensed someone from the Nagen moving fast towards them. So they were chasing the ship. No, it was Cozart. Elias could sense him and as Elias looked out the window, he saw Cozart slow down outside the window and move his hands apart creating a blue sphere, smile at Elias, and then continue on in the direction of the Lighthouse Sector.

"Earth," said Elias out loud as he realized where Cozart was going. "Open the gateway Kabec."

"What?" asked Kabec.

"Just open the gateway. I'm going after him," said Elias.

"That's what they want. If you do that, they'll all be able to attack you," said Kabec.

"He's going to Earth. I have to get there before him. Now open the gateway," commanded Elias.

Kabec looked at Elias with fright before opening the gateway to the ship. . They were not too far outside the Lighthouse Sector now as the ship had been moving many times the allowed Cliern speed to get back. Elias knew for sure Cozart was going to Earth. Going to the Shockwave would be unwise. He went out of the ship and made a beeline for Earth determined to reach there before Cozart did.

Chapter 23: Elias' Revenge

Elias sat on a wooden bench in a random park, his eyes sifting through the scenery. He was wearing the dark black hooded cloak he had gotten from Nayreen because he did not want anyone to recognize him, but his cloak was drawing attention for standing out on such a pleasant, breezy day. A few kids had come up to him and started talking to him before their parents could pull them away. The parents had their kids kept at a safe distance from him thinking he was a deranged homeless man.

While he kept a calm exterior, inside Elias' mind he was filled with anger. He could sense Cozart coming closer and closer to the Earth. Elias waited for him to arrive. He closed his eyes and took in deep breaths.

After another two minutes Cozart flew inside Earth's atmosphere. Elias opened his eyes again and got up going closer to the lake. Everyone around him looked scared and some of them even walked away. Then Cozart came flying down, stopping as he floated three stories above the surface of the lake. The people standing around Elias gasped and many began to run away.

"So, this is your precious Earth," said Cozart. "I certainly expected it to look much better than this."

Elias didn't say a word. Rage was building up inside of him. He refrained from attacking Cozart right away was because he was waiting for everyone around the lake to clear out.

"You know, I thought you'd be a bit angrier at me. After all, I did kill your best friend, Quincey," said Cozart as he smiled.

"I'm going to kill you, Cozart," said Elias talking slow breaths. He was getting upset at the time that people were taking to make their way away from the two.

"My name is Maraye, not Cozart. And I appreciate your sentiments, but I seriously doubt that you'll be able to kill me. No, you're too soft," he said. "If you really wanted to kill me, you would've done so as you passed me." He laughed. "You and your precious Clierns. They weren't so helpful were they? I mean you were merely a few planets away from their borders and they just let Quincey die. It was a shame really. But then again, I'm sure the Clierns won't be missing too much with little old Quincey out of the picture."

Elias' breathing picked up.

"Then of course there's your father. What was it that you said? He told you and your mother he died," said Maraye laughing. "So gullible. Your father was much too powerful to have died so easily. No, he merely needed an excuse to abandon you two. He was sick of you!"

Elias' face was clenched and he was livid.

"Shut up," he screamed.

Maraye looked taken aback. "Make me," he said.

Elias didn't care about the people around him anymore, launching himself at Maraye with such great force that the ground shook as he left it and huge ripples formed on the surface of the lake. He wasted no time with any fancy maneuvers or tricks as he sent an enormous energy burst at

Maraye. Maraye had no time to avoid it and his attempt at deflecting it did nothing as the blast careened into him sending him flying dozens of yards up in the air. Elias continued through with his blast and caught Maraye's head from above with his right hand. Maraye was smoking orange and barely alive as he took quick breaths. Elias looked at him with pure hatred as he held onto his head.

"I told you," whispered Maraye, "you're too soft to kill me."

Elias looked down at the ground where people were staring at the two of them and pointing. He sat there pondering his thoughts for a few seconds before flying high and away at a slow pace.

Maraye chuckled.

"Soft. Just like your father," he said. He continued mocking Elias. "What are you going to do? Send me to the academy?"

Elias continued flying higher while holding on to Maraye's head. After a short while, they were in the middle of space between Earth and Mars and Elias stopped.

"Ah, your friends. They've followed you. I can sense them coming," said Maraye.

Elias flicked his wrist and tossed Maraye ahead of him, letting him go.

"You're softer than I thought. Letting me—"

Elias sent a blast powerful enough to kill ten people at Maraye before he could finish the sentence. In a flash Maraye was dead. Elias stared at the spot in space where he had just been. He was still filled with anger. Maraye had gotten inside his head. He was starting to believe what Maraye had said about his father and the Clierns.

Alera, Kabec, Tasich, Siara, and Samara came near him. He looked at them and they were just staring at him with their eyes open in shock.

"What did you do?" asked Tasich.

"I did what he deserved," said Elias.

"Nobody deserves that," said Tasich. "I know you're mad." He paused. "But—"

"It was your fault that Quincey died. You switched places with Cozart. What gives you the right to tell me what to do? How do I know you're not one of them," yelled Elias now out of control with anger looking ready to attack Tasich.

"Look, I thought he'd be able to help. I didn't know he was with the Nagen," yelled Tasich.

"You're lying," screamed Elias.

He started sending energy blasts at Tasich, who was already smoking neon green, but Alera jumped in the way of them. She deflected them although with great difficulty.

"Elias. Stop it," she screamed continuing to deflect his attacks while starting to smoke purple.

Elias' attacks began decreasing in energy as Alera moved closer and closer to him, deflecting them away. Soon Elias stopped and his arms fell to his sides. Alera was now floating in front of him.

"Stop," she whispered.

Then she hugged him as he floated there beginning to cry. They were all silent and nobody moved for a few minutes. Alera let go of Elias and looked at him.

"Elias," she said.

He didn't say anything as he just stared straight ahead looking past her at space. He wanted to leave. He wanted to go as far away as he could. He didn't want to hear about the Clierns or Earth or anybody. He just wanted to be alone right now. He closed his eyes.

♦

Alera continued looking at Elias. He wasn't saying anything. She waited for him to say something. He looked calm now. Then she saw him close his eyes and she relaxed, but in a split second there was a gigantic flash, Alera blinked, and Elias was gone. When her eyes opened all Alera could see was an enormous white streak that stretched as far in space as one could see.

Alera stared at it looking dumbfounded. It was true. Elias was no yellow diamond. He was the son of an ancient.

"What the...?" said Kabec, his eyes wide open as he stared at the white streak across space.

Siara opened her mouth, but she just stuttered unable to say anything at all.

Everyone stared at the white streak for a minute before it started to fade.

"Alera," said Kabec. "When you unlocked him, what happened?"

"Why?" she asked.

"Because Elias isn't a yellow diamond," said Kabec sounding a bit scared. "He's the son of an ancient."

"I know," responded Alera.

"You knew?" asked Kabec. "How long have you known?"

"Only two days. I had a hunch that's who he was when I saw the ancient language. I can read it," she said.

"But how?" asked Kabec.

"His mom taught it to me," answered Alera.

They all floated there silenty for several seconds more before Kerlan, Raina, and several Cliern special forces came up to them.

"Are you all alright?" asked Raina.

Alera nodded her head without looking at Raina.

"Okay. We need to get you all back on the Shockwave, okay?" Raina said.

They all followed Raina back to the Shockwave and Alera looked back out into space one more time at where Elias had been before she went inside the emergency bay with the others.

◆

Elias opened his eyes after he had stopped and looked back. He had created a bright white streak in space by flying through so fast. He took several deep breaths as he looked around him at where he was floating. Elias was beyond the Cliern's known Universe now having traversed from the Lighthouse Sector in octant six to well past octants one and eight on the opposite side of Sanize. The beacon that was part of his suit was glowing showing him where the closest border lay.

Elias went the opposite way in search of a planet, any planet, where he could be left alone for a few days.

◆

"Is something wrong?" a young woman named Sara asked.

"No, nothing wrong," said an older woman named Isabelle.

Isabelle sensed it. A feat only performed by ancients. Sara looked out the window and saw what Isabelle had sensed.

"Look," said Sara.

"It's a space jump," said Isabelle.

"Space jump?" asked Sara.

"Flying so fast it appears as if one jumped through space. The streak will fade soon," said Isabelle.

"Should we greet the person who did it?" asked Sara.

"Soon. For now we wait," said Isabelle.

◆

Several days had passed since the encounter with the Nagen and Alera was sitting in the Explorer's Library. She was having trouble concentrating on the book she had open. Since their ordeal, the ship's hierarchy had given Alera, Kabec, Tasich, Siara, and Samara time off from their usual lives, but Alera was trying to get back into a normal routine to keep her mind off what had happened to them.

Samara glided into the room and sat down opposite of Alera.

"Siara said you wanted to see the recording I made," she said.

"Hmm. Oh, yeah. But I don't need it now. You don't—"

Samara handed over her HoloTele to Alera.

"Thanks," said Alera.

Alera transferred the recording to her HoloTele and put the pictures on the table's hologram display.

Samara looked at it.

"So Elias' dad was an ancient," she said.

"Yeah," said Alera.

"How?" asked Samara.

"I don't know," said Alera. "But I'm almost positive these markings were made by him."

Samara sighed. She looked back down at the table avoiding looking at the pictures.

"You know, I heard Ramses and Kerlan calling Elias a white diamond," said Samara after a few minutes had passed.

Alera chuckled.

"A white diamond," said Alera shaking her head. She looked back to the pictures and let out a long sigh. Then her eyes opened wide and she looked back at Samara. "Wait. A white diamond. I can't believe I didn't think of it before. How could I be so stupid?"

Alera got up and flew over to another part of the library. She was looking for a book that she had once read.

"What's up?" asked Samara confused.

"I--I've heard that before," said Alera still looking for the book. "I remember reading about it." She kept looking for a few seconds. "Got it!"

Alera took the book from the shelf and exchanged it with the pictures from Samara's recording as she put the book's pages up on the table's display. Alera flipped through until she had reached the portion of the book which mentioned the white diamond. She began to read it again. Next to the writings were three pictures.

"Well?" asked Samara.

"Elias' dad is dead. He had to die," said Alera.

"What? Why?" asked Samara.

Alera gulped.

"Because Elias was born."